Portia Da Costa is one of the most internationally renowned authors of erotic romance and erotica, and a *Sunday Times*, *New York Times* and *USA Today* bestseller.

She is the author of eighteen *Black Lace* books, as well as numerous short stories and novellas.

D1637747

Also by Portia Da Costa

Hotbed

PORTIA DA COSTA

BLACK
LACE

1 3 5 7 9 10 8 6 4 2

Black Lace, an imprint of Ebury Publishing
20 Vauxhall Bridge Road,
London SW1V 2SA

Penguin
Random House
UK

Black Lace is part of the Penguin Random House
group of companies whose addresses can be found at
global.penguinrandomhouse.com

First published in 2001 by Black Lace
This edition published in 2015

www.eburypublishing.co.uk

A CIP catalogue record for this book
is available from the British Library

ISBN 9780352347831

Printed and bound by CPI Group (UK) Ltd, Croydon, CR0 4YY

Penguin Random House is committed to a sustainable future for our
business, our readers and our planet. This book is made from
Forest Stewardship Council® certified paper.

MIX
Paper from
responsible sources
FSC
www.fsc.org   FSC® C018179

Contents

Thanks to 'Teacher' for inspiration
and to June for help with research.

Chapter One
Talons and Pink Taffeta

'*A*nd do you think she'll come?'
The voice was powerful, yet as lush as velvet. It never failed to make Patti horny. She knew she had to reply but her throat was choked with lust and with the thrill of fear that fed it.

'Patti, do you think that your sister will come? Just because you asked her to?' the beautiful voice persisted, revealing no impatience or irritation, although if the roles had been reversed – as they sometimes were – Patti would have been well pissed off and shown it.

'Y-yes, she will ... I'm sure she will ... I asked her, didn't I?' Patti stammered, feeling the blood rush to her head as she bent further over the edge of the big old sink, and tried to find patterns in the cracks that laced its enamel. A map, that was what she needed, a way through the maze. Anything to help her regain control of herself and stop her saying the first mad thing that came into her head. Anything to stop her breaking down, probably within the next minute, and grovelling for even the tiniest bit of contact. She knew full well that her companion much preferred someone with a bit of fight rather than a yes man or a yes girl.

'I know you've got overdeveloped feminine wiles, Patti my love, but do you really think she'll travel all this way, and leave the fleshpots of London – *just* because her sister asks her to?'

The voice was arch now; the burlesque note, so familiar from the onstage world outside this scummy dressing room, was dominant. But Patti knew that the tall figure moving behind her – causing wafts of cool air to tantalise her hot, naked skin – was adept at chameleon changes. She was dealing with a supreme dissembler here. A pussy tease, a prick tease, a God-knows-what tease . . . A wearer of so many false faces that the real one rarely surfaced.

'Yes. Yes, she will! She used to live here, didn't she? Of course she'll come!' Patti gasped, her body coming alive as a stiff, textured fabric brushed against her. It seemed to draw a line of flame across her tender buttocks. Her tormentor was so near now, and had come upon her with consummate slyness, making not a sound despite outrageously high heels.

'Well then I'm impressed. You know how I love a woman who can make another woman come!'

She should have seen it from a mile away, but the double entendre still caught Patti unawares. So caught up was she in the game and her own small, but pretty stupid, lie that she giggled without thinking.

Only to be rewarded with a slash of pain and the breath knocked clean out of her.

'Oh shit!' gasped Patti, still smirking despite the new fire in her bottom cheek, and the hotter, wetter, much dirtier fire in her sex. She could take any amount of spanking and other abuse, but the denial of satisfaction was a truer torture. And Stella knew it.

She was such a bitch! Or *he* was . . .

Oh fuck, thought Patti, grinning despite her pain. What did it matter? Man or woman? Either sex hit just as hard!

'I beg your pardon?'

The voice was changing again now, as the person at the performer's core took over. The real person, the one as addicted to these power-trips as his – her? – willing victims were.

Gotcha! Patti thought as she murmured, 'Nothing.'

'But you *did* speak,' Stella persisted, her voice almost normal now. Whatever *that* was?

'I said "shit!" because you hurt me,' hissed Patti. In defiance, she shifted her position slightly, hoping to make her backside sting less. Either that, or ease the gnawing ache in her sex.

She could well imagine the sight she presented. A pretty woman bare-arsed over the edge of a huge old enamel sink, her short skirt hitched up to her waist, and her tights and panties bunched around her knees. She pictured also, and effortlessly, the person standing just behind her. The regal figure who loved to play with pain and questions.

A fucking drag queen, thought Patti. The great and utterly glamorous Stella Fontayne. How in God's name did I get involved with a drag queen?

'Well, wash your mouth out with soap and water!' The pantomime voice had returned, and Patti could hear the rustle of fabric being adjusted. What the hell was Stella up to now? If only there was a mirror over this bloody great sink.

Why the fuck *am* I so drawn to her? To him? Without benefit of that mirror, Patti could still see the tall figure, who – wig, cocktail gown and all – had stolen her life with just one flash of her unnaturally long eyelashes. Who'd made troubles, both old and recent, seem like nothing.

Is it because of *her*? Patti thought of a certain real woman. Who was one of the troubles in a way – a long-standing one – and yet also a source of happiness.

Admit it, Patts, you know it's the truth. It'd been

staring her in the face all along. Just like the grimy cracked enamel. The answer was so obvious and so tempting that it made her grin again.

I bet *she'd* never wear a fuchsia-coloured taffeta fish-tail sheath dress in a million years, Patti thought, catching a flash of hot pink out of the corner of her eye. I can't remember when I last saw *her* in anything but black.

It made sense, yes, but somehow it insulted Stella. What she felt for Stella wasn't transitional. She – or he – was a person to love for himself not a stepping stone to someone else.

'You're very quiet.' Patti felt the stiff pink taffeta scratch her skin again. Just where it was sorest from the efforts of Stella's hard but elegant hand. 'What are you thinking about, little one?' Patti felt the very tips of a set of long pointed nails slide across her backside, the touch frustratingly light yet like five streaks of acid.

She groaned, no longer quiet, her cunt contracting.

The nails retraced their track, lighter than ever, yet hotter because the nerve ends had been stirred. Patti bit her lips, felt her head go light, endured the tiny spasm in her swollen, aching clit.

'Patti?'

The voice was more revealing than ever now. Patti heard her own name sound deeper, full of real emotion, and felt her body go limp, lose strength, blown away by it. Her cunt wept, the thick slippery liquid sliding out of her like an unfurling flag of lust. She wept other tears too – but not from the pain. Confused, she turned her head to dislodge the drops, and saw again the glittering pink of Stella's costume. There was an electric crackle in the air as it slid to the floor and hit the grubby lino.

She had lovingly tacked and sewn that skirt, then fitted it closely on its wearer. *Very* closely. Precision-tailored, with only a sheer silky basque beneath. It had been fun, that fitting, and her cunt grasped involuntarily, recalling it.

Feeling the long fingernails again, against her jaw this time, Patti knew that Stella was changing even as he touched her. Not his costume this time, but his mindset. Unrestricted by the conventions of gender, he was making the best choice for the moment.

He was a man now, in spite of the exotic, whorish perfume he wore, which as ever threatened to make Patti sneeze. In spite of the red satin knickers that Patti saw flash across the edge of her vision, consigned to the floor, with the dress.

'So, you're absolutely convinced that your sister will come back to Redwych to visit us?' persisted the man who still seemed to be 'Stella', even now.

'Yes! She'll come! I've already persuaded her, I *told* you!' gasped Patti, fighting the hard, stiffened edge of a corset as it pressed against her bottom. Fighting the urge to churn her hips and rub herself, 'I – I'd never let you down . . .' She paused, and heard, through her own pounding blood, a series of tiny distinctive pops. 'Stella . . .' she whispered, watching ten long, hot pink ovals – Stella's false fingernails – drop one by one on to the counter beside her.

'I know you won't, little one,' murmured her lover as his fingertips, shorn of their talons, explored her labia and paddled in her juices.

'Oh, God,' moaned Patti, saliva rattling in her throat as if every gland in her body was open and pouring out liquid. Her clitoris felt ready to burst from the gathered sensation.

'No, it's just me,' said 'Stella', his laughing breath warm in Patti's ear as his erect cock forged its slow way inside her.

Chapter Two
Slow Train

*D*espite living life at what seemed like light speed in London, Natalie Croft had always preferred slow trains.

They took her back to the most exciting part of her childhood. The time when – roughly fifteen years ago – she'd just discovered boys, sex and her own body. To school trips taken on slow trains and coaches, and times when the teachers' backs were turned and she'd explored and *been* explored.

As the present-day train pulled into the first station out of London, Natalie looked out on to the platform and felt the same old girlish thrill. In a lot of ways, she wished to God she didn't have to make this journey, but the train, a sense of adventure and the prospect of seeing Patti – they all seemed to combine and produce a boost of inner energy. It was a sexy feeling, but it bothered her too. Should she really be feeling horny in relation to seeing her half-sister again? Too kinky ... You really shouldn't feel like that about someone you were related to, should you? Especially if that person was a woman.

Shit! I'm thirty! Shouldn't I be able to deal with this

by now? she thought. Looking through the carriage window, she registered a dark-clad shape pass by on the platform outside, but in her heart of hearts she still seemed to see Patti.

Why do I let her get to me this way?

Natalie supposed that it was because they were half-sisters. That 'half' made a critical difference. It meant that Patti was both a mystery to her and closer than a full sister could ever have been. Natalie always felt a disturbing urge to squirm when forced to face the subtle distinctions.

An awareness of being watched made Natalie feel foolish. There was nothing she liked less than looking an idiot, and here she was shaking her head, frowning and pulling faces for no apparent reason. People would think she was a care-in-the-community case.

Looking up, she saw that the dark shape from the platform had materialised in the coach now. A tall, blond man in a long black raincoat was looking around, anxiously trying to decide which free seat to choose. It was airline-style seating here, and there were plenty of single seats, beside other commuters, but no sets of two. The black-clad man was clearly concerned about invading people's space.

Choose me! Natalie thought, then immediately wondered what had got into her. He wasn't anything special. He wasn't young, dark and confident-looking, like her usual prey. He was middle-aged, his sandy blond hair was curly, for God's sake, and he looked like exactly the kind of shy, inhibited, clerical type who still wore a vest, and either lived at home with mother or had a doting housekeeper to look after him.

Probably a teacher. Or a librarian. Or maybe even a don if he's getting off at Redwych.

And yet . . .

Without warning, the tall blond man suddenly looked her way, and, for a moment, his expression was incredibly layered and complex. Natalie saw shyness, a definite twinge of sexual attraction, and something else that passed away so fleetingly that she wondered if she was imagining things. It was amusement, she realised. Inside, he was laughing. She had no idea why but in that moment she wanted to share the joke with him.

Choose me, she willed him, and smiled, hoping she didn't look too obvious.

Her quarry hesitated. His eyes flicked to another seat, then another, as if he were teasing her. He hefted his large, old-fashioned leather briefcase, as if preparing to move on.

You fuck, stop pissing me about! Natalie thought, then thought again, as she saw a blush stain the man's fair complexion. He isn't playing games, you stupid mare. He's just *shy*!

'Excuse me . . . Are you saving this seat for anyone?'

The voice confirmed it. It was soft and diffident, the voice of a mild-mannered man who was shit-scared of women. And yet, somehow, it wasn't unpleasant.

'No, it's all yours. Go ahead,' murmured Natalie, upping the voltage of her smile. He mightn't be her type, but in an odd way he was still quite cute.

It took a few moments for her seatmate to organise himself. He had a coat, briefcase and newspaper to dispose of, and there was very little leg room and even less space on the luggage rack. To Natalie, he began to seem less cute, and more of a fussy pedant as he fiddled with first his coat – which he folded and put on his lap – then his seatback table, and finally a collection of files, books and writing implements.

Bloody hell, he *is* a teacher, thought Natalie, as her companion opened an exercise book and appeared to assess its contents for marking. And a right old tight-arse too, she silently added, watching him rearrange his paraphernalia yet again, then flick through a slim volume of poetry, looking for a reference.

Then she caught sight of his bookmark.

Oh Teacher, you naughty boy, she thought, her irritation with him forgotten. He was keeping his place with what looked suspiciously like a dirty postcard: a sepia-toned photograph of two women in their underwear, one of whom was spanking the other. It wasn't particularly explicit, and Natalie only really caught a glimpse of it, but somehow the faded image got to her. Crossing her legs, she suddenly realised she was wet.

Christ Almighty, woman, what's the matter with you? He's just some prissy schoolmaster with a dubious taste in postcards and you're getting the hots for him! Are you really reduced to fancying someone like him?

But it was true. As she moved discreetly in her seat, she could feel the slipperiness in her knickers, and the sensation that the lips and folds of her cunt were bloated. Already.

How long was it since she'd fucked someone? In her on/off relationship with Alan, the sex had been a bit on the sparse side lately, she realised. Not that it'd really bothered her. She'd been too busy worrying about her status at the magazine. And well I might have, she thought, bitterly remembering the reason she'd wished she *wasn't* travelling.

Take some 'you' time, Alan had said – in his capacity as editor rather than intermittent bedmate. Have a break, Nat. Get some perspective. When you come back we can look in some new directions for you.

Hah! Directions like fucking well sacking me, you conniving bastard! It's no wonder it stopped being worthwhile faking orgasms!

Natalie ground her teeth; her interest in her fidgety companion was momentarily forgotten. Management were such a set of jumped-up little shits, she thought, and Alan most of all. They wanted her out of *Modern Examiner* but they were too bloody cowardly to just say so! Well, she'd show them. She was on the trail of something. Something hot and tasty that could be sensational if her instincts were sound.

Looking down at the newspaper clipping she'd been reading, she saw another male face, one far more confident than that of the nervous academic beside her.

Smug bastard, she thought, touching the face in the picture. Whitelaw Daumery reminded her very much of money men at the magazine, the ones who were intent trimming the financial fat, her salary included. He too was a golden-boy type: rich, successful, squeaky clean, just the sort of noble entrepreneur-cum-minor local politician that the new government lapped up and liked to reward with a fat-cat job on some highfalutin quango or other. She'd get some dirt on this whiter-than-white prick if it killed her! And where better to start than Redwych, where he lived and where she'd been born?

Not sure quite what she'd actually done, Natalie suddenly became aware that she'd knocked Teacher's elbow and made him drop his poetry book. Mumbling some apology, he bent down and tried to get it, his pale, clean-shaven face momentarily brushing her thigh. But the space between their seats and the backs of the ones in front of them was so limited that a tall man like him couldn't reach it.

'Don't worry, I'll get it for you,' said Natalie, immediately aware of some very distinct sensations. The brush of her companion's cheek – possibly even his lips! – against her thigh had restored every throbbing erg of sexual excitement that fretting about work and Whitelaw Daumery had momentarily sidetracked. And the sight of Teacher's hot, confused face made her want to do some very bad things to him. His hazel eyes were wide and popping; he was terrified!

Don't worry, Teach, I'll be gentle with you, she said silently as she reached down for his book and postcard.

In the cramped space available it was impossible to be elegant. Feeling her breasts tingle as she hunched over, Natalie had no intention of sparing Teacher's blushes, so she pressed herself comprehensively against his knees and his thighs as she pretended to search for his poetry text.

God, this is so deliciously squalid, she thought as she found but ignored the book, then made damned sure that Teacher could feel her nipples against his leg. She stared at the smeared plastic seat back, the matted carpet in the seat well, and somehow the very grime and horribleness of it all added an extra excitement. A sudden waft of a pungent yet expensive cologne, coming from the general direction of her victim's crotch, only made her underhand actions feel sleazier. He was a clean man, a nice man, and she wanted to dirty him and grope his blameless body.

Natalie had the poetry book and the postcard in her hand now, but she was deeply aware of how close Teacher's genitals were. She had a sudden mad urge to forget her original goal altogether, and just unzip his trousers and get his prick out. It was hard to see anything really, but a seventh sense told her unequivocally that he had a hard-on. The temptation was immense, but, deciding against it, Natalie straightened up.

'Here you are,' she said blithely, revealing nothing. Let him guess, she thought. Let him imagine. Speculate. 'Tricky little devils but I managed to find them eventually.'

Teacher's face was an icon of confusion. His ears were orchid pink, his pupils dilated and he looked as if he was in deep, deep shock. 'Th-thank you. Thank you very much,' he said as he took the book and card. He looked so nervous and totally thunderstruck that the urge to outrage him was stronger than ever.

As he rearranged his belongings, she slid her hand beneath his coat.

The effect, as she closed her fingers around his cock,

was like zapping him with an electric cattle prod. He leapt in his seat, gave a muffled little gasp, and, under his raincoat, the flesh beneath Natalie's hand reared and stiffened. It felt like a small but very fierce animal disturbed in its lair, and now pressing up against Teacher's trousers trying to get to her.

Natalie felt light-headed. All was not as it seemed. Not what she'd expected. The angry erection she held had nothing to do with the mild, shy man she'd believed she was sitting next to. He felt powerful. Primal. Dominant in a way that bypassed all words and first impressions. All over again she wanted to get down on her knees and suck his penis. But this time it was awe, not a desire to intimidate him.

Yet when she caught his eye, she didn't feel quite so awe-struck. His look of alarm stirred the seductress in her. She had him in the palm of her hand, didn't she? In every way that counted to a man . . .

Or even to a born-again boy.

She squeezed lightly and he swallowed, fear and excitement in his face. He couldn't look away and his eyes were almost black with arousal. Beneath her fingers his cock fought its containment.

The small, fierce animal wasn't so small now, and Natalie held his gaze, as excited as he was. She licked her lips, almost without thinking, and saw his eyes close, almost in a swoon. Message received and understood.

I've got to see this, Natalie thought. I've got to see him. Get his dick out. Touch him. More . . . She debated for a second, wondering if she dare unzip him here in this scummy coach, with other commuters just yards away. Glancing around, she saw there were just enough other passengers to make things dodgy, but still she was tempted. She ran her forefinger along Teacher's zip and heard him mutter something, a soft garbled plea, desperate and breathy.

You want it, don't you? Looking into his shadowed hazel eyes, she saw the answer she wanted. He was game. He would play along. He was up for it. Natalie smiled. He was so 'up' he'd probably find it difficult to walk!

And yet he'd have to. If he wanted her . . .

Releasing him suddenly, she withdrew her hand, picked up her file of newspaper clippings and fished down beside her seat for her bag to put them into.

'Excuse me.' Standing up, she kept her voice absolutely normal. This was a mind game now and she wanted him to wonder if he was simply imagining things.

'Oh, yes. Of course . . .'

Teacher stood too and slid out of his seat to let her pass, upsetting his marking in the process and sending sheets of paper cascading into the aisle. As he bent to retrieve them, Natalie shimmied by, hoping that he would pause to take a good look at her thighs. In silky black tights and a short skirt, they were impressive.

Walking away, she could almost feel hunger in the gaze that followed her. She had no doubt that his palms were sweaty and he was jumbling up his papers; but, even so, she couldn't be sure that he'd have the bottle to follow her.

But she didn't look back. Far too obvious, girl, she told herself as she locked herself into the lavatory cubicle and faced reality in an unreal situation.

If she'd thought the carriage itself was grubby, then the toilet was a new dimension in disgustingness. Everything was shades of grey, except the toilet pan, which was stained with some more organic colours that made her feel quite queasy. It was a relief to put the seat down once she'd pissed.

Running a trickle of tepid water to wash her hands, Natalie stared into the mirror, and wondered if the person she was seeing was real, too.

She looked the same. It was her handsome, if not pretty, face; her sleek, conker-brown hair, groomed into a businesslike ponytail; and her brownish-green eyes. The clothes were the same ubiquitous black she always wore: city top, short skirt, black tights and shoes.

But what she was hoping for wasn't *her* at all. She liked her sex clean and luxurious, with all the nice little trappings that money could buy. An expensive meal, good wine, clean bodies in fresh, crisp sheets. Not hard, fluorescent lighting, grey filth, and a quite unignorable smell of urine. And as a rule she liked to *know* the men she fucked!

Feeling massive second thoughts, Natalie looked around. God, there wasn't even enough room to do anything! The cubicle was tiny, and Teacher was tall, and not insubstantial. They would certainly have to do it standing up. Do whatever it was they were going to do ... Natalie's mind blanked as the train jerked and swayed across a set of points.

Bracing herself, she reached into her bag for a lipstick, then – as best she could – painted her mouth. Scandal-ous Red, it said on the end of the slim black tube, and that made Natalie grin and pull herself together. Highly appropriate, she thought. How much more scandalous could you get than fucking a total stranger on a train?

It was mad. Downright dangerous. Gross and dis-gusting. But even so she could feel her pussy twitching.

As she stuffed the lipstick back in her bag, there was a soft knock at the door, and, as her heart revved up, Natalie saw a fleeting inner image of Patti, her half-sister.

God, would Patti do this? Natalie paused with her hand on the door's locking mechanism. Her sister was so quiet, so imperturbable, so safe, so fucking unimagin-ative. Which was probably why her husband had left her, vacating their pristine suburban bed after only a year or two of marriage.

Suddenly it was the thought of outraging Patti, as much as the man outside, that galvanised Natalie. She slid the lever to unlock the toilet door.

For a heartbeat, she wondered whether it was just someone wanting the loo who'd knocked, then absolute certainty kicked in and she schooled her features into a mask of non-surprise.

Her shy teacher's face was a picture. Almost every emotion a man could feel was in it. Fear. Doubt. Horror. Total lust. This man hated himself – but he was still here. He wanted her even if it meant a descent into hell as a consequence.

The door had been open for only a fraction of a second, but it seemed like an age. Hearing other travellers approach, Natalie said nothing, but grabbed Teacher by the sleeve and hauled him inside.

'I –' he began, his brow furrowing furiously as he could get no further. He seemed incapable of coherent speech – or action.

For a moment, Natalie's doubts welled up. It was the first time this had happened to *her* too, and the weight of responsibility seemed to squash down her libido.

Good God, men! They either knew too much or, in this case, too little. When was she ever going to find one who was just right? Losing her patience, she slid her hand around the back of his neck and pulled his face down to hers.

'I'm Steven ... My name's Steven,' he gasped in the second she drew breath to kiss him.

And I'm Natalie, pleased to meet you, she thought savagely as his mouth opened to her tongue. His own tongue lay quiescent, warm and malleable, but, as she teased and badgered it with hers, she felt his hands come up and curve around her back. His long fingers spread against her through the jersey of her top.

So, not so useless after all ...

Natalie's spirits rose as Steven's grip strengthened,

and finally he fought back at her with his tongue. Pressing her body to his, she could feel the exceptional erection she'd explored back in the carriage. There was no diminution in its size or hardness – in fact it seemed even more imposing. He'd shed his jacket now, and she imagined him walking down the aisle after her, unable to disguise the telltale bulge. She wound her fingers into his thick, soft, curly hair and mashed her lips against his, conscious of smearing Scandalous Red across both their faces.

'Please . . . I . . . what do you want?' he gasped as they broke apart, the lurid lipstick like a badge of sin around his mouth.

'I want to fuck you,' said Natalie. The normal filters she imposed on her speech had vanished. She could say absolutely anything to this man. Do anything to him. She pulled roughly at his shirt, popping off buttons, then explored his chest and pinched a nipple with finger and thumb. She felt as if she were a man and that his reddened lips had somehow reversed their roles.

Steven groaned, his pelvis jerked forward and his head tilted back. Closing his eyes, he seemed to stare blindly heavenwards as if he were a martyr being tortured.

Oh shit! Oh God, don't do this to me, you fuck! Natalie thought, her cunt shuddering at the sudden beauty of this strange, shy man. She'd wanted to dominate him, take what she wanted with barely a thought for his needs; but, in a movement he probably wasn't even aware of, he'd turned the tables on her. Enraged, and aching furiously with the need to fuck, Natalie lunged forward again, then, wrenching at Steven's collar and tie, she kissed his throat and chest just as sloppily and haphazardly as she had his mouth and face. She felt an extraordinary desire to bite, and did so, sucking on his flesh as her teeth closed and nipped.

Steven just groaned again, then bucked forward, grinding his hips in an agonised circle against her.

Oh no you don't, sonny Jim! Natalie thought, pulling back heartlessly, then grabbing at Steven's tie and dragging so he had to look at her. She couldn't believe what she was doing, and yet she was doing it. There was no way he was going to get off without her permission. He was *hers*. He was her object. He gave pleasure to *her*!

'Get it out!' she ordered, aware that her voice was a hiss, and that Steven was blinking furiously. He was obviously disorientated and the thrill of it was so immense that Natalie almost came. She really could do anything with him! Anything at all!

'What? G-get what out?' he stammered.

'Your dick, little boy . . . Get your dick out. I want to see it.'

Natalie knew the words were absurd. He was a tall, grown man, at least a decade her senior, if not a good deal more. He was possibly a teacher or some figure of authority. Yet in her mind she'd instantly regressed him to his helpless adolescence.

And not only in her mind, it seemed.

Obeying her immediately, Steven attacked his belt and the zip of his trousers with a surprising degree of dexterity. Natalie suddenly wondered if he had been deceiving her all along, and this was a game he played all the time; but then his look of pure, horrified lust dispelled that impression. As he reached inside his jockey shorts she almost expected him to say, 'Sorry, ma'am . . .'

The penis he drew out from between his flies was nothing like a boy's. It was a splendid animal, just as big and sturdy as she'd hoped for. The glans was slippery, ruddy and swollen, gleaming with pre-come. Natalie saw Steven's fingers curl round it, lovingly familiar.

And you're a wanker, too, aren't you? she thought, feeling totally evil.

'Don't just fucking stand there,' she said, edging back, feeling the reinforced glass of the opaqued-out window behind her, 'Help me! I want it inside me!'

Abandoning what was clearly his favourite toy, Steven acted swiftly, once again inspiring suspicion. His cock swaying, he dipped down, took up the hem of her skirt and raised it to her waist. About to help him, Natalie changed her mind, dragging up her top and clasping her own breasts through her thin black satin bra. Her nipples were hard as fruit stones, and as she twisted them a jolt of sensation shot straight to her clitoris.

'Hurry!' she gasped, more an entreaty than a command this time.

Steven hesitated, faced with her tights, and then began skinning them down her legs. When he reached her feet, he pushed her harder against the glass, then swiftly lifted first one foot then the other, and flung away her shoes. A second later the black tights followed, landing, Natalie noticed distantly, in a pool of indeterminate fluid on the floor of the cubicle.

Aware of her bare feet treading in the same substance, the hard feel of the glass against her back, and the rank smell all around them, Natalie could never remember wanting a fuck this much in the whole of her life. Impatient with her novice lover and the constraints of her clothes, she dragged down her panties, consigned them to the same dubious fate as the rest of her things, then reached out for Steven's erection to pull it towards her.

The way he bit his lip, his face setting into a hard mask of concentration, made her fear the worst and expect a spontaneous jet of semen. But then the danger seemed to pass and he stayed hard, following her lead and letting her position him just as she wanted him.

'For Christ's sake help me!' gasped Natalie, fighting for purchase against the slippery glass. She still wasn't sure that they were going to be able to manage it, but Steven seemed to catch on, reaching down to take hold of himself, and with his other hand lifting up Natalie's thigh for access. Then, using the weight of his body, along with a lot of jiggling and nudging, he pushed inside her.

And now it was Natalie's turn to raise her eyes to heaven. Penetrated, she reached down to touch her clit and felt as if it were she, and not the train, who was rushing along a track, hurtling towards an unknown, yet also familiar, destination. Her pussy spasmed almost instantaneously, needing nothing from her partner in the way of staying power, expertise or even the slightest bit of movement. He was simply an object, a bar of flesh, around which to contract.

As she climaxed she heard him sigh and say, 'For Christ's sake, please tell me your name! Who *are* you?'

Natalie Croft.

Thirty years old; hair dyed the colour of polished wood; slim, outstandingly flexible body – and a truly marvellous fuck.

Welcome home, Natalie Croft, Steven Small silently bade the black-clad young woman as he watched her disappear in the taxi that had so conveniently drawn up in front of her just a moment ago. Let's hope we'll be seeing each other again soon, my dear.

He'd told her a little white lie, of course, when he'd said he was getting a lift, but it wouldn't do for her to start putting two and two together at this stage of the proceedings. At least not about him, he reflected wryly, thinking of her reading material on the train. Those newspaper clippings suggested an unforeseen yet intriguing complication.

And someone's been lying to *me* too, he thought as he

turned on his heel and made for his car in the station car park. Natalie Croft was a journalist, and, from what he'd seen in the brief time before the journey had begun to get interesting, Steven deduced that she was back in Redwych, her home town, on the trail of a story. About Whitelaw Daumery, of all people.

Steven swore savagely to himself. He despised Daumery, and knowing as much as he did about the man, recent developments had almost made him sick to his stomach. He had no problem with acquisitiveness, or even bending the law to breaking point; and, with secrets aplenty of his own, Steven encouraged and admired games of deception. Rampant hypocrisy, however, was the one thing he could not tolerate. Whitelaw Daumery deserved to tumble from the complacent pinnacle on which he'd set himself up, or, if not to fall, to at least get no enjoyment from his new, high-profile status.

'Fuck him!' murmured Steven, consigning Whitelaw Daumery to an insulated mental compartment and returning his attention to a far more pleasant topic.

There had been no mention whatsoever of Natalie coming to Redwych on a story. Not even a hint of it. He'd been sold an outright fib, he suspected, and the thought of dealing with the little liar who'd told it to him produced a delicious sexual thrill. Playing was always much more fun when there was a real and valid context for it. The striving and the prizes were so much greater.

He unlocked his car and slid inside it, his cock as hard as stone again as he reached for his mobile phone.

Steven Small. Good God, I just fucked a man called Steven Small – standing up in a train lavatory – when, a couple of hours ago, I'd never even set eyes on the guy!

Slumped into the back seat of the cab she'd jumped into in a panic, Natalie felt spaced out and slightly sick as if she'd woken too fast from a vivid dream. She was profoundly relieved that Steven Small couldn't share the taxi with her, because there was not a single thing she could think of that she might have said to him.

One minute she'd been climaxing savagely in a grotty train toilet, her body clenching around his. The next minute, it seemed, she'd been on the station, surrounded by perfectly normal, boring and completely sexless people, bidding farewell to Steven Small, as if all they'd done was share a conversation about the weather over a cup of disgusting commuter coffee.

Shit! I never even took his phone number.

Natalie felt sweaty all of a sudden and realised she was blushing. Before she could stop herself, she glanced into the rear-view mirror and caught the eyes of the cabbie – a female one, unusually – on her. It was almost as if the woman could read the whole story of what had happened in Natalie's hot, pink face. Her exposed, slightly tanned legs were a bit of a giveaway, too. They looked all wrong with her smart suit, but there had been no way she was putting on those tights again.

Just mind your own business and drive, Natalie felt like saying to the driver, as tiredness swept over her. Pretending she hadn't made eye contact, she turned to look out of the window at the fair city of Redwych passing by beyond the glass.

I just dreamed it, she told herself, trying to hang on to that – even though her lack of knickers too was a potent reminder of her sins.

As the taxi sped through the streets of her home town, Natalie could hardly believe the changes that had taken place since she'd last been here. There were so many new houses – all on horrible, stereotypical, upwardly mobile estates – so much urban development, so much bland, corporate grey concrete that looked all wrong with the traditional honeyed stone that Redwych was famous for.

The city fathers want their heads examining, she thought. It was bad enough that Redwych was a runt of a city that had a chip on its shoulder over not being automatically mentioned in the same breath as Oxford and Cambridge, without spoiling what individual character it did have.

Definitely some vested interests at work here, she thought, her mind retuning away from the astounding events on the train and becoming knifelike and professional. She wondered how sound her gut feeling about her possible story was. Her instincts were usually sound, and she had an instinct about Whitelaw Daumery. How much of this desecration of Redwych's stone and heritage was down to him?

Finally dismissing the image of Steven Small's donnish face contorted in ecstasy, she focused on her proposed quarry. Mr Nice Guy Entrepreneur, everyone's favourite businessman, so much in the public eye for being the friendly, upright, honest face of large-scale multifaceted commerce. He was a bit of a housewife's golden boy, too, with his dark, distinguished looks, and his happy family and his many charitable good works.

God, I fucking hate you, thought Natalie, every sixth sense in her rebelling against such a self-defined paragon.

And now the man was to lead this new think tank, this high-profile Committee for Moral Practice in Business. Yeuk! The very name guaranteed, in her mind, that each and every one of the committee's members was an unprincipled hyena with a festering cache of underhand business dealings buried somewhere. Why else would people put themselves forward for something like that? Except as a bluff, as the perfect cover . . .

Unless, of course, it was planned as a springboard to greater things. How long before Daumery stood for Parliament? For high Cabinet office? She imagined that smiling and so falsely open face ranged beside that of the Prime Minister ... Even *replacing* that of the Prime Minister.

I'll get you, you fuck! Natalie thought, feeling an unexpectedly evangelical fervour for her own mission – her plan to bring Mr Nice Guy Golden Boy Daumery down so many pegs that he wouldn't know what had hit him until he was lying in the gutter.

The fact that Whitelaw Daumery looked uncannily like the financial director at the *Modern Examiner* – the very one she suspected was behind the 'rationalisation' of her own position – had nothing whatsoever to do with it, she told herself, feeling her stomach suddenly flutter.

'We're here,' said the cabbie, jolting Natalie unceremoniously out of her zealous reflections.

And it was true. As she popped open the door, and stepped out on to the pavement, she found herself in Northmore Row, in front of the neat suburban house where she supposed she would be living for the next however many weeks it took to achieve her objective. That was assuming that Patti would put her up. She hadn't really asked her, as such.

Her half-sister's house was quite a big one, given that she was divorced, with no children, and nothing in the way of what Natalie would describe as a decent income. Patti had said something about setting up a small dressmaking business of some sort, the last time they'd spoken, but Natalie couldn't see how anything that the unambitious Patti could come up with would finance the upkeep of such a house. It was built of the creamy, gilded local stone, detached and with large front bay windows, very much a 'des res' in spite of being a cliché.

'No one to meet you?' enquired the taxi driver, catching Natalie unawares again. She turned to see that the female cabbie had already unloaded her bags from the boot, and was standing beside her on the pavement, obviously waiting for payment. She nodded to Natalie's luggage. 'Shall I bring these in for you?' she enquired, her expression vaguely amused and challenging.

I bet you just love showing off your muscles, thought Natalie, feeling nasty. The cabbie was chunky, had short hair and was wearing extremely sensible shoes. Most definitely a butch dyke, decided Natalie, and probably making a pass at me.

Well, I've had enough impromptu seductions for one day, sunshine!

'No, it'll be fine. My sister will help me with them. I'm sure she'll be out in a minute. What do I owe you?'

As the cabbie wrote her receipt, Natalie glanced from the front door of Patti's house, to each of the windows in turn.

Where are you, Patti? she thought. You know what time I'm supposed to be arriving. The least you could do is to look out for my taxi.

'Thanks,' Natalie muttered as the cabbie passed over the receipt and a business card. The card read Ruth Hamer Cars, and for a moment Natalie wondered if that was the cabbie's name, or that of yet another dyke who owned the firm.

But, as the cab drove away, Natalie lost interest in the notion of a lesbian taxi firm, and stared again at Patti's upstairs windows. What was the significance of one of the bedrooms having its curtains drawn in the middle of the day?

'What the devil are you up to, Patts?' Natalie murmured, her heart suddenly beating as fast as it had done on the train.

Chapter Three

Adventures with a Window Cleaner

Whatever Patti was doing, Natalie realised that her sister clearly wasn't alone. There was an extended aluminium ladder propped up against the house, adjacent to the bedroom with the closed curtains, and at the foot of the ladder was a plastic bucket, draped with shammy leathers.

In spite of her weariness and disorientation, Natalie laughed out loud.

God, no! Surely not! Quiet, oh so straight Patti was having a slice of afternoon delight with her window cleaner of all people! It was like something out of a cheap British sex farce from the sixties and Natalie immediately thought of words like 'knockers' and 'bonking' and 'nookie'.

Oh, Patti, honestly! Couldn't you have just a bit more imagination than that? thought Natalie, still inwardly sniggering.

But a white van parked just a little way along the kerb seemed to confirm her sister's lack of sexual discrimination. On its side were the words DYSON'S

WINDOW CLEANING SERVICES in a fairly horrible Old English style typeface.

'I can't believe this,' muttered Natalie as she lugged her bags to the porch, then reached out to push the doorbell button.

Then she hesitated, feeling an unsettling, almost sick flutter of anticipation somewhere around her solar plexus. Instead of ringing the bell, she very slowly and gingerly tried the door, and, against all her expectations, it swung open, the cool, shady hall inviting her onwards.

She's mad, thought Natalie, stark, staring mad. Leaving the door open ... This isn't London but they still have opportunistic crime, even here in the refined realms of academe. But, then again, they might well have plenty of opportunistic sex here too? It happened in the most unlikely places these days – even on trains.

Forget that, it didn't happen, Natalie told herself again.

Setting down her bags with the same intense care with which she'd opened the door, Natalie looked around her. Nothing much had changed here. At least not superficially. The narrow white-painted hall was tidy enough, but not as immaculate as it had been last time Natalie had visited. The only thing that looked out of place was a very shabby leather jacket, obviously a man's, that hung on the coat stand along with various macs and coats that Natalie knew belonged to Patti.

What the hell do I do now? Natalie thought, and, as she dithered, the door to the kitchen swung open a few inches and from the gap padded a large, black-and-white cat.

Something else new!

Natalie was taken aback, as much by the strange animal as by the existing situation. Since when had Patti had a cat?

The cat plodded forward, and rubbed itself enthusiastically against Natalie's bare legs. Natalie had never had a pet, but somehow instinct guided her. She reached down and caressed the animal's ears, and it responded by purring loudly and butting hard against her hand.

'Shush, cat!' she whispered, mindful of what she suspected was going on upstairs.

The cat seemed to understand her, giving her leg one last boink with its head, before ambling away and going back where it had come from. In the doorway, it turned, gave her what she could have sworn was an amused look, then disappeared.

My God, a mind-reading cat! Whatever next? Natalie thought, then was almost immediately distracted from her new friend by a faint sound emanating from above her.

Should I shout and make a noise? Follow the cat into the kitchen and give it some Whiskas or something? Go out and come in again, slam the door loudly and shout 'Anyone home?'

Instead of all these, she abandoned her bags, slid off her shoes, and padded silently up the familiar staircase, barefoot. On the landing, she paused, the hairs on the back of her neck prickling and her ears straining to hear the slightest sound, then was rewarded by what could only be described as a sigh of pleasure emanating from a partially open doorway of Patti's bedroom.

Oh God, thought Natalie, feeling her face curve into a huge smirk. Oh God, she really is doing it. She's screwing the window cleaner!

Natalie crept forward, pressing her hand against her chest, the beating of her heart seemed so loud. She didn't want to disturb what was surely going on beyond that tantalisingly open door.

There were clearly two voices now. Low, husky, slightly fractured voices. The sounds of two people too involved in what they were doing to worry about niceties of diction and eloquence.

'Please . . . Oh God, Dyson, please!'

Natalie recognised the voice of Patti, but sounding quite unlike she'd ever heard her sound before. Patti was usually so soft-spoken, her voice low, amiable and easy-going, but now she was pleading, the words broken, almost feral. There was the sound of struggling, the movement of fabric, the kicking of limbs.

Natalie moved forward, keeping herself as narrow as she could, and parallel to the door so that she could see and not be seen. She felt almost afraid to look but could no sooner have stopped herself than have stopped her heart beating.

In the curtained room, there were two figures on the wide, rumpled bed. One was unmistakably the curvy shape of Patti; the other was a man, a muscular *young* man, whose curly dark hair straggled down to his shoulders. The pair were clearly making love – although not yet fucking – but neither was naked. The young man – Dyson the window cleaner, Natalie presumed – was wearing a thin, bedraggled-looking shirt in some kind of white cheesecloth-like material. It was clearly his only garment, because when he knelt up, looming over his partner, his strong, compact buttocks were quite bare.

Patti was wearing the remains of a slip, or perhaps a teddy, as a bodice of tattered lace clung to her generous breasts without really covering all that much of them. But whatever the thing had been it had been partly ripped off her, and her belly and crotch were exposed. Natalie felt her own sex lurch when she saw where the missing scraps of fabric were.

Patti's wrists were tied with it, fastened together to the brass bed head above her head. Her body was half twisted and she was staring at her window-cleaner lover over her own arms, her eyes enormous and beseeching.

It took just a fraction of a second for Natalie to take in the scene before her. Patti's tousled hair, her moist, open pussy; the young man's burly back beneath his thin shirt, his black curls, his freedom of movement as opposed to Patti's bondage.

Oh, yeah, sis, way to go! cheered Natalie silently, her heart flipping and swooping with envy until she remembered her own less than salubrious escapade on the train. It must be the season for it, she thought, pressing her hand against the mound of her own sex. Edging forward a bit, she moved as close to the pair of lovers as she dared.

Fortunately, Patti and her young man were completely absorbed in each other. Natalie reckoned that she could probably have walked right into the room and sat down on the dressing table stool and they would never have noticed her. Not that she was sure she would have wanted to be that close. Not without being part of the action too.

'Please,' murmured Patti, her usually placid voice husky and wheedling. As Natalie watched, she saw, with a mixture of slight disgust and a horrible empathic stirring, that Patti was wafting her crotch towards Dyson and trying to entice him to do something to her. Natalie had an odd feeling that it might not be simply intercourse that her sister wanted, but something dirty, far more obscure, and rather perverted.

Right on!

'Please what?' enquired Dyson, rocking back on his heels and revealing a gigantic erection that almost made Natalie gasp aloud and reveal herself.

The man was huge. Unable to stop herself, Natalie squeezed her crotch hard, trying to imagine such a monster pushing its way into her. At a rough estimate, he was bigger, even, than Steven Small had been, and a penis like that would stretch a woman, might even hurt her if she were not ready for it. Relaxed. Wet. Open. The way Patti so very clearly was.

'Rub me! Fuck me! Do something, for Christ's sake!'

Patti answered, moving her hips faster now, as if the action itself might bring her some relief.

'You're a greedy bitch,' said Dyson, laying hands on his own flesh rather than Patti's. He was quite well spoken and his voice sounded affectionate, but he didn't oblige his partner. Instead, he began a slow, luxurious masturbation, caressing his thick shaft with a fair degree of creativity, his fingers exploring the entire length of it and circling delicately around the fat, bulging tip. Holding his glans between the pads of two fingers, he effected a rolling motion, as if assessing a fine cigar, and a low, ragged groan escaped his lips.

Still half unable to believe what she was seeing, but nevertheless admitting that she was loving every second of it, Natalie marvelled at the unknown Dyson's mastery of his own sexual anatomy. Some men came if you as much as laid a finger on them – then blamed the woman for it! – but this young, dark man of Patti's, like Natalie's own blond teacher before him, seemed to be able to extend his own pleasure to a fine, controlled degree. Something that obviously delighted him and was driving Patti wild.

'Oh God, oh God, oh God,' she groaned, thrashing on the tangled sheets and bringing up one knee and crossing it over herself in an attempt to stimulate her quim without using her hands. Natalie noticed that, at some time, Patti had been wearing stockings, very dark fine denier ones, but now all that remained of them were a few twisted fragments tangled round her knees, calves and feet. When had Dyson torn them off her? Natalie wondered. Would that be before or after he'd tied her to the bed with the shreds of her own underwear?

Momentarily abandoning his splendid erection, Dyson took hold of Patti's ankles – one in each large but oddly sensitive-looking hand – then adjusted his position on the bed until he was kneeling squarely between her thighs. She wriggled again, but he subdued her. Not only with his grip on her but, as far as Natalie could see, with the power of an intense and focused scrutiny. He was staring directly at her stretched-open sex, as if monitoring the puffy, reddish flesh for the tiniest of reactions. Natalie could almost feel the heat of his gaze on her own pussy, and, unable to resist her need any more, she clasped her hand between her legs.

'Dyson, you shit! I'm going mad here!' cried Patti, heaving her lush body about as far as she could within her bonds, both living and of fabric.

Dyson's only reply was to laugh softly, then rub first one, then the other of Patti's shapely feet against his penis. If Patti truly objected to the way she was being treated, Natalie knew that he was almost inviting her to kick out and hurt him, but instead she ran her bare toes to and fro over his length.

'I want you, Dyson,' murmured Patti, in a more coaxing tone this time, as she swept the sole of her foot slowly up and down his erection. 'I want *this*,' she said, as he released her ankles and she was able to hold his shaft lightly between both her caressing feet.

'You certainly want something,' replied Dyson, reaching behind him, as if searching among the rumpled bedding for some object that Natalie had not yet seen. He seemed, for the moment, almost indifferent to Patti's attempts to pleasure him, and oblivious to his own aroused state. His erection stood proudly out in front of him, impressive by any standards, yet he barely looked at it. Natalie could not imagine the average man being so detached. They were mostly extraordinarily proud of their equipment, even when it was only deeply average!

Still searching, Dyson turned away from Patti, casually brushing her off as he did so. She made a small sound of irritation, but he ignored it, retreating slightly so she could no longer reach him.

'Ah, here we are,' he said after a moment, bringing

out the object of his search – a chunky cylinder about eight inches long, fashioned from what looked like flesh-coloured rubber and very thoughtfully shaped.

Yowsah, it's a dildo! thought Natalie, unable to stop herself from grinning. A sex toy. A faux penis. Perhaps even a vibrator?

It wasn't that she'd never seen such a thing before: she'd seen plenty and she even had one tucked away in her luggage somewhere. But it was much more exotic to see one in this particular context. Was it Patti's own toy, or had Dyson brought it with him, hidden in his bucket?

At this thought, Natalie had to forget her sex for a moment and clap both hands over her mouth to keep herself from giggling. Happily, Patti and Dyson remained completely self-absorbed.

'How about this?' said Dyson softly, moving around so that he was to the side of Patti, and his genitalia were out of her reach. He laid the dildo gently into her cleavage, nestling it into the V between her inadequately covered breasts, and then he began to move it back and forth in a simulated fucking action.

Patti groaned. Just as plaintively as if it were a real penis sliding between her breasts. Natalie saw her sister's eyelids flutter, and watched her begin to writhe again, and marvelled at how deeply Patti seemed to be able to throw herself into her fantasy. It was a skill that Natalie wasn't really sure that she herself possessed. She was normally too much of a control freak to really, really let go.

Pausing for a moment, Dyson laid aside the dildo, and put both hands on the top of Patti's bodice. In a swift, quite brutal gesture, he ripped the lace right down the front and laid bare Patti's breasts, her midriff and her rounded belly. She was completely exposed now, the scraps of fabric that clung to her no longer offering even the slightest bit of protection. Not that they'd probably ever done that anyway.

Patti groaned again, then opened her eyes. For a moment, her expression seemed to clear and sharpen. 'I'll never forgive you for this, you know!' she said, sounding petulant. 'That was my best teddy, you selfish little bastard!'

'Oh, don't complain so,' said Dyson, reaching for the sex toy again. 'I'll buy you another.'

Patti gave him a look of fleeting disdain – which seemed to suggest that Dyson's looks might be his principal asset, and that there wasn't a big income to be made from window cleaning – then closed her eyes again, slipping instantly back into her fantasy.

Cupping one large breast, Dyson applied the tip of the dildo to its nipple. He circled the teat slowly with the rubber monster, manipulating the rosy flesh until it looked so puckered and engorged that Natalie imagined it must be almost painful. Feeling a wave of empathy, she cupped her own breast, and found the nipple tumescent beneath her bra and her jersey top. The sensation, when she touched it, was breathtaking, and, as she closed her finger and thumb on her tender little teat, her knees went dangerously weak. A moan escaped her lips, but luckily it didn't matter. Patti's moans were easily loud enough to drown it.

'Oh Dyson ... Oh Dyson ... Yes!' she exclaimed, moving her lower body about on the bed while her young tormentor continued to tantalise her breasts. He was switching from one to the other now, each time holding the breast on which he was working quite hard. Natalie could see his fingers digging into the pale, opalescent flesh, and see reddened marks left by the pressure. The more he preyed on Patti, the more exciting it was to watch, and, to her astonishment, Natalie found herself unable to resist massaging at her crotch through her skirt. For a moment, she tried to imagine what *she* must look like this time – standing on her sister's landing, fondling her own tit and squeezing and massaging herself helplessly. The inner vision was such a turn-on that she had to bite her lip again at the immediate surge of pleasure.

Back on the bed, Dyson was changing his tactics.

Abandoning Patti's breasts, he held the dildo to her lips, forcing her to let it into her mouth.

'Suck it, Patsy,' he murmured, putting his face close to Patti's and making it difficult for Natalie to see their expressions. Not that she needed to. Her mind supplied the details.

'That's it, Patsy, take it in ... Suck it. Lick it. Do it properly.'

He appeared to kiss Patti then, pressing his lips to the corner of her mouth, right up against the rubber. 'Make it wet,' he went on, kissing her again, pressing a tiny peck to her cheeks and her brow. 'Make it really wet ... because you know where it's going next, don't you?'

With this, he released his hold on the dildo, forcing Patti to hold it with her lips. Her cheeks tautened with the strain as he ran his hands possessively down her body, lingering momentarily to maul her breasts a little, then moving on and down comprehensively until he reached her ankles. These he took hold of, then pulled wide apart.

Patti struggled, her eyes huge and rounded, her lips and cheeks working and twitching with the effort of holding the dildo in her mouth.

'There, stay like that,' he said, quite harshly, then he bent close again, and whispered in Patti's ear. Natalie couldn't hear what he was saying, and the possibilities were as frustrating as anything she'd experienced so far today. She could only imagine the obscenities he was suggesting. And surely they were pretty fancy ones – because Patti's eyes bulged, she gobbled uncouthly, and her bare hips lifted.

After a couple of minutes, and in a sudden, startling whirl of motion, Dyson straightened up, plucked the dildo from Patti's mouth – and then, without warning or ceremony, pushed it smoothly into her cunt while pressing his thumb against her clitoris.

Natalie could not have said, afterwards, who she would have deemed to be more shocked in that moment: Patti, who screeched, bucked upwards from the bed, her whole body jack-knifing in an intense and very graphic orgasm; or herself, as she buckled over, fist crammed in mouth, hand working furiously to rub her twitching, throbbing clit. The last thing she pictured clearly was a triumphant, laughing Dyson, pumping hard, prick in hand, his glans directed fairly and squarely at Patti's parted lips.

Of the three of them, Natalie was relieved that she was the first to recover. Hardly daring to breathe, she crept back down the stairs, listening as the moans and groans and creaks from the bed began again.

Way to go, sis! she thought, somewhat reluctantly, realising that a lot of her preconceived ideas about Patti and her sex life had just been shattered.

Patti had always been the quiet one, the slightly reserved one, the one who never much seemed to like the word 'fuck', much less the act itself. But that had changed now, clearly. Sister Patti loved fucking and a damn sight more!

Some other things were just the same, though, and Natalie was glad of that. When she carefully pushed open the door to the sitting room and went inside, she found that the usual bottles of drink stood on a small silver tray on the sideboard. Without stopping to look around, she walked straight across, poured herself a good slug of whisky and drank half of it.

'Jesus Christ!' she murmured, vaguely registering that it was a decent Scotch, not the supermarket blend Patti had foisted on her during her last visit.

Still half turned on, Natalie slumped into an armchair.

Today was the maddest day of a life that was generally not uneventful.

This is all crazy, she thought, closing her eyes for a moment. She knew she'd run away from London with her ideas for an important story only half cocked, but now she'd got here – in fact even before she'd got here – she'd found that the tight-arsed university city of Redwych had suddenly turned into a hotbed of lust and depravity. She wondered if Daumery had some dirty sexual secrets too, in addition to the financial sleaze she sensed was there.

But he looked so clean-cut, so wholesome in a handsome, older-man type of way. She could imagine him as the distinguished one with slightly greying hair in a shaving-gel commercial. She couldn't really picture him playing with dildoes and tying up his beautifully groomed lady wife.

Natalie opened her eyes and looked around, seeking something normal to get her mind back to its focused, analytical centre.

Patti's sitting room was as untidy as ever, although in a slightly new and interesting way. There was evidence everywhere of this famous business of hers, the home dressmaking service she'd told Natalie about, and which Natalie had admitted to being unimpressed by. There was a complicated-looking sewing machine at one end of the dining table, and the rest of the space was covered with fabric swatches, badly folded patterns in bulging paper packets and other paraphernalia. Quite a lot of what looked like finished garments were laid over the backs of chairs, and hanging on a free-standing rail.

'My God!' murmured Natalie, getting up and walking across to take a closer look at one particular item that had caught her eye. Who the hell was Patti sewing for? A pantomime dame? Or just an extraordinarily large woman with a rather flashy dress sense?

She picked up what appeared to be a cocktail dress.

It was long, with a fairly full skirt and a high, almost crew-type neck. The silky fabric was a vibrant royal-blue colour, shot through with an iridescent aquamarine thread.

Not exactly understated, Natalie thought, holding the bizarre garment close to her face to investigate the distinct whiff of perfume that rose from it. The scent was sharply exotic and spicy, an unsubtle pile-driver of a perfume that was so strong it almost caught in her throat. Unexpectedly, as she breathed more of it in, it turned her on.

'Gorgeous, isn't it?' said a familiar voice, just behind her, and Natalie dropped the blue dress and spun around.

Patti stood in the doorway, smiling a smug, creamy smile that Natalie had never seen before, and wearing a pink silk kimono that was just as unfamiliar. Natalie was used to seeing her in something shapeless made of towelling.

Natalie shrugged and moved forward to meet Patti, who also advanced. They hugged awkwardly, and Natalie reflected for a second how difficult it had always been to be physically comfortable with Patti. She always felt as if she had to hold back, and not be *too* loving.

'It's ... different,' she said, returning to the subject of the dress as they drew apart. Anything to distract her from the fact that Patti was clearly naked under her beautiful robe, her curvy body still warm and glowing from the attentions of her friend the window cleaner. Natalie was just wondering where the energetic and imaginative Dyson was, when she heard a vehicle start up outside, obviously his van.

Almost biting her tongue to keep from asking the burning questions, Natalie brushed her fingers over the rich, silvery blue cloth of the oversized gown. 'My God, Patti, who the hell are you making this for? A drag queen?'

There was a pause – in which Patti smiled broadly and pushed her tousled honey-brown hair back behind her ears. The action made the pink kimono gape and Natalie caught a flash of her sister's right nipple.

'Actually, yes,' Patti said at length. 'All these clothes *are* for a drag queen. His – or should I say her? – name is Stella and she's my best customer.'

'Far out! How the devil did you get hooked up with someone like that?' Natalie felt genuinely curious, genuinely mystified. It had been an age since she'd spent any length of time back here in Redwych, but it seemed the last place on earth to support a drag scene – and, even then, Patti was the last person whom Natalie would have expected to be involved in it.

'She . . . *he* answered my ad in the paper. She wanted some new costumes and, as they're not exactly the sort of thing that you can get in M&S or Next, she asked me to make the dresses up to her specifications,' Patti said, with a shrug of her shoulders that made her breast bounce in their silk containment. Clearly looking to change the subject, she nodded at Natalie's whisky glass. 'I see you've started without me, but would you like a top-up?'

Natalie nodded, and Patti did the honours, pouring a generous drink for herself, too. Another first, as Natalie had rarely ever seen her sister drink before nightfall.

The next few minutes were prickly. The two of them exchanged the stock questions that always passed between two siblings who hadn't seen each other for a while. Natalie felt gradually more and more irritated with Patti, as it was clearly she who was the one more at ease with the situation.

I should be the cool one, Natalie thought. I live in London. I've got the career and the social infrastructure. And here she is, lounging around wearing next to nothing, after having just had wild kinky sex . . . Goddammit, I can still smell that randy window cleaner on her!

In the end, Natalie had had enough.

'Patti, who the hell is that man you were just fucking?'

'I beg your pardon?' Unfazed, Patti laughed as she answered Natalie's question with one of her own.

'The guy who just drove off. The one who came from upstairs. The one you had sex with!' To her horror, Natalie felt herself blushing and she felt hot and sweaty in her black city jacket.

'How on Earth did you know I'd had sex with him?'

Oh fuck! There was only one way to know that – which meant that Natalie would have to own up to having watched them.

'I heard you shouting. It sounded like sex to me.'

'He could have been attacking me. Trying to murder me.' Patti was grinning from ear to ear now, and Natalie felt like slapping her one, just as she'd frequently done when they'd been children fighting over shared possessions. 'If you heard me shouting, why didn't you come up and try to help me fight him off?'

'Don't talk bollocks, Patti, I know what sex sounds like. I have had cause to shout a bit myself in my time.'

A vision of the toilet on the train flashed before her eyes for a moment. Steven Small's tortured face, twisting in silent ecstasy as he climaxed; her own face, seen in the cracked mirror, her features as contorted by pleasure as his, her fist stuffed in her mouth to stop herself from yelling and cursing as she came.

'You watched us, didn't you?' Patti challenged, getting up to top up their glasses. 'You snuck up the stairs and watched Dyson and me having sex . . .'

'Of course I didn't!' Natalie felt even more furious now, and even hotter. She felt hornier, too, catching sight of Patti's pubes as the glorious kimono fluttered and floated. 'What the hell sort of person do you think I am?'

'An investigative journalist, sis, that's what I *know*

you are,' said Patti smugly, sitting down, and briefly flashing Natalie again as she rearranged the silk robe. 'But it won't do you any good this time. Dyson isn't anyone famous: he's just my lodger. Oh, and he cleans my windows, which is how I came to meet him.'

'Fuck you, Patti,' said Natalie grimly, swigging at her drink and nearly choking on it in the process.

Patti said nothing, but then she'd won. She didn't need to speak.

For a few moments, neither of them said anything, but eventually Natalie broke the ice.

'God, I'm knackered! And I don't know why. Back in the Smoke I'm rushing around all over the place, doing a thousand things at once, working till all hours. And all I've done today is sit on my backside on a train.'

It wasn't strictly true, but, in spite of Patti suddenly making her sex life an open book, Natalie didn't feel like making any true confessions of her own just yet.

'Travelling is always tiring,' said Patti mildly. 'Would you like something to eat?' She strode towards the door and the kimono floated dangerously again. 'Or did you have something on the train?'

What the hell does she know?

Natalie felt a sudden surge of alarm. Patti was grinning again, and it was a strangely knowing grin, as if she were privy to what had happened in that cramped toilet cubicle. And yet how could she? It was impossible.

Stop being paranoid, Natalie told herself, then she said to Patti, 'No, I haven't had anything to eat since breakfast.' She got up and tried to smile as normally as she could at her sister. 'Don't go to any trouble though, Patts: I'll have a sandwich or something. Whatever you've got. I'll come and help you.'

Looking forward to doing something really mundane for a change, like buttering bread and making tea, Natalie followed the trailing wake of Patti's kimono down the passage into the kitchen.

'When did you get your cat?' she asked, remembering her unexpected feline welcomer.

Later, when Patti had gone out and left her with only Ozzy, the cat, for company, Natalie began to wish that she'd tagged along. Patti had urged her to, but beneath the offer Natalie had sensed some diffidence. As if her sister was looking forward to something that she was protective of, something that she didn't want Natalie to share.

Natalie's suspicions had been further roused when Patti had taken a phone call. A mobile had rung and Patti had plucked it from among her sewing gear, excused herself awkwardly and disappeared.

Natalie had been curious as to why her sister had needed a mobile phone, but she supposed it was to contact her dressmaking clients when she was out and about. Although, in that case, why the sudden, exaggerated need for secrecy?

Natalie had got another shock when she saw how Patti had dressed to go out.

The word 'hooker' had immediately sprung to mind. Patti had been wearing clothes Natalie had never seen before, and had never ever expected to see. Since when had her cautious, modest sister – who had never previously worn anything that was likely to draw undue attention to herself – suddenly started wearing high, black patent court shoes, thigh-skimming leather mini-skirts and tight cotton bodices that clung to her generous breasts?

When Natalie had expressed astonishment, Patti had merely said, 'I just got fed up of being a frump. I fancied a new look.' Sliding her arms into a leather jacket – another innovation – she'd given Natalie a peck on the cheek and left her to her own devices.

And she's got a new life, too, thought Natalie now, remembering the expression on Patti's face as she'd left.

Her sister had been aglow, nervous yet excited, her eyes bright, her cheeks flushed. She's definitely up to something, Natalie decided, shaking her head and feeling hideously old maidish.

High heels. Nights out. A lover. Patti's world's changed, it seems, in every way possible. And mine's still the same, except for one instance of fucking a stranger on a train.

Natalie ate quickly, fed Ozzy, who was clearly an opportunist and had latched on to her as another source of cat food, then retired to the bedroom she always stayed in. She didn't want to run into the other new resident – Dyson, the window-cleaning lodger – and, as Patti had said nothing of his possible whereabouts, nor mentioned any timetable of his comings and goings, there was no knowing when he would turn up and make life embarrassing.

I wonder if they talked about me, Natalie thought as she flicked with little interest through the channels on the small portable television in her room. Did she tell him, before he left, that she suspected I'd already arrived and that I'd been watching them? The possibilities were appalling yet in a sick way quite exciting. Dyson had looked delicious, and eminently fuckable. And primed by Steven Small, on the train, she now felt hungrier for more and more sex than she'd done in a long time.

Aware of the nagging ache of lust, Natalie imagined Patti and Dyson giggling together as they touched each other. They would laugh because they were screwing and having fun, and she was in the house, knowing that they were screwing and having fun. Knowing that she could hear them. Even see them. There was no way to divine whether she'd managed to convince Patti that she hadn't seen them. After that first confrontation, it seemed the subject was firmly closed. Goddamn it!

Leave it alone, Nat, she told herself, snapping off the undiverting television. You're here to do a job, not speculate on either Patti's sex life or your own.

Dragging her laptop out of her luggage, Natalie made a few notes on her proposed project, then hooked the machine up to the unused phone jack in the corner of the room. After one or two abortive attempts, she finally managed to log on to a free Internet provider and send a few emails to her most useful contacts. In the oblique terms that journalists often employed, she sent out requests for more background information on Whitelaw Daumery, in order to supplement the meagre dossier she'd already assembled. For such a high-profile figure, there was surprisingly little in the public domain about his personal life. A web search yielded very little more, but Natalie had to admit, it had been a half-hearted attempt, and she could have found much more if she'd really committed herself to delving deep. Despite her earlier resolutions, it was still proving hard not to be distracted by thoughts of sex.

When she'd shut down the computer and was putting it away, she heard a sound downstairs. For a moment she panicked, then realised it was someone putting a key in the lock, not a burglar or a mugger or some other intruder. The solid footsteps on the stairs told her it was Dyson, who'd come home, and not Patti; but after listening, and almost holding her breath so as not to attract his attention, Natalie heard the young man go out again, not long after, and the door slam.

Is he going to meet her? Natalie thought, throwing herself back on to the bed, her limbs restless and any tiredness she'd felt earlier dissipating. The nagging, undeniable demon of sex had roused again and her fingers almost itched with the need to masturbate.

Snapping off the bedside lamp, she lay in the darkness, allowing her imagination to go its merry way. She had no idea where her sister might have gone, but in

her imagination she saw her in some narrow passage-
way, such as existed in the old, academic part of the
town. Patti was leaning with her back against the weath-
ered stone wall of one of the venerable buildings that
the tourists admired so much, and she was clearly
waiting for a lover, and racked with the same desire
that Natalie felt. As Natalie pushed her hands into the
trousers of her pyjamas, Patti braced her back against
the wall, raised one long, slender leg, and clasped a
hand to her own crotch.

While Natalie massaged her clit, she imagined Patti
doing much the same, only less directly. In the fantasy
her sister was massaging herself, but through the leather
of her skirt. She was touching her breast, too, fingers
plucking at a nipple through her thin cotton top.

'Oh, God,' murmured Natalie absently, shimmying
further down the bed, and opening her legs wider. In
the alley of her mind, Patti widened her stance, too,
moaning quietly as not one, but two figures advanced
on her through the gloom. From the right came handsome Dyson, clad in his leather jacket and jeans, and
from the left – holy shit! – came the mysterious, confused and confusing Steven Small, wearing the long
black overcoat he'd been wearing when Natalie had first
seen him on the railway platform.

Oh Teacher, what a nice surprise, she thought dream-
ily, wriggling her bottom as a new jolt of pleasure
skittered through her. The appearance of the shy academic in her fantasy had upped the ante somehow.
Unexpectedly boosted the fun of it. She groaned loudly
and an orgasm took her completely by storm, dashing
out of the shadows as the simulacrum of Steven Small
darted forward, his diffidence forgotten, and ripped
open the flimsy cotton top worn by her fantasy alter ego
Patti . . .

As her cunt grabbed thin air, Natalie almost fancied
she could feel his teeth on her nipple.

Chapter Four
The Inquisition

*I*t wasn't a location she'd ever been summoned to before.

The grimy old warehouse was deserted and even in daytime, in the sunshine, it would have been an eyesore. But now, at night, and glistening with rain from a sudden, unexpected downpour, it was downright menacing. Patti shuddered and pulled her jacket closer around her as she approached, over uneven ground, what looked as if it might be the entrance.

'Good luck,' Ruth had said as she'd hung out of the taxi window. 'And have fun!'

Fun!

It was all right for that taxi-driving dyke to tell her to have fun, thought Patti, feeling sweat break out in her armpits and her groin, despite the sodden summer chill. She's not the one who usually gets herself into these situations. She's not the one who's going to have to face the inquisition.

And it will be that, Patti admitted to herself, pushing open a large, heavy door that was only just clinging on to its hinges. She'd told a white lie to Stella – well, a slightly greyish one – and now she would be questioned as to her motives as well as being taken to task for her various transgressions. The transvestite's throaty laugh, and the tone of 'her' words on the phone, had told Patti in no uncertain terms that what lay ahead of her would be gruelling, and, while her heart was pounding, in her gut she could hardly wait.

The footing was rough inside the warehouse, as well as outside. Abandoned machinery, small and large, cluttered the high echoing expanse of what might once have been a huge workshop, and what hadn't been left as useless had been torn out, leaving great, uneven areas of concrete floor like gaping dirty grey wounds. There was very little illumination in the place other than scattered shafts of it that filtered in through broken windows high up in the walls. It came from the arc lighting that still lit the old industrial estate, and within the building it made the hanging chains of abandoned hoists glisten.

A small 'snick' sound made the hairs on the back of Patti's neck stand up and her cunt tingle as if she'd been goosed by some phantom hand. She peered into deeper shadow at the far end of the workshop, and saw the tiny glow of a cigarette's tip in the darkness.

Or is it a cigar? Cigarillo? Whatever? she thought, conscious of seeking even the smallest distraction. Patti thought of the times that she'd seen the person who was waiting for her smoking. Making elegant, undeniably sexy gestures with those thin, long, aromatic tubes, which were probably equally as deadly as the more common-or-garden brands of fags, if not more so. Either way, it was a sure sign that the smoker was either excited or wound up, or often both.

'Good evening, Patti,' said a familiar voice, its owner still swathed in the dark. There was a faint disturbance in the blackness, though, the impression of movement, of a lighter being secreted in a pocket.

'Good evening, Stella,' replied Patti as boldly as she

could under the circumstances. She'd told that lie and now she had to pay for it. The lie had been small, really, nothing more than a fib, but with Stella just a tissue of an excuse would do.

There was a heavy rustle in the darkness, and, although she couldn't see it, Patti sensed a smile on the beautifully made-up face of her nemesis. Stella was in that mood tonight, Patti could tell. It made her both shit-scared and almost breathless with desire. The fear and the lust rushed through her veins, with her blood, like a venom. Her knees felt wobbly and she had to swallow again and again to ease her dry mouth.

'Is that all you have to say for yourself?' enquired Stella, as the shadows acquired form, and – high heels clicking loudly on the concrete – the transvestite moved forward and became visible.

Patti got just a glimpse of some kind of long black garment before she remembered to drop her eyes reverently. She was in the wrong; it was no use compounding her errors with insolence. Well, not today . . .

'I – I don't know what you mean . . .'

'Oh, I think you do,' replied Stella, prowling now, and beating out an ominous staccato rhythm with her heels. Patti wondered for a moment how the tall woman managed to walk so confidently, in what were probably four-, possibly four-and-a-half-inch stilettos, on the warehouse's rough, damaged footing. She'd found it ankle-twistingly difficult herself, and she was a real woman, born to a life of high heels and generally unsuitable footwear.

'Yes, sweet Patti, you do know what I mean,' said Stella, not waiting for an answer. Out of the corner of her eye, Patti saw the thin cigar go spinning away, barely smoked, and the next moment she was looking directly into Stella's eyes, her chin held firmly in a grip that few women could have imposed.

'Is it . . . um . . . still that business about Natalie?' she offered, dazzled by the face that filled her vision.

Stella Fontayne could not have been described as classically beautiful, but her ambiguous face wore a mask of glamour that made notions of conventional feminine good looks redundant. There was no way, in a million years, that she could have passed for a real woman, but she was a spectacularly handsome transvestite. Her make-up was flawless, vivid and boldly stated, yet by no means a caricature, and Patti had never once, in all the times she'd seen Stella in drag, seen even the faintest trace of dark razor stubble. She knew that the transvestite was a natural blond, but, even so, she might have expected a hint of shadow.

'Of course it is,' Stella replied, releasing Patti, but still holding her, it seemed, with the force of her gaze. The huge dark-rimmed eyes that floated before her face were like lasers tearing all deception wide open. 'I thought that I impressed upon you, when we spoke, that this wasn't a matter to be taken lightly. You told me a lie, Patti, remember that. You told me an untruth when you promised nothing but the truth.' The drag queen smiled as if enjoying the judicial reference.

Patti wanted to shake her head. For a moment she was tired of games and she just wanted to say 'Forget it! You don't need this . . . Just get on with it!'

But she didn't. She could hardly think straight. Her body felt as if it were on fire, burning up with the need to get started on the dark road that lay before it. Without thinking, she brushed her hand against the front of her skirt, against her crotch, as if the fleeting pressure might bring her aching quim some ease.

'She was coming here anyway, wasn't she?' challenged Stella. 'It was nothing to do with you, was it? She hasn't come to Redwych because you asked her to at all, has she?'

It was the truth, but they'd been through all this.

Stella was just rubbing it in. The transvestite had picked up perfectly on the skewed mix of enmity and affection that existed between herself and Natalie. She wondered if Natalie herself was aware of these muddled feelings. She'd certainly never mentioned them overtly, and Patti felt that, for her own part, she had been half asleep, in so many ways, before she'd encountered Stella and then emerged from an emotional chrysalis.

'No. Not really. She's never done *anything* because I want her to,' Patti admitted, knowing it was true. She felt a brief flare of resentment, then a hot, hot feeling of joy. Oh, she'd get her own back, sometime soon, and it would be sweet!

'Oh Patti, is that so? What a pity ... I might have rewarded you if you could have persuaded her to – shall we say – *participate* in a few interesting local activities.'

Stella smiled, her fuchsia-painted mouth as much a threat as a promise, and Patti suddenly wanted to make even more outrageous claims. Like, Just touch me once and I'll bring Natalie to you. Or, Squeeze my breast, or touch my clit and I'll persuade her to walk naked before you, kneel before you, take your cock in her mouth.

But it was no use making things worse than they already were. Although 'worse' wasn't the right word here. What lay ahead would be all the 'better' the greater her transgression was. And this kind of better was something of which Natalie had no comprehension – in spite of her cleverness and her worldly, city veneer.

'She might participate anyway,' Patti said, the choking excitement in her throat taking all the weight from her words. It sounded as if she were whispering, panting, just breathing heavily like some bitch on heat. 'Just because she thinks she's missing something. She's like that. She can't bear it if I'm getting something that she isn't.'

Stella turned and walked away for a moment, and

Patti got a better look at her. The transvestite wore a long, black leather coat that rustled evocatively where it swung from a tightly cinched waist. A black oversized beret crowned her dark-red wig. Patti had been right about the shoes, too. Towering heels made Stella's calves look as sleek and hard as a dancer's, and her dark nylons gleamed like sharkskin where the stray light caught them. On her long, narrow hands, she wore black leather gloves.

'And do you think you'll be getting something?'

Stella's voice had a purposeful quality. There was something deep and rich and genuine about it, in spite of the hints of camp and burlesque. As always, she was playing her part with total conviction. It was still a game, but, in another sense, quite real.

'I don't know. It's not up to me, is it?'

Patti shivered, wondering if she'd gone too far, but Stella laughed again.

'No, my sweet, it isn't.' She came closer again. Just as Patti had prayed for her to do, she cupped Patti's breast and squeezed it. 'It's up to me, Patti, my love. And I do think you should "get something" . . . I think you should get quite a lot. You need to be taught a lesson for telling me such outrageous lies.'

Swaying forward, Patti tried to press her aching nipple into Stella's gloved palm.

'Oh no, no, no!' exclaimed the transvestite, pulling back. 'No treats for you just yet, my sweet. Not after being such a bad, bad girl. You have to perform for me first, before you get your jollies.'

Perform? For 'me'?

Patti felt a fluttering between her legs, and a perceptible rush of moisture dampen her knickers. She looked around. Stella had said 'for me' but, within the games they played, a 'performance' usually implied an extended audience.

Where were they, these people who took their

pleasure in watching her suffer? These men and women she didn't know, but to whom she so often bared her all?

As if the thought summoned the substance, there was a sound – a heavy, multiple, crunching tread – and two figures appeared in the doorway. Menacing in the low light, they came forward, walking carefully but with purpose, and, as they came fully into view, Patti gasped.

The sight of men wearing full-face leather hoods wasn't new to her – in fact on nights like this it was almost commonplace – but, each time she saw it, the shock resurfaced. Anonymity was the watchword at these little gatherings, and almost the only person who was never masked was Stella Fontayne. Even Patti herself had had occasion to don the threatening leather headgear, when she had been on the administering side of the equation, but the glamorous transvestite, their leader, never hid herself behind anything more than a purely ornamental eye mask.

I suppose it's because 'her' entire existence as Stella is a mask, Patti thought fleetingly as more figures – some well dressed, others scruffier, but most of them hooded – appeared and made the echoing area seem crowded. The bigger the audience, the greater was the intensity of the experience. Patti felt almost nauseous, the yearning was now so powerful.

There was no way she would be allowed to touch herself until one of her Inquisitors indicated that he – or perhaps she – wanted her to. But that only made her cunt ache more heavily. The crotch of her panties was soaking now, and her swollen labia slipped and rubbed against the wet cloth as she adjusted her footing slightly to try to get some ease.

A soft 'tut-tutting' sound indicated that Stella had seen the way she'd moved, and disapproved of it.

'What did I tell you?' the transvestite asked quietly. She nodded, indicating that Patti could answer her.

'No pleasure until after I've performed,' she said, forcing out the words because her mouth had gone suddenly dry, as all moisture in her was draining towards other areas.

'Quite so.' Stella inclined her head, and listened to a whispered comment from one of the newcomers. Sometimes, the other Inquisitors never spoke at all during these encounters, as if the choreography were all pre-planned. At other times, they all spoke up, directing the action. But mostly it fell to Stella to be the spokeswoman.

'Put your hands on the top of your head, my dear.' Stella was obviously conveying the suggestion of the man who'd murmured something in her ear. The man – a fairly well-dressed individual of solid build – leaned forward again, and offered some new ideas that were apparently so ingenious they made Stella smile beatifically. 'Oh, that's nice . . .' she purred, and the well-dressed man moved forward.

A waft of strong cologne almost made Patti feel dizzy, but it was the sensation of being manhandled that most affected her equilibrium. Her new master took hold of her hands for a moment, removing them from their position on top of her head just long enough to take off her leather jacket. This he flung to the dirty floor of the warehouse, before attacking her cotton top and ripping it open without unfastening it. Patti wanted to protest, but she knew it was forbidden.

When her top was hanging torn and open, the man then tackled her bra. This he wrenched down, and wedged underneath her breasts, making the elastic cut cruelly into her and force them upwards into graphic prominence. Although she wasn't supposed to, Patti moaned with pleasure at the sensation of being displayed and used so carelessly in front of others.

For the next two or three minutes, the man who had ruined her top played with her breasts. He pinched her nipples, pulled them around, then cupped the flesh of her breasts and jammed them upwards, rubbing the individual mounds against each other in rough circles. Then he crouched down and took one nipple in his mouth, subjecting it to fierce, sustained suction while he rolled its twin between a finger and thumb.

Patti couldn't help herself. She gasped and sobbed, spreading her thighs a little and moving her hips. Her cunt grew more heavy and ponderous with every suck and tweak; it seemed to be gaping down there, a mile-wide chasm beneath her skirt.

'Oh, please,' she whispered, her pussy melting and fluttering. She closed her eyes to conceal her consuming shame and hunger. It was a pointless gesture because her moving body betrayed her.

'Enough, I think, my friend,' said Stella, taking the man by the shoulder and pulling him away from Patti. 'Can't you see that the little slut is enjoying herself too much?'

Without the man pressed against her, and supporting her, Patti swayed. A couple of the others moved to either side of her and held her by the shoulders, their fingers gripping her hard as they kept her on her feet. One of them reached across, and, against Stella's instructions, fondled her tit again. The transvestite didn't caution him, but her eyes grew narrow, warning, and the handling ceased.

'Test her, somebody,' Stella said after a moment, the words deceptively soft and casual.

Patti trembled. She hated this, and yet she loved it, too. It was so demeaning to be revealed as exactly the horny little slut that Stella accused her of being. Surreptitiously, she parted her legs and scrunched her eyes even more tightly shut.

A rough hand fished around under her skirt and pushed it up to lodge around her waist. The same hand then took hold of her thin panties and literally tore them off her. She felt the burn of the fabric as it abraded her buttocks momentarily, then cold air against her moist pubes. She imagined steam, from its heat, revealing her state.

Footsteps told her that the ruined knickers were then carried to Stella, and she imagined the transvestite inspecting their sodden gusset, then inhaling their tell-tale odour.

A softly breathed 'Oh, yes . . .' only confirmed her supposition.

But, if she'd thought her willingness would win her any clemency, she soon realised she was entirely mistaken. The hands that held her seemed to pinch her all the more cruelly, the fingers digging into her skin. Just as she was about to protest, she felt herself dragged along as if in response to some unseen visual direction of Stella's. A few seconds later, she was pushed unceremoniously face down against a bench of some kind. She could just imagine how her naked bottom was raised and prominent. It wasn't a big one, but, uplifted and presented like this, it seemed an enormous target.

She wondered what they would aim at it.

There was a long, long pause in which she lay there, ignominiously displayed, her cunt weeping and her bare breasts pressed against the cold, rough, gritty surface of the bench. It took her all the self-control she possessed not to groan out loud, or demand that someone touch her.

Presently, it seemed her prayers were going to be answered.

'Would someone like a go at her before we start?' Stella asked conversationally. 'It seems a shame to waste all that heat and juice.'

For a moment, Patti felt herself transported back to another scenario, some weeks ago.

Faced with a similar question, she'd squatted over the face of a man bound face upwards against a table, waiting to have his thighs whipped and his penis tormented. She could still feel the energy of his tongue as he'd licked her to orgasm, his enthusiasm unaffected by thoughts of the ordeal that had lain ahead of him. He'd slurped and lapped at her as if she'd been his first meal after a fortnight of starvation.

Hands on her bottom brought her winging back to the here and now. Someone was pulling her buttocks apart, and this time she did cry out. She wanted a cock inside her, but not that way. It was too much, too invasive, she was still very much unused to it. The sensations were too confusing and she wasn't yet sure if she enjoyed them.

'Not there,' said Stella softly, as if reading her silent pleas. 'No buggery. Not just yet.'

Patti shuddered again, realising that she had nothing to be grateful for. There was a quality to the transvestite's voice that suggested she was merely reserving something special for herself. Pressing herself down against the bench, Patti tried to imagine the solid girth of Stella's cock forging its inexorable, inevitable way inside her bottom.

'Oh, no,' she gasped, appalled that she'd actually voiced the words out loud.

'There isn't such a word as "no",' the transvestite whispered, suddenly at her side. 'Not for you, my dear, at least.' Patti felt a gloved hand slide beneath her chest and manipulate one of her nipples very lightly. At the same time her other assailant continued to maul and tug at her bottom cheeks. Maybe he wasn't being encouraged to fuck her there, but he was still determined to have his share of fun with her firm, pale flesh. She almost choked when a hard, callused finger pushed in through the ring of her anus.

The word 'no!' rose again, as a scream this time, but, abandoning her breast, Stella twisted Patti's face around to the side and kissed her on the lips. As the finger ravished her bottom, the drag queen's warm tongue explored the depths of her mouth.

Patti felt an intense orgasm begin to rise inside her, only to have it cut off agonisingly when – at some unseen and unheard signal – the kiss and the finger in her arse were both withdrawn. She was left high and dry, immolated by her own need to climax. She cried out 'No!' again. She just couldn't help it!

' "No" doesn't exist,' reiterated Stella, her voice steely now, yet still somehow humorous. 'How many more times do I have to tell you? You have no rights here, my dear. Not in these circumstances. There is nothing that we want to do to you that you can refuse us. Do you understand it?'

Patti nodded. Tears of frustration seeped out from the corners of her eyes. If they weren't going to let her come off, why didn't they just get on with it? Just lay about her bottom with whatever they were going to use to beat her? Feeling the way she did, she hoped it would be something severe, something that would make an impact – if she couldn't have pleasure, she would have pain, and as much as she could bear.

Low sounds, deliberately muffled, taunted her. They were making their preparations, but refusing to give her any hint of the type of punishment that lay ahead of her. She had no idea if they had brought their implements with them, or whether they had been secreted, here in the hellish place, well beforehand. Who could tell how carefully, and how far in advance, Stella planned things? Sometimes she set up scenarios weeks ahead of their execution; at others, people were summoned on the spur of the moment.

Even as she tried to anticipate how they might punish her, Patti was taken by surprise when a cock nudged at her sex, and, with no other preparation, pushed quickly into her. She gasped as her unknown lover thrust into her with a series of quick, inelegant jabs, stretching the mouth of her vagina with a penis that was quite short but extraordinarily wide in the girth. Aware that Stella didn't want her to climax just yet, Patti fought the pleasure, trying to analyse the quality of the flesh within her. Had she had this man before? Had she ever orgasmed on this stubby cock? Masturbated it? Sucked the semen from it?

But the effect it was having on her made it impossible to question or quantify anything. Contrary to the rules of this unspoken game, Patti disobeyed with a fingertip pressed delicately against her clit – and climaxed.

Squirming against the bench, her quim convulsing, Patti shrieked with shock when a line of pain burned across her buttocks. The man who was shafting her continued to move and thrust, but someone else – not Stella this time – had moved alongside them and applied a single, accurate cut with what felt like a willow switch, right across the crown of her bottom. As she jerked at the fire of it, her struggles and moans triggered her 'lover' into climax. She heard him grunt 'Oh, God' then grab at her hips as his own pelvis bucked.

It was all over in a second or two, and, as he withdrew, she felt his sticky cock trail sideways across her buttock.

'Anyone else?' enquired Stella, and through her inner haze Patti heard the 'snick' of the lighter again. Despite everything that made her smile inwardly, Stella must be really turned on to light up again so quickly. The transvestite might be able to project the most marvellous façade of detachment and uninterest, but, to those who knew her, the demon weed revealed her feelings.

Patti forgot these observations, however, when another voice – gruff and disguised – spoke up in claim of her. A moment later, another penis was pushing rudely into her body and, to her secret delight and smugness, a hand reached around to fondle her quim.

Stella might have decreed 'no pleasure for the slut' but not all the participants were inclined to completely obey her.

Generous though this lover's intentions were, his lust and his hair-trigger reactions got the better of him. Within seconds, he was pounding into her and coming with a great hoarse shout. His inaccurate fingers had done nothing to slake her need, and merely stoked it again, to a higher, more rarefied pitch.

Stella asked again if there were more takers, but this time Patti sensed that the members of the assembly were keen to move on. It was the more arcane pleasures that they'd really come to witness.

As she lay there, with her bare bottom presented, Patti wondered what Natalie might make of this situation. Her sister had been shocked, earlier, Patti knew that. Natalie always posed as the world-weary *cosmopolitaine* who had seen everything and done everything, but instincts honed over the years, and a knowledge of her sister's personality that Natalie would most vigorously deny, told Patti that in reality Natalie was really not all that experienced. The little scene with Dyson had actually embarrassed her, despite her claims to the contrary.

But will Nat ever get a handle on this? Patti thought, adjusting herself discreetly across the bench, widening the gape of her legs to give a better view of her sex. How could she ever convey the excitement and the vertiginous thrill of being demeaned, displayed, exposed like this? Presented as an object. A collection of flesh and orifices, of pulsing glands and fluids to be enjoyed and abused. Even examining the concept, Patti felt her cunt begin to flutter. She wanted to reach around, pull herself further open, and exultantly exhibit her sticky sex and her tight little anus. She wished again that her nice, rounded bottom were bigger and more voluptuous – offering more scope to the skilled and enthusiastic marksman.

'Shall we begin?' Stella suggested, and, after a murmur of affirmation, the beating started.

The single cut, earlier, had in no way prepared Patti for the shock of being punished. There was nothing that could prepare one for it, as every time the experience was different. It varied with the implement used – in this case willow switches seemed to have been passed around – the strength and the angle of application, and the way the recipient's body was feeling to begin with.

Beginning to groan, despite an intention not to, Patti felt that she had been well prepared for tonight's session. She'd felt quite strong, keen and up for it when she'd arrived. Gritting her teeth at a particularly sly cut that came winging in across the under-slope of her bottom, hurting horribly, she nevertheless believed that she could go on for a long time tonight, and rise up and up through the layers of pain and exposure to a new level of ultimate pleasure.

By now her bottom – and her thighs – were so tingling hot and throbbing that she could quite imagine steam rising from them in the cool night air of the warehouse. And yet with each cut, she could not help but lift herself into the next blow in order to magnify its impact. A number of times, she involuntarily reached around to clutch at her sizzling buttocks – effectively halting the proceedings – but each time she was glad when one of the participants stepped close and pulled her hands away, either roughly or with a strange, nurturing tenderness.

When at last it seemed they had finished whipping her, Patti smiled, despite the tears and spittle that streaked her face and had ruined her make-up. She had already got something that she'd wanted this evening. At least it felt that way. Her bottom was a fiery, aching mass of sore redness, and, in her perceptions, it had at least doubled in size.

Once again, she realised that she was holding herself, her fingers warmed by the heat in the flesh they were pressed against. Someone prised her hands away, and this time she realised it was not a solitary individual that had come forward, but the entire group.

The hooded, anonymous men were clustered around her now and, when she opened her eyes and turned her head, Patti saw that the ones in her field of vision had unzipped themselves and were rubbing furiously at pricks that pointed directly at her bottom. She could well imagine that all the rest of them were exposed and masturbating too.

One by one, she heard them grunt, and often swear hideously, then unleash their semen upon her. The impacts were minute, yet, even as delicate as they were, they stirred her pain. She began to moan and shift herself about, seeking her own release.

'Are you ready to come, my dear?' whispered Stella from very close by, and Patti wondered for a moment if the transvestite had her cock out too. Probably not, as she mostly liked to preserve the illusion of being a woman for as long as possible.

'Yes,' Patti gasped through clamped jaws, as another man came all over her.

'Then that's what you shall do!'

Patti sensed, rather than heard, the transvestite summon one member of the group to the fore. The others hauled her up from the bench, turned her, then sat her hard down on it, provoking a scream as her wounded buttocks were scraped against the wood. She cried out again when she was dragged forward right to the edge, and her thighs were wrenched apart and her pelvis was tilted to give access to her sex.

At a nod from Stella, the chosen one stepped forward. He was a younger man, slim and lithe, and Patti fancied she knew him despite the hood. His cock was large and he was working it slowly between long, elegant fingers that were not those of a manual labourer, as were some of the others.

'Take her,' commanded Stella and the man who was to finally service her stepped forward, adjusted himself gracefully and slid, in one neat thrust, right into her.

Patti began to gasp as pleasure gathered in her around the hub of the young man's cock, but then Stella was right by her side, and cupping her face between her leather-gloved hands.

'Come now, my dear,' the transvestite whispered, just before she pressed her mouth to Patti's.

And Patti obeyed her, just as a fingertip pressed delicately against her clit.

'So, shall I help her?'

Patti climbed painfully to her feet, wiping the last traces of semen from her lips with her fingers, then thoughtfully licking at them. She looked up at Stella, who was lounging, splay-legged, in one of the large leather chairs in the comfortable study at 'her' home in the nicest part of Redwych, but the transvestite still seemed lost in the tail end of her climax.

Noticing a tiny smudge – at last – against the corner of Stella's lipstick-covered mouth, Patti fished in the pocket of the long black coat, which they'd thrown across another chair. With the utmost reverence, she repaired the perfection of the red-painted edge, and, when she was about to draw back, she was stopped in her tracks when Stella grabbed her wrist.

Beautiful hazel eyes held Patti's gaze just as fiercely as a strong hand held her arm. Stella might well still be post-orgasmic, but, even so, her mind was as rapier-sharp as ever.

'What do you think?' she asked, her grip closing

delicately to the edge of pain, then relaxing again. 'Would you like to?'

'I – I don't know,' said Patti, feeling her own desire – which she'd thought was so drained and sated that she'd not want sex again for at least six months – begin to stir. 'It might be tricky. She's good, you know, and even without help she's bound to find something.'

Stella continued to hold her, continued to stare at her. Patti had never known anyone who could look you in the eye so steadily and so long without even a hint of a blink.

'I mean ... well ... you know Whitelaw Daumery don't you?'

Patti knew it was probably a lot, lot more than that. She suspected that Stella – who had a finger in more pies in this town than most people even knew existed – had done, or was maybe even now doing, business, perhaps far from ethically, with the so-called crusader for 'moral practice'.

But she daren't say that, of course, even though she also knew that Stella was aware that she knew!

'I can take care of myself,' said Stella at last, her eyes alight with mischief. 'And it might be fun to set your sister running and see just how far she gets.' She adjusted her grip on Patti's wrist and drew her fingers forward. 'It's no skin off my nose what happens to Daumery. The man's a pig. I'm becoming tired of him.' She drew Patti's fingers between her painted lips and began to slowly suck on them.

As Patti felt the evocative suction take effect on parts of her body other than her fingers, her knees went weak in an instant. But, even so, her mind, like Stella's, was working, and she couldn't help but speculate.

She suspected that Daumery and Stella were involved in ways other than financially. Ways that she too may be entangled in ...

Had Daumery been in the warehouse tonight? Was

he one of the leather-hooded men who'd fucked her? Sprayed her with his semen? Laid a sharp willow switch across her bottom?

It was possible. More than possible.

And wouldn't it be fun, even if it was also dangerous, to see if clever Madam Natalie could unearth *that* fact as well as any fiscal or ethical wrongdoings on Daumery's part?

She was just about to suggest this to Stella when the transvestite relinquished her fingers.

'Let's talk about your sister later, shall we?' the drag queen said as she pulled Patti inexorably down towards her lap again.

Chapter Five

A Comrade in Arms?

S he felt like a fish out of water.

Natalie had been born in this town, and lived the greater part of her early life in it, but, standing at the bus stop waiting for a bus for the first time in what must have been ten years, she suddenly felt like a stranger and an alien.

Even her clothes were wrong. It was a nicer day today, as if the rain last night had washed away the unseasonably cool weather. The less well-heeled tourists and the students who seemed to predominate, even out here in the suburbs, were all dressed as if they'd just landed in Ibiza. Natalie felt that her black jeans, zippered cotton jacket and sleeveless top were far too smart and structured, even though to her they were casual. Everyone else was in a vest, lurid shorts – baggy or cycling – and a baseball cap. There was also a horrid proliferation of flip-flops!

'This is mad!' she muttered, reaching into her bag and fingering her mobile phone. The temptation to phone the taxi firm she'd used yesterday – Butch Ruth's Sapphic Taxis or whatever – was really tempting. But, much as it galled her, the fact was she wasn't on a *Modern*

Enquirer expense account on this jaunt. This was a wild-goose chase entirely of her own devising, and she was reliant solely on her own funds and resources. London living had left her nothing to squirrel away, and, for the first time in years, she was genuinely hard up and there was no money to spare to pay for cabs.

'You're the bloody journalist – find it out for yourself!'

Patti's words, from over breakfast, still echoed ominously in Natalie's ears. She had asked Patti if she knew anything about Whitelaw Daumery and her sister's reply had been not only grumpy but also peculiarly facetious somehow. Natalie had experienced a strong urge to pitch in and have a real go at Patti on a variety of fronts, but she knew it wouldn't do to alienate her sister while she was relying on her for free board and lodgings.

'Fuck this for a game of soldiers!' muttered Natalie, rather louder than she'd intended, as she made an executive decision to walk into the city centre rather than hang around festering while she waited for a bus. A couple of pastel-clad old ladies, also waiting, gave her an outraged look, but, used to the hard face of London hostility, Natalie ignored them. She began striding out purposefully towards the nucleus of civic and academic buildings that were clearly visible, nestling in the natural hollow in which Redwych had first been established. She was glad now that she'd put some flat shoes on. It shouldn't take too long, and the going was downhill.

After a while, Natalie almost began to enjoy herself. It was a great day, a cliché of blue skies and high fluffy clouds, and, despite the uncertainty of her situation, she felt free and light and fresh, somehow, for the first time in ages! In an act of liberation, she reached up and pulled out the little covered band that held her ponytail in place, then shook her head to loosen the residual tension in her scalp. Fluffing her hair with her fingers, she knew she should be running her mind over the facts she'd already gleaned about Daumery, and beginning to form an angle for her story, but, when she slipped on her shades against the warm, morning sun, she really felt as if she was all of a sudden on holiday.

What would make this really choice, she thought, after a while, would be to have a man on hand, too. A leisurely walk, a boozy lunch, then back to a hotel, or maybe his place, for sex in the afternoon. Maybe something a bit kinky? Patti wasn't the only one who was allowed to spread her sexual wings.

Dismissing thoughts of her sister and the infuriating mood that Patti had been in this morning, Natalie easily summoned up the face of Steven Small again. And his unexpectedly splendid body!

Every time she thought of her escapade on the train, Natalie could still hardly believe what she'd done. And yet it *had* happened, and her reluctant stud was somewhere in this town and, amazingly enough after his performance yesterday, presumably tutoring the young of Redwych in the ways of righteousness.

And English literature, if his books had been anything to go by.

It should be easy enough to find him – she was a journalist after all; rooting out information was what she did every day. He was probably even there listed in the bloody phone book, for Christ's sake. If she wanted more of him, all she had to do was get in touch and take her fill!

And maybe she would do just that. But first she had another man to meet.

Before too long, and against her expectations of her own stamina, Natalie found herself entering the venerable collegiate part of the town, with distinguished and hallowed architecture all around her. Despite her intention not to be seduced by it, she found herself goggling around like the most naïve of Japanese tourists, drinking

in all the history and tradition and downright quaint-
ness of the city she'd been brought up in. It was a
beautiful place, she had to admit, and admiring it, as
she did now, she could almost feel sympathy for those
elite factions who got so upset because Redwych always
fell just a whisker short of Oxford and Cambridge in
terms of prestige.

The offices of the *Redwych Sentinel* were in the main
business and shopping thoroughfare, and it was only as
Natalie mounted the steps and pushed open the stiff old
double door that she began to have doubts about her
welcome. As a member of the public, she supposed she
would be admitted if she had some legitimate entrée,
such as an interview, or maybe to place a small ad or
order a photograph. But if any of the news staff discovered she was an employee – albeit precariously – of
an elitist metropolitan current-affairs magazine, she may
be told to shove it in no uncertain terms. She could just
imagine the choice journalistic epiphets. 'Stuck-up London bitch' was the very mildest she could expect.

So the best course of action seemed to be to present
herself as a friend of Alex Hendry – whose byline
covered the local entertainment scene, environmental
issues, and probably the births and obituaries column
for all she knew. He must be a cub reporter, from out of
the city, she surmised. His name certainly meant
nothing to her from the days before she'd left Redwych,
and, with a vested interest in journalism, she'd studied
the *Sentinel* slavishly.

But, come to that, why should his name mean much
of anything to Patti?

'Oh, all right then,' her sister had said this morning,
with a studied weariness. 'I've never met Whitelaw
Daumery, nor met anyone who knows him. At least not
to my knowledge ... But I do know someone who
works at the *Sentinel*.'

And what was this 'not to my knowledge' remark all

about? Natalie reflected, thinking with hindsight how odd that had sounded. Did it imply that she met a lot of people under anonymous circumstances? Maybe she even had anonymous sex with people whose names she barely knew? If so, it was clearly a developing family tendency . . .

Natalie found herself grinning again, but she quashed it when the very prim, uptight and overlacquered receptionist deigned to look up from her word processor and turn towards her.

'May I help you?'

Natalie felt her psychological hackles go up immediately. She wanted to crush this officious little bitch with a killer verbal volley, but somehow she couldn't be bothered to spoil her own day by going that way. Instead she just smiled and said, 'I'm here to see Alex Hendry, please.'

The receptionist didn't smile back. 'Do you have an appointment?' Her overstyled hair seemed to crackle with hostility.

Remaining cool, Natalie said, 'Oh, he'll see me. I'm a personal friend.' Her adversary started to bluster, but she pressed on, 'Just tell him that Natalie Croft is here to see him, and that I'm Patti Simmon's sister. I'll guarantee he'll just come racing out here!' She resisted the urge to study her fingernails nonchalantly.

It was a total bluff. Alex Hendry was probably some boorish provincial hack who'd say 'Who the fuck?' and instruct this battleaxe here to tell Natalie to get lost.

And yet somehow the ploy seemed to work.

Muttering just a little, the receptionist applied herself to the fairly antique-looking switchboard system, conveyed Natalie's message, and then said, 'He'll be right down.' The way her drawn-on eyebrows had shot up showed she was just as surprised as Natalie at the response.

Feeling foolishly pleased with her small triumph,

Natalie roamed the tiny, uninspiring foyer. I don't know what I'm feeling so triumphant about. He's probably a greasy little geek with bad breath, and if he was any kind of a real journalist he'd have done an exposé on Daumery himself, yonks ago!

But, when Alex Hendry arrived, Natalie got an even bigger surprise than when she'd learned he was coming down to see her.

'Hello, Natalie,' said a warm, amused voice as a figure right out of *GQ* stepped out from behind the counter. Alex Hendry's smart, modern suit, silk shirt and surgically styled hair were a million miles away from the too-tight-leather-jacket-and-polyester-slacks image that Natalie had anticipated. Against her expectations, and slightly against her wishes, she found herself instantly fancying him.

'Patti said to expect you,' murmured Alex, leading her to the door. 'Why don't we go and get a drink? My favourite pub is just round the corner.'

Natalie nodded, nonplussed. She felt annoyed with herself for losing the initiative *and* her ability to speak for the moment, but the venomously jealous look on the receptionist's face compensated somewhat.

As she followed him along the pavement into the oldest part of the town, Natalie began to get her powers of perception back. She'd tried to ring this character herself this morning, but got no answer from either his desk or his mobile phone. How come Patti seemed to have direct access to him?

'I tried to ring you,' she said, as Alex led her into the Curlew, an ancient public house with a low and wavy ceiling and painted black timbers that were the genuine article rather than corporate kitsch. 'Didn't you get the voicemail I left?'

'Sorry,' said Alex, turning towards her. His eyes were green, vivid even in the subdued light, and their brilliant twinkle seemed to enhance his dark, roguish looks.

He had a vaguely Celtic or even Hispanic look about him and a pale skin combined with glossy black hair. Natalie imagined him as having either Basque or Catalan genes.

'Phone's on the blink,' he said with a disarming grin. 'Takes some messages . . . Loses others . . . Yours must have been one of the unlucky ones. I'm sorry . . .' His smile broadened. 'But at least you've found me now.' He licked his lips. 'I hope it was worth it.'

You clever little fuck! Natalie thought. 'Let's hope so, but for that you can get the first round.'

A short while later, when they were drinking lager and Natalie had outlined her project to him, Alex Hendry was still smiling, but somehow also mocking her.

'Don't you think that, if there was anything concrete to be had on the guy, I would have had it already?' he said, confirming exactly what Natalie had thought herself. 'I hate Daumery. He's a sanctimonious prick and a hypocrite – and I certainly could do with a big story to get me out of this backwater.' He took a long pull at his lager, straight from the narrow-necked bottle, and something about the careless action made Natalie's cunt clench with lust. 'Why should I help *you* at the expense of helping myself?'

Playing for time, Natalie took a swig of her own beer.

Bad idea. Putting the contoured bottle to her lips produced an instant flash image of herself, on her knees, opening her mouth to receive Alex's shapely, contoured prick into her mouth. The picture was so vivid that involuntarily she glanced down at his crotch. When she looked back up again, his eyes were on her, having tracked her revealing glance. To her embarrassment he chuckled and adjusted the way he was sitting. As if she were warily watching a poisonous snake, in case it struck out at her, Natalie looked down again.

He was hard. His prick twitched inside his trousers.

'Goddamned beer. It always does this to me,' he said

conversationally. Unlike Natalie herself, he seemed unconcerned, completely unembarrassed at being visibly turned on.

Natalie swallowed, tried to focus. It was difficult, though. For a moment she couldn't remember why she was here in this pub in the first place. All she wanted was to take this snappily dressed young stud outside, into a back alley or somewhere, and fuck him senseless!

It was just like 'Teacher' on the train all over again . . .

'I could put a good word in for you at the *Modern Enquirer*,' she suggested, saying the first thing she thought of. It was nonsense, of course. She didn't have any say there at all now, it seemed. And, even if she'd still been Alan's golden girl, the *Enquirer* didn't recruit that way, anyway.

Alex gave her a long, twinkling look. Everything about him said that he knew she was bullshitting him, but that he also found it not just hilarious, but deeply sexy. And the fact that he *did* find having her in such an unaccustomed position of disadvantage erotic seemed to have precisely the same effect on Natalie. If she'd wanted him a moment ago, she was desperate for him now.

Still not saying anything, Alex took another swig of his beer, then looked down for just the briefest second at the outline of his erection.

Natalie felt faint for a moment. Sick with lust and shame and a dozen other less definable emotions. She experienced a profound sensation of being dirtied; of wallowing in sleaze; of being the horniest of horny sluts. She was violently angry with herself, and fairly miffed with Alex Hendry, but she felt that if she didn't have sex – soon – with this attractive but despicable man, she would simply drop down dead.

'You fuck!' she mimed, then spoke up just a little more audibly. 'I'm not a prostitute! I'm not going to sleep with you to get your help! I'll do without, thank you very much! I can manage.'

All Alex did was smile, and fingered the neck of his beer bottle suggestively. Natalie saw red.

'How many times do I have to tell you? I'm not fucking you just to get a few pathetic scraps of information!' she cried, outraged, even though she'd done that very thing more than once before. She was also aware of outraging a brightly dressed American tourist couple at the next table. There were pointed transatlantic mutterings about getting her removed from the premises. She felt like telling them to fuck off as well as Alex.

'I don't need to go to bed with you to find out what I need to know,' she told him more quietly. 'It might take a bit longer but I'll manage very nicely on my own. I *am* a journalist!'

'Then fuck me because you want to,' he said even more quietly, his silky tone making the 'F' word inaudible to the easily offended tourists. 'I've decided to help you anyway, whether we have sex or not.'

Natalie wanted to smash her beer bottle and do serious physical damage to the smiling, handsome, unashamedly laddish face in front of her. There hadn't been many times in her life when she'd actually wanted to hurt someone, but now was one of them. It took a huge effort of will to quell her impulse to scar him.

'Big of you,' she said, 'but, as I said, I can manage. For information *and* for sex.'

Alex chuckled and stared at Natalie's right hand. To her horror, she realised that she too was fiddling with her bottle in a thought-provoking way.

'There's nothing hornier than the thought of a woman playing with herself,' he said.

Natalie's knuckles went white, and the urge to bottle him surged up like fire forced through a pipe. But again she managed to contain herself. It was on the tip of her tongue to tell him about her escapade with Steven Small on the train, but then she thought better of it. Any account of that quick, frenzied, almost animal encounter would only make her sound like even more of a slut than he already thought her.

'I don't have to play with myself to get what I want.'

But, up until the time on the train down here, how much of a lie had that been? Her relationship with Alan had fizzled out, and she had been masturbating quite a bit, hadn't she? Every day, in fact. Sometimes more than once . . .

But now she felt revivified. Energised. The thought of playing with herself actually felt good all of a sudden. And the thought that she could – and would – have sex whenever and wherever she wanted did too. Patti was bonking herself senseless with her window cleaner and probably with other guys, too. Why shouldn't she, Natalie, do the same? She'd had Steven Small yesterday, and she suspected she could have him again at the drop of a hat if she could be bothered to find him. But why not have this man, too? This handsome young bastard who as a journalist could loosely be termed a 'comrade in arms'? Dear God, it wasn't as if she didn't fancy him!

Feeling she'd procrastinated long enough and that it was time to take the initiative, she stood up. She gave Alex a square-on look, but said nothing. Clearly intuitive, he stood too, smiling a smile that Natalie wryly noted as slightly awed.

Either that or he was a fucking good actor!

'Where can we go? Do you live near here?' Natalie asked briskly when they were out in the street. It seemed important that she be seen to be making the choices here. She didn't want this clever, confident man to get the better of her; the sex had to be on her terms. Sneaking a glance at him, she wondered how old he was. Younger than she was by several years, she guessed, but that didn't seem to matter. What was important was getting him to make her come.

'I don't live too far from here,' he said, then gave her a wolfish look. 'But I do know somewhere closer – if you don't mind roughing it a bit.'

'Whatever,' said Natalie, thinking of the train toilet yesterday. Wherever they did it, nothing could be more sordid than the smell of urine and soggy paper towels crushed underfoot.

Thinking of the odour of that grimy cubicle, it suddenly dawned on Natalie that, before having any kind of sex, she needed to relieve herself. But how to convey that to Alex without seeming at a disadvantage again? He was a man, and could utilise any secluded spot, the lucky bastard!

Within minutes it seemed they'd found that place exactly. They'd slid between two buildings and were in an enclosed yard somewhere in the oldest part of the city centre. It reminded Natalie of the fantasy she'd brought herself off to last night. Of Steven and Dyson screwing Patti in an alley. The situation here in reality was just as insalubrious as the scenario she'd imagined had been. The only difference was that it was daytime, and the sun was shining, high above, between the roofs of the buildings that loomed over them. In the shadowed corners, though, it still seemed comfortingly dark.

The yard was quite small and claustrophobic, and dominated by a medium-sized, dark-green van that stood parked against one wall. A high wooden gate with a padlock stood at the far end – through which the van had obviously been driven in – and there were only tiny, high windows in the buildings around that overlooked the yard.

Nobody could see them.

And above the noise of city traffic, and machinery operating nearby, nobody could hear them, either.

Natalie looked at Alex. He was smiling slightly, and

watching her. In the grubbiness of their surroundings he was an anomaly in his sleek suit and expensive shoes, and she had a sudden, wayward yen to shock him out of his air of well-groomed superiority.

'I need to piss,' she said, and, not allowing herself to hesitate, she went over to a corner of the yard, where crumpled newspapers and other rubbish spilled out of a cluster of bins. Unfastening her trousers, she started to slide them down.

'Let me help you,' said Alex, for the first time looking a little alarmed.

Have I pushed a special button of his? thought Natalie, hesitating, her fingers on the waistband of her panties. It seemed she had. Alex hurried to her side, and, as she made to push her knickers down, he reached for her, squeezing her crotch roughly through the thin white cotton fabric.

'Ah!'

The jolt of pain and pleasure was so intense it almost made her head spin and her swollen bladder release its contents into her underwear. She squirmed against the hand that abused her, wanting the pressure to stop – and yet revelling in it. She moaned again, as her cunt seemed to gather itself in readiness. Alex's middle finger moved cleverly and a little bit of urine spurted out and wet her gusset.

'Let me piss!' she groaned, still moving, working against the finger.

'Nobody's stopping you,' he said, his voice low and urgent, revealing that he wasn't quite as in control as he seemed. Moving against her, he rubbed her thigh with an enormous erection.

'No way,' hissed Natalie, knocking his hand away, whipping down her pants and trousers and squatting in the corner. The stance was awkward, but the release of her water almost triggered her orgasm. As her bladder emptied she also had the satisfaction of seeing Alex step away in order to avoid getting his immaculate trousers splashed. Once at a safe distance, he began to knead his groin. Groaning softly, his eyes closed, their expression no longer laughing.

Natalie remained crouching for a few moments, trying to regain mastery of her own body. She felt a strong urge to just rub herself to climax then and there, hunched down among the rubbish – the drive to do something even more outrageous was growing all the time.

'Oh, God,' murmured Alex vaguely as she straightened up, stepped away, then kicked off her shoes.

A sudden image of Patti with young Dyson formed before Natalie's eyes, propelling her hands in the task of unfastening and removing her clothing. Insane as it seemed, she wanted to stand lewd and naked in this horrid little yard, and exhibit herself – for the sole reason that her sister had never done it.

Within a few seconds, her clothes were on the cobbles and Natalie's body was bare in the muted sunlight. Boldly, she slid a hand between her thighs and began to rub lightly at her slippery sex. If Alex wanted 'horny', he could have it – big time.

'You are really something else,' Alex said, advancing on her. As Natalie continued to rub herself, he took her face in his two hands and kissed her, his large, energetic tongue quickly exploring the interior of her mouth.

After a few moments of this, Natalie was gasping, both from the kiss and the imminence of orgasm. Alex pulled back, his unfocused look saying he too was losing it.

'Let's get in there,' he said brusquely, nodding to the van.

'What on Earth do you mean?'

Get in the van? How could they? Did he have the key?

'I've got a key. It belongs to the *Sentinel*,' said Alex,

fishing in his pocket and bringing one out. 'I was having my car fixed the other day, and they let me borrow it.'

'I'm not screwing in the back of a filthy old van!' protested Natalie, even though, somehow, the idea did have a perverted appeal. Had Patti screwed in a van?

Alex shook his head. A classic chauvinistic response to the vagaries of women. 'Where else were you proposing we do it? On the cobbles? Among the rubbish? Standing up against the wall? It's bloody hard, I can tell you.'

He's probably had women here before, thought Natalie, finding that idea exciting too. She could just picture Alex's naked buttocks tensing and jerking as he thrust into a woman against that hard wall. Or maybe he'd leaned against it himself while someone sucked him off.

As she visualised this, Alex was unlocking the van. As the back door of it swung open, he stepped back, made a bow, and gestured that she climb in.

Why the hell not? Natalie thought, stepping forward, then putting her foot on the cold and gritty running plate.

Inside it was dark, it being a solid panel van, but Alex snapped on a little access lamp. There was a pile of coarse-looking sacks that might have been wrapped around newsprint or something, and, slamming the door closed, he took hold of Natalie quite roughly and pushed her towards them.

The sacks were just as scratchy as she'd expected beneath her back, but what Alex did next wasn't quite what she'd anticipated. Instead of ripping open his trousers, climbing aboard, and shoving himself into her as his urgent erection seemed to predicate, he simply tossed aside his jacket and got down on his knees in front of her.

Then without further ado, he crouched right down, used his hand to part her thighs, then thrust his face right in between them and into her sex.

'Oh, God, yes!' cried Natalie involuntarily as he began to lick and nuzzle at her. Almost immediately he had his lips clamped around her clit and was sucking it as if it were the source of life itself. It took only seconds to produce a massive wrenching orgasm.

The sensation was immense, addictive, inhibition-smashing. Natalie was faintly aware of her heels bashing against the floor of the van and making a terrific noise that must be clearly audible outside. All she could do was continue to kick, and grab at Alex's hair and force him to stay in place and sucking. She felt some kind of gel or wax on her fingers but it was of no consequence, no importance, beside her pleasure. Scooting herself closer to him, she jammed her sex as hard as she could against his face.

Another orgasm crested almost before the first had faded and she realised she was shouting too. Calling out obscenities in a voice that didn't sound like hers at all. The way she cursed him would have sounded at home in a scene from *The Exorcist*!

Eventually she could take no more, and she fell back. Alex lifted his face from between her thighs and, squinting blearily at him, she could see tears in his eyes. Not of emotion, she realised, just pain where she'd almost pulled his hair out. His face was wet, too, where she'd smeared it with her juices.

Suddenly, all that Natalie could do was laugh at the sheer hilarious absurdity of their situation. Here they were, a pair of grown-up, quite sophisticated people and they were rolling around in a van like a pair of hormone-drenched teenagers. What the hell had happened to her story, her mission? Under ordinary circumstances she'd have had the bloody thing researched and half written by now, but all she could seem to focus on was her supercharged libido.

Natalie sat up and hugged herself as the laughter consumed her just as completely as the pleasure had.

She felt tears pop into her eyes now too – tears of uncontrollable, hysterical glee!

Alex, too, was seeing the funny side of things. He knelt up, chortling, and ran his hands through his dishevelled hair, as if to check that most of it was still attached to his head.

'That hurt, you bitch,' he said, but the words were affectionate. Moving to crouch beside her, he reached across and kissed her soundly on the lips.

Aware of her own taste on him, vividly salty, Natalie responded with enthusiasm. A second later, she was on her back again, Alex on top of her, and between them they were scrabbling open his fly and his boxer shorts, in search of his prick.

Finding a pretty respectable-sized rod, Natalie wished for a moment that he would stand up and exhibit it to her. She had a mad urge to gauge it against the one she'd enjoyed yesterday. Steven Small's penis – a penis that hadn't reflected its owner's surname at all.

Still, Alex felt big enough to her questing hand, certainly adequate enough to fill her as much as she wanted filling. And, with a bit of shuffling, hip shifting and guiding, it was only a second or so before she felt him push inside her.

'Oh, fuck, yes!' he muttered, not moving at first, but just seeming to settle himself inside her. Natalie had no complaint with that: she'd come already. It was nice just to lie there for a moment, getting her breath back, feeling stretched and filled. Wrapping her legs around him, she slid her hand inside the back of his trousers and clasped his buttocks. His muscles were taut, hard and toned, and his cock seemed to swell as she embraced him.

Slowly, he began to rock their bodies together, not exactly thrusting, but getting the same, marvellous effect in a subtler manner. As his body knocked and knocked against her, Natalie felt her clitoris absorb the impact and her pussy shimmer and clench around his hardness.

He felt so good. She was going to come. She couldn't hold back.

As she climaxed again, her nails sank involuntarily into the muscular rounds of his buttocks. Laughing through her pleasure, she knew that once again she was hurting him. But she didn't care, because all that mattered was delicious extinction.

'So, have you met the delightful Natalie?'

The person on the end of the line didn't introduce herself, but, then again, she never did, nor did she need to.

'Hello, Stella,' Alex said, spinning his office chair around to shield the conversation from the rest of the newsroom. He was pretty safe here in his cubbyhole, but he *was* surrounded by journalists, after all, and any one of them would be more than interested in the affairs of Stella Fontayne.

'Yes, of course I have. You know I have!' he said testily, recognising the beginning of the usual uncomfortable by-play. Even after all this time, talking to Stella, and being in 'her' company, set his hackles rising somehow. It was a response that deeply disquieted him, and that he didn't like to analyse.

Stella chuckled, the sound low, intimate, and almost filthy. Alex picked up a pencil from his desk and felt like snapping it.

'And what did you think of her?' the transvestite went on, her voice arch and lightly challenging.

My God, what do I think of her?

If he were to be honest, Alex was still in shock from the way the situation with Natalie Croft had rapidly escalated. When Patti had told him about her sister, he'd rather liked the sound of the hard, successful journalist from London, and the idea of having sex with her had been immediately on his agenda. But he hadn't expected it to happen so soon, or be so spectacular!

And he certainly hadn't expected Natalie to want him under *those* circumstances. He thought about the games he'd quite slowly come around to, the sexual settings he'd never expected to enjoy in a thousand years because of the sheer squalor of them, and he realised that today he'd found what might be termed a 'natural'.

Natalie Croft had needed no persistent persuasion in order to fuck him in the back of a filthy delivery van, or to let him kiss her or grope her within half an hour of meeting him. In actual fact, she'd been the one to make the running.

He wondered what Stella would make of this. Or whether, as was so often the case, she was already ten jumps ahead of him.

'I like her,' he said eventually. 'She's feisty. She's direct. And she's very beautiful – in a hard, London type of way.'

'Just like you.'

Fuck her! Fuck him! Whatever!

The pencil snapped.

Alex gritted his teeth, and tried to ignore all the crossed signals firing inside him. He looked around, thinking what his colleagues might do with the information he had on Stella Fontayne. The big stories they could write, even the lowliest and most unambitious of them. It was an exposé *he* could have had a ball with if his expensive tastes hadn't put him at Stella Fontayne's mercy.

He looked down at his beautiful suit – now just a little worse for wear after that tumble in the van – and thought of the many other similar ones he possessed, thanks to Stella Fontayne. Then there was the car, his flat, all his electronic equipment – wide-screen television, DVD, every possible fashionable gizmo. He would never have had any of these things, or he'd have had them and they'd have been repossessed long ago, if he hadn't been on Stella's secret payroll. His own life in itself would have made a fabulous story for Natalie, or any other journalist, if he'd just been even marginally well known.

Stella was laughing again. Alex wanted to smash the phone down but he didn't. He would give in and let 'her' know how much this sort of teasing really troubled him. How the erections that Stella's flirtations induced both scared and sickened him.

'Well she obviously thinks I'm beautiful too,' he said at length, 'because she let me fuck her, half an hour after I met her, in the back of that delivery van!'

If Alex had been hoping to shock Stella, or make her envious, he realised almost immediately that he was mistaken.

'Oh, bravo!' the drag queen purred. 'My dear Alex, I am *so* impressed! You must give me full details, right now. I must know all of it!'

Alex longed to just say 'fuck off' and put the phone down, but Stella's hold over him meant that was impossible. Instead he said, as mildly as he could, 'I'm in the office, Stella. It's difficult to talk. Can I phone you a little later, on a different line?'

There was a short silence.

'Yes, perhaps that would be better,' Stella said eventually. 'That way we could enjoy it more . . .' She paused again, and Alex braced himself. 'But in the meantime, just give me a few little titbits to be going on with.'

'What?' Alex could barely hear his own tight, strangled voice. 'What do you want to know?'

'Did you lick her pussy, Alex? And what does she taste like?'

Biting his lip, Alex suppressed a groan of resignation. Inside his silk boxer shorts, his cock stiffened violently, and he knew that when this was over he would have to retreat to the lavatory and masturbate.

In a low, low voice, and with his hand at his crotch, beneath the desk, he began his account.

Chapter Six
Transformations

*S*he supposed she was already a 'she', already 'the divine, the glamorous, the sensational Miss Stella Fontayne!' – even though she hadn't even put on her dress, her high-heeled shoes and her wig yet.

'Here's looking at you, kid,' Stella Fontayne murmured, winking encouragingly at herself in the mirror. A tiny frisson of fear flickered somewhere behind her breastbone, even now, after all these years painting and charades, but she quashed it, then took up her long-handled lip brush. Smoothing on the pearly, rose-tinted lipstick that she'd chosen to complement tonight's outfit soothed the last of her nerves and as she first blotted, then pouted, she knew the colour was good on her. It suited both her skin and the colour of her eyes, bringing out the fugitive green tints within the hazel, and highlighting the creamy porcelain of her heavy but faultless make-up. It would probably even look OK with her un-made-up skin, she supposed, which was even paler, if anything. How strange that what was classed as beauty in a woman was deemed to be washed out and unhealthy when one lived as a man.

Too many hours spent in libraries and classrooms,

she reflected wryly, and not enough time outdoors being butch and athletic. Long, long hours hanging out in unhealthy, dimly lit nightclubs hadn't helped, either.

Not that she had any regrets on that score. Some of her happiest ever moments had occurred in the least salubrious of surroundings.

Pushing an errant strand of blond hair beneath her close-fitting stockingette wig cap, Stella reached for her chosen wig of the evening. She was transforming into a brunette tonight, and the head of hair she eased on, then gripped carefully into place, was one of her favourites. 'Big hair' but not grotesquely so: the curls were soft, shiny and not too structured, with a layered and feathery fringe that masked the critical interface between real forehead and false hair.

'Absolutely luscious, darling,' she proclaimed, turning her now dark head this way and that, and patting a few last tendrils into place before she stood up.

Stella moved to her full-length mirror, and, as always, she paused for a long hard look at the conundrum of her half-dressed body.

Too much 'restructuring' of her natural shape had never appealed to Stella. She took no hormones, nor did she corset herself too tightly. Mostly, as now, she wore loose, silky underwear and relied on well-cut outerwear to trick the eye into an impression of a good female figure. The sense of freedom beneath her clothes was intoxicating, and one of the great pleasures of dressing up. There was nothing to match the sensation of an unfettered cock in French knickers, an erection swinging free and rubbing constantly against tactile fabrics like silk and lace.

She shaved, of course, and with surgical precision, but, being fair-skinned and having light-coloured hair to start with, she had never found it to be the onerous, tyrannical task that plagued some drag queens. The transition between the sexes had always been an easy passage for Stella, and she often wondered whether, if it had not been that way, she would ever have even bothered to make the effort.

'Stop screwing around, girl!' Glancing at her watch, she realised how little time remained before she was needed to preside at the club.

Even so, she couldn't resist the urge to briefly fondle herself. A swift rub stiffened her inside the pliant pale-blue satin of her underwear and she felt a little silky pre-come start to ooze from the tip of her cock. That would mean a stain, of course, on her pristine panties, but the very thought of that made her shudder and get harder. It was oh so sleazy, oh so dirty ... For a moment, she considered bringing herself off inside her panties, then wearing them soiled for the rest of the evening.

Stella gasped, her prick on a hair trigger, her hips swaying. She was perilously close to the edge, but, knowing herself of old, she held back and didn't push on through to climax. This way was much, much better. After an entire evening of slow stimulation inside her finery she would explode with pleasure when the time came; so, pinching the tip of her cock just behind the glans, she tamed the sensations back to a manageable level and her tumescence subsided slightly.

Even so, as she slipped into the beautiful royal-blue gown that Patti had just had biked around to her, Stella had several heart-stopping moments. The shimmering cloth of the skirt had body to it, and the lining had a fullness and stiffness that would tame any stiffness of her own, but it was those very qualities in the garment that jostled her aching prick.

'Well, it's going to be an interesting night, old girl, isn't it?' murmured Stella, winking at her transfigured reflection in the mirror.

But then, aren't they all? she thought, smiling to herself as she slid her long, but narrow feet into her shoes, snatched up her bag and wrap, and then ran quickly downstairs to the chauffeured car that was waiting to transport her to her nightclub.

For the first time in a long time, Natalie felt like just plonking herself down in front of the telly and spending the whole evening in mindless-moron mode. Anything to avoid thinking about what was happening to her.

It was scary. For the first time in her life, she'd lost her focus. Her eyes were no longer on the prize, and, instead of pitching into the Daumery story, she'd frittered her time away obsessing about Patti. And, instead of pursuing the corrupt chairman of the Committee for Moral Practice in Business, she'd simply pursued – and screwed – almost every man who'd strayed across her path!

But even slobbing around Patti's house doing nothing proved more difficult than Natalie had anticipated. Dyson the window cleaner was in residence in the living room. Barefoot and clad in just a scruffy pair of jeans, he wasn't lying on the settee watching football or television soaps as Natalie might have expected. Instead, he was deep in the grips of what looked astonishingly like some kind of studying. Books were spread out all over a table that had earlier been covered with Patti's sewing, and, when Natalie looked in on him, he peered at her through a decidedly bookish pair of spectacles.

Feeling uncomfortable around him – mainly because he was a man, and in her path! – Natalie stayed out of his way. First she had a bath and washed her hair, then she retired to her room with a sandwich and a bottle of water to begin some preliminary work on her proposed article.

At least that had been the plan.

Dear God, who am I to investigate anybody else's sleaze? she thought desperately, nearly knocking her water over across her laptop. Nobody on Earth could be sleazier than I've been these last couple of days!

If she closed her eyes she could still smell the musty, petrol-laced air in the back of that grotty old van. Still feel the pile of old sacking she'd lain on scratching her back. Still feel the suction of Alex's clever lips encircling her clit . . .

All thoughts of Whitelaw Daumery, and ways she could use the information she'd already gleaned, evaporated out of her mind like mist. The only things she could think about were men's beautiful bodies, their importunate demanding hands, their long, hard pricks, and, in Alex Hendry's case, their devilish, mobile, never-tiring tongues.

Jesus Christ, that man can really give head!

Natalie shuddered and clutched her dressing gown around her. She stood up and walked round the room. The temptation to masturbate was becoming a nasty, pervasive habit, and she felt it stronger than ever now. The law of averages decreed that after all the orgasms she'd had that afternoon in the back of that goddamned delivery van she should be completely pleasured out now. With her body relaxed and sated, her mind should be free to analyse and investigate and put facts together in unexpected but newsworthy patterns.

But theory and practice were two different things. She still felt horny and her mind was total mush. She had to bring herself off or she'd go crazy! Either that or she had to find a man to do it.

The image of Dyson flashed immediately into her mind, but the last vestiges of her good sense shouted, 'No! No! No!' It wasn't that she didn't think he was up to the job – she'd seen him in action, after all – or that she didn't fancy him. Because she did. But, with all the pre-existing distractions, she just couldn't face the additional complications of seducing her sister's boyfriend. At least not while she was living rent-free in Patti's house.

Oh, you're a hard bitch, Nat, she told herself a second later. You put on this act, this 'take what you want when you want' act . . . But underneath, the real reason, at least just a bit of it, is that you don't want to hurt Patti's feelings.

How soft does that sound?

Natalie sat down again on the bed, amazed at this new, gentler emotion she suddenly felt for Patti. They'd always been unspoken rivals – at least *she* had, Patti had seemed more easy-going – and always cared for each other in a prickly sort of way, but this strange tenderness she was experiencing was a real shock.

Wondering what her sister had in the house in the way of beer or wine – a little shot of alcohol might clarify things right now – Natalie got up again, went to the door, and was just about to open it when someone knocked on it from the outside.

'Oh, fuck!' she cried, clutching her chest where her heart was pounding.

'Thanks, I'd be glad to,' said Alex Hendry glibly when she opened the door.

Natalie felt a confusing mix of irritation, surprise and sudden, rampaging lust. The last time she'd seen Alex Hendry, earlier that day, she'd told him that he had to completely forget about what had happened in that yard, and in that van. It'd *never* happened.

And yet seeing him here – looking like an absolute babe, she had to admit – it was impossible to expunge the memories from her mind. He was wearing yet another devastating suit, in a dark aubergine shade that made him look tanned and fit and hip. His grin was infuriating and yet all Natalie could think of was the marvellous body beneath the cool clothes, and the most inventive tongue she'd ever had the pleasure to be licked by nestling behind those smugly curved lips. She wanted to kill him. But not before she'd hauled him into her bedroom and made him service her!

'What're *you* doing here?' she demanded, becoming uncomfortably aware of Dyson standing bare-chested behind Alex. The window cleaner's sharp, intelligent eyes were taking in every detail.

'Don't worry,' said Alex, his voice an easy drawl that enraged her even further. 'I haven't come to fuck you, just to take you out. Are you up for that?'

Natalie heard Dyson laugh softly, and, much as she would have liked to smack Alex in the mouth, she refrained, and looked beyond him to give the window cleaner her most chilling glare.

'I wonder if we could have some privacy – if you don't mind?' she snapped, angry with herself for losing her cool so easily.

'My pleasure,' said Dyson, shrugging and turning to walk away. As Natalie watched him along the landing, she noticed that his ancient jeans were torn across the backside, and the bare skin of one buttock was visible. In spite of everything, she felt her gut clench and her sex jump with interest.

My God, I'm a Pavlov's dog, she thought despairingly. Show me a biscuit and I start drooling!

When she returned her glance to Alex, she saw that his smirk had widened. The bastard had clocked her checking out Dyson's arse! Grabbing him by the arm, she dragged him into the room, then almost jumped back because the space was too small and he was already far too close.

'What the fuck do you want?' she reiterated, watching with satisfaction as Alex smoothed the fabric of his sleeve where she'd crushed it.

'As I said,' he said patiently, 'I've come to invite you out. It's business, though, not pleasure. I've an invite to a club where you might make some useful connections.'

'What sort of club?'

She couldn't imagine learning anything useful to her story among crowds of bodies, noise and smoke.

'Well, that's a tough one,' said Alex, sidestepping her to cross the room and sit down on her bed. Fastidious as ever, he inspected the quilt before he sat down, removed a couple of Ozzy's cat hairs, then plucked at the knees of his trousers to prevent them stretching and spoiling their line.

'What on Earth do you mean? It's either a club or it isn't . . .' challenged Natalie as her visitor finally sat down.

'Well, Fontayne's probably isn't what you think of as a club. There's no rave music, no DJs, and no ecstasy.' He paused, his dark eyebrows lifting. 'Well, not the pharmaceutical kind, anyway.'

Natalie made a sound of disgust and turned away, acutely aware of the thin and unsubstantial nature of her dressing gown. She was naked beneath it and she was beginning to feel an overpowering urge to lift the flimsy hem and acquaint Alex with that fact.

'So what is it? A working men's club or something?'

'No, just a sort of old-fashioned private drinking club. There's music, a bit of cheek-to-cheek dancing – and often a cabaret. It's quite exclusive in its own quaint sort of way.'

'It sounds like a blast,' said Natalie sarcastically, even though – against her will – she was intrigued.

'Oh, it is. You'd be amazed. It's not always necessary to live in the Smoke to be cosmopolitan.'

'And why do you think going there will help me? What can I find out? Who goes there?'

'Everybody who's anybody in this burg.' Alex's dark eyes were twinkling. 'Even though they might not want the general public to know that.'

Natalie's internal radar started pinging. 'Well, if it's such a disreputable dive, why haven't you done a story about it? Turned over the stone to flush out the bugs?'

She narrowed her eyes and looked at him more closely. Was he uncomfortable somehow? Had she struck a nerve?

Yes! She had! Alex's confidence suddenly seemed a little friable round the edges. He smoothed the crease in his trouser leg, pinching the dark plum-coloured fabric between his fingertips.

'It's not in my interest to do that just now,' he said, all the playfulness gone out of his voice. He *was* anxious about something, and Natalie sensed that she'd discovered a real Achilles' heel in him.

She felt the urge to push, to find out what Alex Hendry was trying to evade mentioning, but a sudden flash of instinct told her that she might ultimately get more out of him by biding her time. Keep him on your side, kiddo, she told herself. He was a fellow journalist, after all, and, if she turned him against her, he could well annexe her story for his own purposes.

'Whatever,' she murmured, then reached for her water bottle, and took a sip to buy herself a little time.

'So, are you going to get dressed?' Alex enquired. Holding out his hand and wiggling his fingers, he indicated that he'd like a sip of her water. Natalie handed him the bottle, experiencing a strange pang of intimacy at seeing his lips against its mouth, and the way his throat moved as he drank. Again she felt the desire not to go out with this man, but to stay in with him. The bed was there, after all, just a couple of feet away. And Alex was already on it.

'All right,' she said, 'I'll give it a whirl.' Her eyes flicked towards the quilt next to him, and once again Natalie could have kicked herself for giving away her feelings.

Alex chuckled. 'I thought we were going to forget that ever happened.'

'We are! I meant your naffing club!' Natalie snatched the bottle back off him and drained the last drops.

'Look, how smart is this place? I need to know what to wear.' She looked at Alex's divine suit. It was clearly very expensive, possibly Hugo Boss, or Paul Smith, maybe even Armani – but underneath it he was wearing a simple V-necked T-shirt in a slightly paler shade of the same vinous colour. Obviously not a black-tie venue then . . .

'Smart casual would be great,' he said airily. 'Anything, really, as long as it's not denim.'

'I wouldn't dream of it!' said Natalie, aware that she was getting herself into a state of nerves. She grabbed a few things at random from among her half-unpacked suitcase and the wardrobe where she'd hung up her most crushable items. Turning again, she looked pointedly at Alex, indicating he should leave the room while she changed, but, instead of getting up, he just leaned back, his grin widening.

Bastard! Natalie thought, then losing her patience with him she whipped off her robe and flung it over the back of a chair. What the hell! He'd seen – and tasted – virtually everything anyway. What difference did it make, his seeing her naked now?

But his intense scrutiny made her extremely hot, and she felt herself starting to sweat before they'd even set off out. Feeling as acutely embarrassed as if he were watching her pee again, she grabbed up a stick deodorant and rubbed some quickly into her armpits.

Bastard, she thought again, almost throwing it back on to the dressing table.

Next, she stepped into a pair of black lace knickers. They were the first she'd put her hands on, and rather tinier than she would ideally have chosen. At the moment, big, safe, 'old lady' knickers might have been the best option, but it was too late now, and she was acutely aware that the thong back of these panties left her buttocks entirely bare.

Alex said nothing, even though Natalie half wished he had said something, so she could shout at him.

Adjusting her knickers to try to make them cover slightly more of her pubic hair, she discovered something else unfortunate.

Where were all her bras? She was sure she'd picked one up, but it seemed not – and she couldn't for the life of her remember which drawer she'd put them in. It seemed important to seem decisive and purposeful in front of this watching man, so, in order to avoid a lot of searching and rummaging, Natalie simply reached for the top she'd chosen – a sleeveless, boat-necked black 'shell' in a shiny, slightly stretch fabric – and tugged it on over her head. Her breasts weren't huge, so lack of support wasn't a problem, but the clingy top shaped revealingly to her nipples.

Natalie felt blood surge into her face and neck, but she tried to ignore it as she continued dressing. A black, knee-length, two-layer skirt with a slightly ruffled hemline showed off her legs nicely, and the remains of some tan – part natural, but mostly fake – meant that her shins had a bit of a golden glow that rendered tights or stockings unnecessary. Feeling decidedly underprotected, though, she shoved her feet into a pair of strappy black sandals.

'Very nice,' murmured Alex as Natalie sat down at the dressing table. Annoyed with herself for her sudden clumsiness, she ignored Alex's scrutiny and struggled with her hair for a minute or two, finally managing to coerce it into a groomed-looking knot. Then she began to apply a bit of make-up.

Glancing beyond the mirror, she realised that Alex was still watching her closely. She felt half naked still, in spite of being dressed, and decided to keep the make-up ultra-simple. Anything more than just the bare minimum would make her feel tarty even if she didn't look it, so she confined herself to a bit of taupe eye shadow, soft brown eyeliner and mascara. Her lips she covered with a natural pinkish gloss. It wasn't a 'power' look, but a 'safety play' seemed wiser.

'Well, what are we waiting for?' she demanded at the same time as flinging some tissues, a tiny notebook and pencil and one or two essentials into a small black leather shoulder bag.

'My God! A miracle!' exclaimed Alex, unwinding his long legs and standing up. 'A woman who doesn't take a decade to get ready.'

Natalie felt like making some sharp remark about chauvinism, but she refrained. It would give her the advantage if she didn't always rise to the obvious bait. Instead she said, 'Let's go!' and gave him a brilliant smile.

'Don't you even want to spend a penny?'

Natalie felt herself blushing vividly again as she thought of squatting in the corner of a scruffy yard, her waters gushing out of her as Alex looked on. 'No. I'm OK,' she said, knowing as she said it that she was probably making a big mistake.

Alex's vehicle was a cutting-edge but slightly precious-looking four-by-four. It was Japanese, and, like his suits, seemed well beyond the price range of a badly paid provincial reporter. Natalie thought about that phrase he'd used – 'not in my interest to do that just now' – as they sped through the busy evening streets of the city's waking nightlife, and wondered just what *was* in his interest.

Was he taking kickbacks *not* to be a good journalist and uncover certain unsavoury truths? He seemed intelligent ... Maybe he could have dug just as hard and persistently for stories as she did, but was he being paid to do otherwise? If Daumery didn't pan out, maybe Alex could be the source of other angles.

Pondering, she'd hardly noticed where they were going, and, when she became aware of their surroundings again, she found that they were pulling up in a quiet street in the northern part of the city. Not the so-called posh area, she noted, but in the less wholesome quarter that was Redwych's unofficial red-light district. If a toffee-nosed university community could be said to have one of those.

Fontayne's looked nothing like a nightclub. In fact it looked like nothing at all, other than a faintly seedy and dilapidated, but otherwise nondescript, terraced town-house. It was rather large, but that was about all that could be said for it. Only a small wall plate, by the door, identified it at all. Having parked the four-by-four, Alex murmured into the speakerphone above the plate, and almost immediately the door swung open.

In the foyer they entered, a middle-aged woman in a smart but rather old-fashioned evening gown sat at a desk, with a ledger open in front of her and a computer terminal to one side. Beyond her, flanking a staircase, stood a couple of enormous muscle men dressed in black ties.

Just as Alex said, thought Natalie, a private drinking club, complete with bouncers.

'Good evening, Mr Hendry,' the woman behind the desk said, smiling warmly, if not downright flirta-tiously. 'One guest, is it?' When Alex nodded, she turned to Natalie. 'Would you care to sign in, madam?'

Natalie did so, and a moment later they were ascend-ing the stairs, followed by the watchful eyes of the bouncers.

Fontayne's was a strange old place, as far as Natalie could see. A mixture of fading kitsch tat and *fin de siècle* luxury. There was a lot of red plush, rococo and gilding. Natalie could not believe such an establishment still survived in the twenty-first century.

'It's a bit of a dump, isn't it?' she hissed to Alex as they reached the landing, where another bouncer stood at the curtained entrance to what was obviously the main club. Music drifted from beyond the panels of heavy red velvet – something soft and jazzy, understated but strangely appealing.

Alex just smiled, stepping back as the bouncer held aside the curtain for them and allowing Natalie to precede him into the club.

It was darkish, and the atmosphere was unhealthily smoky. Beneath the stylish, Americanised noodlings of the jazz pianist – who was sitting to one side of the room at a baby grand, which was in turn set next to a small stage – there was a steady, murmuring hum of conversation. In an atmosphere of subdued, almost bottled-up excitement, groups of people were sitting at tables, drinking, talking and smoking. They looked fairly ordinary at first glance, and through the obscured gloom, but as Natalie's eyes adjusted she felt a fresh surge of interest.

The clientele was a fascinating melange of not only club styles, but also sexual preferences, it seemed. At the table nearest to where she stood, there was a group of three very conservative-looking business types, but they were accompanied by three women dressed in the trashiest of street hooker style. Natalie saw short vinyl skirts, boob tubes, exaggerated make-up. She almost laughed out loud when one of the women adjusted her long and rather shapely legs and a pair of white stilettos came briefly into view.

Further into the club she saw people dressed in leather – both sexes – and a smattering of gorgeously handsome gay men in tight T-shirts and ripped denims. Scattered among these and also sitting with the straightest of the straight, she saw at least half a dozen drag queens, their sequins and lamé glittering in the darkness.

I wonder if Patti's client's in here, Natalie thought, remembering the glamorous blue frock as Alex indicated that they thread their way through the tables in search of one of their own. The room seemed full, but he went forward confidently as if he knew they'd find a space.

He led them to a table near the stage. There was no RESERVED card on it, but somehow Natalie got the impression that others had been warned not to sit at it. She wondered again what Alex might have done to deserve such special favours. This was one of the best tables in the house, yet it seemed to have been held for him.

When they were seated, a cocktail waitress approached them. She wasn't a bunny girl as such, but she wasn't far off. Her legs were among the longest and sleekest that Natalie had seen, even on London catwalks, and her skirt was pelmet-length beneath a tiny white net apron. She leaned and whispered in Alex's ear, and when he nodded she trotted away again, with purpose.

Natalie saw red. 'Er ... any chance of actually *asking* me what I want to drink?' she began, then stopped just as abruptly, her eye caught by a flash of movement a few tables away.

Patti!

Natalie leant forward so she was slightly shielded from her sister's eye line, yet at the same time could still see her. Patti was sitting with a small group of men and women whom Natalie had never seen before, but who all seemed to know each other very well. Patti looked flushed and excited, and – to Natalie's slight chagrin – extremely glamorous, despite the fact that her clothes and make-up were nothing out of the ordinary.

What was different about Patti was a sort of subtle gleam, an indefinable aura. She looked sexy, powerful and knowing, somehow. Quite unlike the Patti that Natalie had been familiar with prior to this visit.

'It's Patti,' Natalie whispered to Alex, while keeping herself hidden. 'What the hell is she doing here?'

'She's a member. Didn't she tell you?' In the darkness Alex's handsome face looked slightly mocking, as if he felt sorry for her because she didn't comprehend the blatantly obvious.

'No! She's hardly told me a fucking thing about anything!' Natalie said crossly, plucking at the table-cloth. 'But there's plenty going on with her, obviously, the devious bitch!'

Alex chuckled, but at that moment, before Natalie could either look back at Patti or make any further comment, two things happened. The cocktail waitress arrived with a bottle in a cooler and two glasses, and the already dim house lights began to lower even further. Natalie glanced round, hoping to catch Patti's eye this time, and let her sister know she was here and that she'd want to know, before the evening was out, what she was up to. But the light was already too dim, and Natalie's attention was distracted yet again by a fleeting glimpse that she caught of another face, a couple of tables beyond Patti. It was just an impression though, just on the edge of her vision . . .

Whitelaw Daumery?

Surely it couldn't be him. Not in *this* place. Not Mister Squeaky Clean in this cheap den of tawdry iniquity?

Natalie peered into the shadowy mass of seated fig-ures, but she could no longer see anything. The spotlight that was now focused on the stage eclipsed the rest of the room.

'And now, for your pleasure and delectation,' the pianist announced, 'our hostess, the divine, the glamor-ous, the sensational Miss Stella Fontayne!'

The instant the spotlight flared, Natalie forgot about Whitelaw Daumery.

Stella? Oh, bloody hell, this was Patti's drag queen! The new customer who had a fondness for shimmery fabrics. The tightly focused spot illuminated a circle on the small stage and a second later a tall, colourful figure stepped into the light. A man/woman wearing the very same rich blue dress that Natalie had last seen in her sister's living room.

But this was a drag queen like none that Natalie had ever seen before – a million miles away from the hard, glittering Barbie-like creatures in the audience and from any performers Natalie had seen on television and in clubs and at parties. She'd heard them crack risqué jokes on girls' nights out and as kissograms; she'd seen them lip-synch to gay music and to show tunes. In all these cases, though, they'd been overblown, over-sequinned, over-eyelashed, and lurid, almost barbarous caricatures. She'd never seen one who was really beautiful – like the diva who now stood before her, basking in the unwavering attention of a clearly adoring audience.

'Good evening, ladies and gentlemen,' said 'Stella', her smile slight and rather mysterious as she scanned the club with glowing, darkly outlined eyes. 'And welcome to Fontayne's . . .'

Stella's voice was clearly an acquired one. Specially cultivated for the role. But again there was no grotesque exaggeration. The feminine tones overlay a rich, vibrant baritone and Natalie suspected some serious dramatic training at the heart of the performance. As she watched and listened, unashamedly entranced, she felt herself forgetting all about Daumery, about Patti, about Alex Hendry sitting beside her, and about all her worries about her story, its possibilities for success or failure and her fears for her job at the *Modern Examiner*.

This is pure entertainment, she thought with an astonished smile as she listened to the transvestite's light banter with the audience and to a succession of unexpectedly sophisticated and only slightly dirty jokes.

'Now then, it's about that time, my dear friends,' said Stella after a while, turning to nod to the pianist, 'the time when you have to indulge me – and listen to my singing.' There was a murmur of approval rather than a groan, but the transvestite went on, 'Well, it *is* my club, after all.' She paused and smiled, then nodded again to her accompanist. 'There's a saying old, says that love is blind . . .'

Natalie had no real idea of what she was going to hear, and as Stella purred through the half-spoken, half-sung introduction, it took her a while to recognise the song . . .

'There's a somebody I'm longing to see . . .'

It was 'Someone To Watch Over Me'. A famous standard. A sweet, almost schmaltzy ballad. There was nothing particularly raunchy and suggestive, nor was the vocal delivery in any way camp.

Stella had a voice that was just as beautiful and unexpected as her appearance. A man's voice, yes, but trained, Natalie realised, in just the same way as the drag queen's speaking voice was. It was the voice of a new, composite creature that was both man *and* woman – and maybe, somehow, better than either one of them.

Oh, get real, Croft! Natalie told herself, laughing inside at her own whimsy, even as she enjoyed Stella's accomplished interpretation of the song. There was something knowing yet also touching about the well-known old lyric, and the way the transvestite performed it. Natalie felt hot all of a sudden, looking at that compellingly painted face and listening to the persuasive, light yet full-sounding baritone. She wanted to get close to Stella Fontayne suddenly; wanted to get to know what made a person like that tick.

Jesus Christ, I don't believe it! I'm starting to fancy a man who wears a dress!

Patti hadn't wanted to miss Stella's set, but there were other priorities to attend to, and other needs to be served. Much as she loved the old songs Stella sang so well, she'd heard them many a time before, and would hear them many more times, without a doubt.

The thing she was most concerned about was missing more of Natalie's reactions to the club and its denizens. It would have been interesting, to say the least, to observe her city-smart, cynical sister being oh so cleverly reeled into the sticky irresistible web that Stella was spinning.

Patti gave a tiny sigh of regret then allowed her 'other priorities' to claim her.

She was not the only patron of the club to have crept away in the darkness. Others had left the entertainments on offer out there to enjoy the more arcane ones available to certain 'special' members of Stella's clientele – those who were a part of the inner circle, the privileged elite.

Patti wasn't the 'victim' in tonight's entertainment. At least not for the moment ... Things could always change and mostly did. For now, she sat to one side, on the lap of one of the several hooded men in the room, allowing him to fondle her quim as they watched the first of several tableaux of the evening. His fingers were skilful and she was already very wet. As a second digit slid inside her and his thumb circled smoothly on her clit, she groaned and kissed his neck just beneath the stitched leather edge of the hood.

The room in which they were all assembled was shabby and old-fashioned in décor. It was lit by only an assortment of mismatched table lamps, and furnished with an equally hotchpotch collection of battered armchairs, and less comfortable upright chairs culled from a variety of dining suites. On these chairs, and in a circle, sat about twenty people: some women, some men, about half of them wearing hoods and the other half freely exhibiting their identities – and in some cases a whole lot more!

Everything had been removed from the centre of the circle, leaving clear space, and the only concession to modern convenience and luxury at all was a generously stocked bar at the far end of the room. Some of the participants were drinking; others didn't seem to need it. Everyone's attention was focused on the activity in the cleared area.

A woman in her fifties, grey-haired, but still attractive, and dressed in a glorious, white, heavy silk shirt and black trousers and black high-heels was having her way with a naked and hooded man.

Patti rather enjoyed seeing the boot being put in by the other foot for a change. There were more female submissives in the group than males – as was often the case, she'd gathered – but most people were like her, and switched according to how the mood took them. Even the mighty Stella had been known to put herself on the receiving end for a change. A rare treat, if you were lucky enough to be invited . . .

The naked man was blindfolded as well as hooded, and Patti shuddered in empathy. The vulnerability of his situation made her melt around the fingers that invaded her. She closed her eyes for a second and put herself in his position of blackness, delicious fear and total availability. There was nothing to be done in such a situation but to accept, to wait, to hold fast and endure. And yet it was a form of freedom, too. No decisions to make and no effort of thought involved. You were just a body, a column of pure feeling and sensation – perfectly submissive.

The fingers inside her suddenly flexed, stretching her, and as the thumb squashed down on her clit she gasped, completely back in her own body and attentive to the man who was masturbating her.

As her legs kicked and the pleasure surged, she heard the masked man groan too, as if in sympathy.

Chapter Seven
The Private Room

When the lights went up at the end of Stella's set, Natalie felt disorientated. There had been something curiously intimate about the transvestite's singing, a personal quality that had reached out to Natalie and made her feel that the songs had been chosen especially for her. She felt as if – even in the space of a few numbers, 'Someone To Watch Over Me', 'Stormy Weather' and several other standards – she'd come to know Stella Fontayne and had established a direct connection with her. With him. Whatever . . .

It took a few moments for Natalie's brain to re-engage, then the clamouring thoughts rushed back in again with a vengeance.

Patti!

Whitelaw Daumery!

Natalie turned around, scoping out the club, inwardly cursing the low lighting and the smoke haze. Where she'd seen Patti, and she thought she'd seen Daumery, new patrons had already taken their seats. Goddamnit, she'd missed them! They'd both gone.

The sound of someone discreetly clearing his throat to attract her attention reminded her that she wasn't here alone. She turned towards Alex, who was studying her with a slightly amused expression on his face.

'You'd completely forgotten I was here, hadn't you?' he said, not unpleasantly, then reached out and drained the glass of wine that he'd poured while Stella had been singing.

Natalie was glad of the low light this time because it was true: she had forgotten him. Hastily, she took a sip from her own glass, then drank more deeply. It was a soft white wine, not the cheap champagne substitute she'd been expecting. The taste was mellow and fruity, yet a little complex. A good wine in a place where there shouldn't have been any. She finished the glass.

'Admit it,' persisted Alex. 'For a minute there you had no idea who you were here with.'

Holding out her glass, Natalie shrugged. 'It's this place . . . The tranny and all . . .' When Alex had topped her up, she drank again, quickly. 'And I'm sure I saw Whitelaw Daumery over there just before the lights went down. I could swear it was him.' She glanced around, subconsciously wondering if just the name might summon her quarry, but the new occupants of the table were now laughing as if they too were mocking her. 'You never mentioned that he was a member here, either. Why on Earth was that, might I ask?'

'I don't know everyone who comes here,' Alex replied easily, not rising to her. 'Although I do know someone who's almost always here. Someone who could be a big help to you if you play your cards right.'

'Who's that?' demanded Natalie, drinking quickly again. She was aware that the wine was already making her a little light-headed, and that she would have to find the ladies' room sooner rather than later.

'Who do you think?' said Alex, and without warning he was on his feet, and pulling her up too.

Natalie shook his hand from her arm, but nevertheless followed him as he led the way through the tables, through the laughing, murmuring people who encircled them, and towards an unmarked door at the far end of the room.

Into the lair of Stella Fontayne, I presume, thought Natalie as they passed into a dimly lit corridor. The walls were painted with a beige emulsion, now discoloured, and hung with one or two cheap prints, but the general air was one of a bleak lack of maintenance. At the far end of the corridor a spiral staircase gave access to both the ground floor, and to floors above. There were also several doors, just as anonymous as the one they'd already passed through, and Alex knocked on one of these, then waited for an answer.

'Come in,' said a voice. It was muffled by the closed door, but still unmistakably the same one that Natalie had heard just a few minutes ago, singing 'Unforgettable'.

The room they stepped into was even darker than the club, lit only by a single Tiffany lamp strategically placed on a cluttered dressing table. It was also even shabbier – if that were possible – than the corridor behind them. Overstuffed armchairs were draped with heaps of shimmering dresses, cosmetics littered the discoloured melamine of the dressing table, and a big old sink stood in the corner, both its taps dripping. The general impression was of a shabby yet almost oriental glamour, and the sight of a slightly drunken-looking black-lacquered screen in the corner reinforced this. Natalie half expected Shanghai Lily to come slinking around from behind its painted panels, but instead the voice of Stella Fontayne issued forth, low and amused.

'Good evening, my dears, how did you like the set?'

Alex answered first.

'Sensational as ever, Stella,' he said, 'although I'm not sure about the change in the intro to "Blue Moon".' He turned to Natalie and winked. 'Did you just forget the words or what?'

'You cheeky young fuck,' countered Stella with a
laugh, her mannered voice curling happily around the
obscenity. 'What would you know about song lyrics,
Alex? You're a philistine. Don't you recognise artistic
licence when you hear it?'

'Is that what you call it? I thought it was just the first
signs of senility showing up,' replied Alex, laughing
himself.

Stella continued to chuckle but didn't rise to the bait.
Natalie could hear faint evocative rustles coming from
behind the glossy black screen and she couldn't stop her
imagination from running wild. She pictured a broad-
shouldered, narrow-hipped male body encased in a
luxurious corset, forced into a new shape by nylon net
and whalebone. Did Stella wear lace and satin underwear? Did her cock swing free within the delicate fabrics, or did she bind it close to ensure a perfect
bulge-free line to her gowns? How uncomfortable was
that when, inevitably, she needed to urinate?

Croft, you're a pervert, Natalie berated herself
silently. But all the same, she could tell where the
thought had come from. Her own need to pee was
becoming increasingly acute, and as Alex took her hand,
then sat down in a big, saggy armchair and drew her
on to his lap, she had to suppress a gasp at the fierce
jolt in her bladder.

Why, oh why, do I keep getting myself into this
situation? Natalie thought, feeling sweat pop out in her
armpits. It was almost as if she enjoyed it. As if she got
off on the unique discomfort of needing to pee. The
thought of *that* only made her hotter than ever.

'So, what do you think of my club, Natalie?' enquired
Stella. There was a soft whoosh of cloth and the shimmering dark-blue dress was draped over the end panel
of the screen. 'I suppose it seems tame to you by London
standards. A bit of an anachronism.'

'No, it's – it's great,' Natalie stammered, feeling at a

loss for something to say in this weird environment. Her own lack of confidence in her sense of place concerned her. Usually she was so sure of herself, even in the weirdest situations. Snap! Snap! Snap! Always on the ball. Effortlessly getting a feel for the people and their surroundings, as well as how to describe them. She prided herself on asking the right questions, the cleverest ones, the ones that got just the newsworthy answers she wanted. But here, in this shadowy room in the pervading yet hidden presence of this provincial drag queen, she felt completely wrong-footed and out of touch with herself.

'Great, eh?' murmured Stella, clearly unimpressed by such a nonspecific response. 'So what's your usual music preference? Techno? Garage? Acid jazz?' She paused. 'Or perhaps you prefer the classics.'

Natalie wondered for a moment what Alex had been saying about her. It was obvious that he had briefed Stella, or else why on Earth would the transvestite even know her name. She was about to answer sharply when a surge of sensation made her gasp. Hidden from their hostess, Alex had started taking liberties . . .

'I like all kinds of music,' Natalie said tightly, trying to control her breathing and stay still even though Alex's hand was right up her skirt and his fingers were touching the gusset of her flimsy thong. 'Anything really. And I do think you've got a marvellous singing voice. Even if you don't sound exactly like a woman!'

From behind her hide, Stella chuckled again and a silk robe that had been hanging from the corner of it disappeared. Natalie tried to use the moment of distraction to knock Alex's hand away from her crotch, but, exhibiting a strength she wouldn't have expected in him, he quelled her and pressed his fingers fiendishly against her belly, just above her pubic bone. Her need to pee escalated into the stab of a thousand hot needles and she had to pant for a moment. The only way to escape from him was to create a fuss that Stella would hear.

'I do the best I can,' said the transvestite, as the silk rustled and she obviously slid into her robe. 'Under the circumstances . . .' For just a second the pitch of her voice dropped slightly and Natalie gained an impression of the voice of the man who was Stella. It sounded familiar somehow, and her brain began the process of placing it – but then Alex's fingers pressed again and she couldn't think any more.

Straining every muscle, Natalie fought the sensations and held in her gathering waters. She bit her lip, and, as quietly as she could, she tried to shove at Alex and push herself free of him. As she mimed furious obscenities into his face, he only smiled at her.

'Are you two all right out there?' said Stella suddenly. 'Not getting up to any mischief, are you, Alex? I know what you're like.'

'No, nothing going on here,' Alex said blandly as, with a deft twist of his wrist, he got his hand on the inside of Natalie's thong, his fingers probing. 'What kind of man do you think I am? You know I'm a perfect gentleman.'

If she hadn't been in such a state, Natalie would have laughed out loud at such a bunch of corny clichés, but as it was she had all on to cope with the turmoil in her body. Alex had two fingers between her labia, and was slowly and relentlessly rocking them against her clit. Her arousal was soaring, her slit was drenched and her heart felt as if it had risen into her throat. The bastard was trying to make her come while she was still supposed to be having a conversation with Stella.

'You're no more a gentleman than I am,' retorted the transvestite, her laugh knowing, as if she could see what Alex was doing. 'But don't mind me, my dears. You just have fun if you want to. I won't watch. I'll just have five minutes behind here and relax with a ciggie.' After a moment, Natalie heard the click of lighter, then saw a plume of smoke drift up from behind the screen.

This was surreal. What had she stumbled into? Natalie wasn't narrow-minded, quite the reverse. She saw herself as permissive and liberated, even a bit degenerate after her seduction of Steven Small on the train and what she'd done in that secluded yard with Alex.

But this was different. To casually allow herself to be played with in the presence of a third party she'd never met before? It was unthinkable.

And yet . . .

Maybe she'd crossed over into a world where things like this were thinkable, natural, a matter of course.

But the feminist in her rebelled. These two were exploiting her, weren't they? Alex was copping a feel of her quim and Stella, despite her make-up and her pretty wig, was still a man getting his jollies from hearing a woman being masturbated. And he had the bloody cheek to sit there smoking while he listened to it!

'Stop it, you bastard!' she hissed at Alex, struggling against him, but getting nothing for her efforts but an excruciating jab of sensation in her swimming bladder. She gasped, clenched every muscle, and then kicked her legs as his fingers circled diabolically on her clit. From behind the screen Stella 'tutted' in mock disapproval.

'Get off me, Alex,' Natalie persisted, her voice cracking slightly against her will. She couldn't stop her legs moving or her hips weaving. One of her sandals slid free of her foot and clomped to the floor. 'I didn't come here for this! I came here to find out things . . . About Daumery . . . You said it would be useful!' She squirmed hard, both in protest and in pleasure, but Alex's arm around her waist closed like a vice. Between her legs he pinched her clit and lightly twisted it.

'You fuck!' she cried, bucking like a fish on a line,

terrified that she might wet herself, yet also, and nastily, wanting to. So she could ruin her tormentor's flash suit!

'Whitelaw Daumery, eh?' said Stella after a moment, another plume of exhaled smoke rising up. 'What gives you the idea that coming here can help you find out anything about him?'

Tears of frustration and befuddlement threatened Natalie's make-up. She could barely see, barely think; she was aching to pee, aching to come. She felt so excited she wanted to rip open her top and caress her breasts as Alex played with her clitoris. Her grip on her objectives and her methods was disintegrating.

'He was out there, in the club,' she said faintly, shaking her head to try to clear her thoughts. It no longer seemed worth the effort to fight against Alex. 'I saw him. Do you know him?' She forced some effort into her voice to let Stella Fontayne know that she was addressing her. That she could still function as an intellect, not just a mass of firing nerves and pumping glands.

'Was he? Fancy that,' Stella said whimsically. 'I never realised.' There was a sound of movement from behind the screen, a swish of fabric. Hyper-aware, Natalie sensed a tension and excitement in the air that didn't emanate from her own chaotic flesh. She had a flash vision of a long stiff penis held between fingers tipped with long scarlet nails. Her pussy spasmed and ejected a little slick fluid on to Alex's massaging fingers.

'Look!' she said fiercely. 'If you don't stop and let me find a toilet, I'm going to piss all over you and your fancy suit, OK?' Summoning the last of her strength, she shook herself free of Alex and sprang to her feet. 'Where is it? Where's the loo? There must be one around here.'

Both Alex and Stella were laughing now. Broad, loud, male laughs. Expressing a vile, chauvinistic age-old amusement at the plight of the 'little woman' in distress.

If Natalie had had a knife about her she would have gone for first one, then the other of them. Gladly!

'Through there,' said Stella, and, as if the two of them were telepathic, Alex nodded towards a door that Natalie hadn't noticed before, in the shadowed darkest corner of the room.

Natalie fled, overcome by her own body, but still enraged. She had a horrible feeling she may already have wet herself.

The lavatory beyond the door was tiny and basic. Stella obviously washed in the sink in her dressing room, as there was nothing in the cubicle but the high, old-fashioned pedestal with an overhead cistern. Natalie had no doubt that they would be able to hear her pissing through the insubstantial-looking door, but she no longer cared. When she pulled down her knickers and hunkered down on the seat, she groaned with frustration when the relief she craved wouldn't come. Her bladder was so irritated by Alex's fingerings that she couldn't seem to relax and let her tortured urethra open.

'For Christ's sake,' she hissed through gritted teeth, wriggling on the ancient wooden seat, feeling a low, subversive drag that made her sex pulse. On an instinct, she reached down and stroked herself, at first gingerly, then harder, and harder, until she was masturbating furiously.

It took just a couple of seconds for her to come, like a rocket soaring up out of the squalor of the tiny antiquated lavatory, and for her pent-up water to gush blissfully, increasing her pleasure. As she jerked and rocked, she heard her own harsh cry ricochet revealingly around the four grubby walls. Alex and Stella would hear her too, but what the hell! Fuck them!

Natalie sat for a long while, slumped on the seat, getting her breath back and coming down through layers of white shock. She felt exhausted. Elated. Disgusted with herself yet somehow also liberated. No one would ever be able to accuse her of being a tight-arsed control freak ever again!

The only thing that bothered her now was her total lack of progress in finding out about Daumery. Wasn't that the supposed goal of all this, the destination at the end of this tortuous trail? Not for the first time, she realised that there was a part of her that was forgetting how to care about the job, and about her status at *Modern Examiner*. She had no idea what she would do other than be a journalist, but somehow the treachery and double dealing she'd been subjected to suddenly seemed more significant and less a force to be fought than one to be walked away from, with indifference.

'You're getting soft in your old age, Nat,' she whispered to herself as she pulled up her knickers and smoothed down her skirt. Grateful for the private and confined space, she shook her head to clear it of all the nonsense.

'Look. About Whitelaw Daumery,' she said briskly as she stepped out of the lavatory. Then she stopped short. The cluttered dressing room was deserted.

Where the hell were they, Stella and Alex? They were gone, and the scruffy room had a stillness about it that was almost creepy. As if no one had ever been there at all, and she was lost in an alien place like Alice through the Looking Glass.

A cracked looking glass, thought Natalie when she'd washed her hands in the sink and she was leaning towards the big dressing-table mirror, checking her face and hair. After smoothing a few straggling wisps of hair back into her sleeked-back style, she decided she looked OK, if still a little flushed, then looked down at the jumble of cosmetics, tissues, cotton-wool buds and other ephemera that were strewn across the ageing and dis-coloured plastic surface.

Clearly, Stella favoured high-end make-up brands to create her façade of womanhood. Natalie saw the distinctive packaging of Versace, Shishiedo, Laura Mercier and several other top names, and when she opened a few eye shadows, and twisted up lipsticks she found the colours were all far more subtle than she'd expected somehow. But what *had* she expected? Bright, brash, lurid dawbs? It was clear that Stella was not a common-or-garden drag queen. She was glamorous, yes, but not cheap in any way.

What the hell am I doing?

Dropping the mascara wand she'd been just about to touch up her own lashes with, Natalie leapt to her feet. She was sitting here like an airhead, fooling about with make-up and not thinking at all about Stella and Alex's disappearance or where they might be. She ought at least to suss out Alex's whereabouts. He was the one who'd brought her here, after all.

Out in the corridor, the faint sounds of music and conversation seemed to suggest she return to the club. That was probably where Alex and Stella had gone anyway. And yet the row of enigmatic doors seemed to tempt the journalist in her. What secrets might lie beyond them? Or down that vertiginous-looking staircase at the end of the corridor. She walked along and looked down, seeing another corridor below. It was in darkness, but there was a tiny glimmer of light, suggesting an open door somewhere down there.

A gut feeling compelled her to descend – even though she had no idea who or what she might find down there.

After nearly slipping twice on the slippery wrought-iron steps, and wondering how the hell Stella managed, with even bigger feet in even higher heels, Natalie reached the lower corridor. Here there were sounds of conversation too, but from fewer voices. She couldn't tell what was being said, but the tone was far more focused and intent than the general mêlée from the club.

There was an intimation of excitement too, an almost wicked expectation.

Tiptoeing, Natalie came to the door of the room from which the light was issuing. It was subdued light again, lamps probably, and she wondered briefly what any part of this strange shabby establishment would look like in broad daylight. A total dump, no doubt. The door stood slightly ajar, and she was able to peer in without fear of being seen.

What she saw, however, made her jaw drop and her heart race. Even though, strangely, she'd been half expecting something like this.

There were about fifteen people in the room, possibly more, and they were sitting around, in a loose circle, watching a performance. Just as Natalie moved forward a little there was a gasp of appreciation.

A man who was naked apart from a leather hood that covered his entire head was standing in the light of a small spotlight, his hands clasped behind his neck. Around him patrolled a greying, middle-aged woman, carrying a stick or switch of some kind. After a moment, she swished it, then hit the man across the front of his right thigh. He cried out piercingly, and his mouth, which was the only part of his face that was visible, looked wet and red as if he'd been biting his lips in pain. Which well he might have been doing, thought Natalie, horrified, yet fascinated, because the lengths of both his thighs were crimson and striped with weals. Almost as ruddy was the huge erection that danced before him.

My God, S&M – this is wild!

Part of Natalie wanted to laugh, thinking in terms of tabloid headlines, KINKY SEX GAMES IN SUBURBIA and the like. There was a general world-weariness that metropolitans affected which poured scorn on such activities – and yet there was another part of her, the greater part of her, she realised, that was breathless with excitement and fascination.

This was 'it', but what did 'it' feel like? Why was it a turn-on? Would it turn her on too?

The last question had already been answered, it dawned on her. She was as horny now as she had been a short while ago, with Alex's hand between her legs. She wished that hand were *still* there. As the hooded man moaned, she pressed her cupped fingers against her crotch.

The grey-haired woman wasn't at all impressed with her victim. She cut him again, this time across his backside, then began flicking his cock very lightly with the long, thin switch. 'You're not supposed to be enjoying this,' she told him, and Natalie thought that the voice sounded more amused and affectionate than that of a strict dominatrix. Although what a strict dominatrix was really like she had no idea. Her own experience was culled from a few art-house films and television programmes that she suspected didn't tell the true story at all.

The man groaned again, then, as the switch slid delicately under the head of his cock, he made a low, broken choking sound, and his hips started jerking. Gouts of white spunk shot from him and, dashing away the stick, he gripped his shaft and began to pump.

Before Natalie's wide eyes, the hooded man's orgasm seemed to go on for an age. He looked agonised, but, surely, he was enjoying it. His face was twisted with the intensity of the sensations, and, though his eyes were hidden, she sensed they were closed; the impression his body gave off was one of the sweetest pleasure combined with a deep and bitter shame.

By coming so soon he had clearly failed his mistress.

What's the sense in this? thought Natalie. How does it work? Up until a few days ago, nothing in her own sexual history related to these . . . these games. And now she seemed to be able to understand it. Or at least her body understood it. Despite bringing herself off only minutes ago, she was aroused again.

At that moment, the strap of her bag slid off her shoulder and it fell to the floor with a bump. The sound was small, but in the room beyond all the faces she could see turned towards the door.

'Come in, Natalie,' said a familiar voice, and Natalie realised that at least she had found Stella Fontayne again.

There was nothing for it but to bite the bullet and join in whatever these people were engaged in. Natalie pushed open the door and stepped into the erratically lit room.

The first people she recognised – after Stella, who was opposite her, wearing a leather eye mask and a gorgeous black silk kimono – were Patti, and then Alex. Her sister was sitting on the lap of a man wearing a leather hood, similar to that of the beaten man; and Alex had shed his designer jacket and was sitting slumped in his chair with one hand clasped tightly against his crotch. He was at one side of Stella, and Patti and her paramour were on the other.

Natalie caught Patti's eye, wanting to ask a million questions, but not knowing how to frame them. When she opened her mouth, Patti pressed a finger against her own lips in a 'shushing' gesture. Natalie was about to persist when she took a second look at the way her sister was sitting. Was it her imagination or was Patti actually sitting on the man's cock? As if in confirmation, the couple adjusted themselves; Patti's short skirt rode up, and Natalie got a clear view of her sister's naked mound pressed against her companion's opened trousers. As Patti wriggled again, her lips parted in a gasp while the man's hands slid up her body and clasped her breasts proprietorially.

Natalie suddenly felt sick and faint yet horribly fascinated. It dawned on her again that, until she'd arrived and caught her sister cavorting with Dyson, Natalie had mostly tried to avoid thinking about Patti having sex. Unsuccessfully, a lot of the time, she realised now, but the odd, idle thoughts that had drifted into her mind had always had the quality of fiction to them. They'd seemed fantasy-like and unreal. But there was nothing notional or imaginary about seeing Patti writhing now. Natalie could almost feel what it was like to be her sister, to be astride that unknown man, her naked buttocks pressed against his belly, and his thick penis lodged inside her like a ramrod. Even as she looked on, the masked man added the final touch. He slid one hand down Patti's body and then wiggled a finger in between the lips of her sex. Patti began to moan as the finger flexed and circled.

Natalie knew what that felt like. She'd felt it herself recently. Glancing towards Alex, she saw he was smiling and watching her closely; his own hand seemed to squeeze in time to the efforts of the man stroking Patti.

I must be dreaming all this, thought Natalie, looking around the circle, and seeing masked and unmasked faces, some looking at the beaten man, some watching her, some looking at the now-thrashing Patti. This can't be happening. Surely I'm back at Northmore Row, in bed, having an erotic dream.

'Don't be shy, Natalie, we're all friends here.'

Stella Fontayne's voice snapped Natalie from her dream.

This was real. All real. The man in the mask had been beaten, had come, and was standing with his head bowed, waiting, presumably, for the next humiliation. Patti was still bouncing up and down on the prick of her own masked man.

'Alex, leave your dick alone and get Natalie a chair!' commanded Stella, turning to Alex beside her and knocking his hand away from his groin.

Alex in turn murmured a good-natured, 'Fuck you, Stella!' but rose from his seat and dragged another chair from against the wall. He set it between his and Stella's, then grinned towards Natalie. He said nothing, but his eyes seemed to dare Natalie to join the circle.

All right, fuck it, I will! thought Natalie, walking around the outside of the circle to take her place. She didn't look at Stella, Alex or Patti. The effort of looking calm and cool and as if she saw sights like this every night took all her energy. As she sank on to the chair she felt as if her legs had been just about to give way. She smoothed down her skirt as she settled herself. It seemed important not to set a precedent of exposure. If Patti wanted to show her quim to all and sundry, that was her business, but Natalie had no intention of doing the same, regardless of whatever blandishments were pressed upon her.

Stella Fontayne seemed to read her mind.

'Don't worry, Natalie, no need to participate when it's your first time,' the drag queen said. Her voice sounded as kind as that of a good teacher on the first day of school, and for a moment Natalie experienced a rush of total disorientation as her brain floundered, trying to make a connection. She wanted to scream with a frustration that wasn't just sexual. All of a sudden there was a link here, something obvious that was staring her in the face, but it wouldn't fall into place and her own inadequacy made her feel furious.

What is it? What the fuck is it? I should *know*!

But then the fugitive association was gone, dissolved by Patti's wild, gulping cry of orgasm.

Still unable to look at her sister, Natalie scanned the ring of faces, what she could see of them, and those of the man and woman still standing in the centre. There was an almost imperceptible leaning forward in all the participants, a hunger in the body language, even in those who were masked. They seemed to be feeding on

Patti's exposure – as much on the emotional quality of it as the physical. She was out of control, regressed to the primal, a puppet to her own involuntary spasms.

To Natalie's right, and in contrast, Stella Fontayne looked almost placid. The painted face was serene, interested yet untroubled. Natalie could see only the oblique glitter of the transvestite's eyes behind the leather domino, but the line of Stella's jaw was very pure and relaxed. Beneath the perfectly applied foundation, her skin appeared very, very smooth. Would the stubble be detectable to the fingertips, however? For a moment, Natalie was almost on the point of reaching out for an answer. The muscles of her arm gathered themselves, but then a sound from her left distracted her.

'Oh, yeah,' moaned Alex, back in his chair and with his hand once more at his crotch. His eyes looked heavy and glazed with desire, yet his attention was very squarely on Patti, who seemed to be rising to a second climax before the first one was fully resolved.

Even as Natalie watched him, Alex turned towards her for just a second and winked. Then, returning to the main attraction of the moment, he deftly unzipped his flies, brought out his cock and began to wank in full view of the circle. In the weird light, he looked huge, bigger even than he'd seemed to Natalie during their time in the yard and the van.

As Patti kicked, shouted 'Oh Christ!' and finally seemed to subside, the focus of the circle's interest was suddenly Alex and his attentions to his prick. Even the hooded man in the centre seemed to sense what was happening. He turned towards Alex as if by instinct and his tongue popped out and circled his red, bitten lips. Despite all he'd gone through, and experienced, the man still clearly hungered for more. For the taste of a fellow man's cock . . .

Glancing between the two men, Natalie saw a sudden

flash of alarm disrupt Alex's display. His eyes widened for a moment, and she wondered what it was he feared so much. Was he a homophobe? Did he fear for his macho image? How strange was that in such a clearly perverted milieu?

Instinctively, she turned back towards Stella, and it didn't surprise her that the drag queen too was watching the interaction between Alex and his hooded admirer. A tiny smile played around her perfectly defined lips. Tiny, but full of mischief.

Oh boy, she knows he doesn't like it and she's wondering whether to encourage it.

Natalie forgot her own qualms for a moment, and found herself caught up in this new development. My God, she thought, I see the attraction now . . . What they all like so much. Or maybe what Stella likes so much. She's playing them all off against each other, balancing their desires and kinks for amusement's sake. Does she ever participate, I wonder? Does she ever lose it? Put on a show? Cede control to someone else in the group?

'You!' said Stella quietly, sticking out one long, dark-stockinged leg and nudging the hooded man on his bare calf with the pointed toe of a large but very elegant court shoe. 'We're finished with you now. Go to the corner, stand with your hands on your head and contemplate your shortcomings.' The drag queen laughed, but it wasn't a cruel laugh. Natalie thought she detected a degree of fondness in it. 'And there certainly are plenty . . .' She slid her toe a little higher, then withdrew it.

The hooded man began to blunder towards the edge of the circle, and contrary to Natalie's expectations, two of the participants moved their chairs aside, then guided him towards what was obviously the designated 'punishment corner' of the room, where no furniture stood. As they slid their chairs back into place, it seemed he was already almost completely forgotten.

All attention now was centred on Alex.

'I think you need some help, my friend,' murmured Stella, reaching down to get her cigarettes, a lighter and an ashtray from where they'd been hidden beside her armchair. As she leaned over, Natalie saw the silky artificial curls of the transvestite's wig slide aside to reveal the nape of her neck. The skin looked white, and vulnerable and feminine, but at the same time the column of the neck was strong, and a man's. Natalie felt a strange twist of attraction, and a sudden urge to bend over and kiss the exposed patch of skin.

'Rochelle, why don't you oblige?' Stella said, slipping a long, black cigarette between her lips, and deftly flicking open the lighter one-handed. She touched the tip of the cigarette into the flame and drew on it long and luxuriously. 'I'm sure Alex would appreciate your expertise.'

Rochelle, it seemed, was the dominatrix who'd just been beating the masked man. She locked eyes with Stella, and for a moment Natalie saw defiance in her face. Then she shook her head and laughed softly. Nodding acquiescence, she turned to face Alex, took a step towards him, then sank down on to her knees. Pausing only for Stella's signal – a nonchalant gesture with the long, dark cigarette – she leaned forward and buried her face in Alex's crotch. Her reddened lips opened like a flower as she took him into her mouth and began to suck him.

Alex groaned again. He closed his eyes and his handsome face twisted into a contorted grin of pure contentment. With one hand he gripped the arm of his chair and the other he wound into Rochelle's wiry, silvered hair to direct her efforts. Rochelle, for her part, applied herself to her task with noisy enthusiasm. The noise of her sucking, slurping mouth, combined with the rustling and scraping of Alex's shoes as he writhed in his chair, sounded deafening in the claustrophobic atmosphere of the dimly lit room.

Natalie watched, captivated by the sight of something so familiar as fellatio seen in such different circumstances. She'd sucked off enough boyfriends in her time, and sometimes found herself getting off on it without benefit of any pleasure for herself, but seeing someone else do it was entirely novel to her.

How ugly it looked, and yet what a turn-on. Rochelle's cheeks bulged out of all proportion with the size of Alex's cock, and she grew red in the face. Her fine, haughty eyes were almost crossed with effort, and perhaps the pain of Alex's fingers gouging into her scalp. Natalie remembered her own fingers pulling Alex's hair as he went down on her, and the tears that had brought to his eyes. The only tears he was likely to be shedding now were tears of pleasure. As he began to gasp, another woman – a blonde with short hair, a tight black dress, and wearing a leather eye mask just like Stella's – moved to the other side of Alex from Natalie and began to kiss him. Her tongue plundered his mouth, just as his prick plundered Rochelle's.

All of a sudden, a hand touched her arm and she gasped. She turned and found Stella watching not the juxtaposition of mouths and cock but her face.

'Would you have done that if I'd asked you to?' The transvestite looked at her steadily, her eyes not wavering once, even as she took a drag from her narrow black cigarette and exuded a long, evocative plume of silvery smoke from the corner of her shimmering rose-painted mouth.

'I – I don't know . . .'

Would she have done it? Part of her wanted to. Part of her wished she was down there now, her cheeks rounded like a hamster's, her throat almost choked with a hard, mindless, thrusting penis. She wanted to feel a strong male hand gripping her head, smell the rank smell of man in her nostrils.

And yet . . .

She looked down at the long, well-cared-for hand that still lay lightly on her bare arm.

That was a strong male hand, for all the beautiful, long nails that tipped each finger. How would it feel to have those talons buried in her hair? How would it be to suck a man, yet see that ersatz woman's face looking down on her as she did it? To taste salty male flesh, yet smell the sweet, feminine fragrance that wafted even now from the enigmatic body beside her?

As she looked up from Stella's hand, and into her dark-lined eyes, she realised that it may not be all that long before her curiosity was satisfied.

Blowing a perfect smoke ring, the drag queen mimed the single word, 'Soon.'

Chapter Eight
On the Trail

Natalie looked down at the sheet of pale-pink paper, with its cryptic list of dates and phrases, and suddenly saw what had been staring her in the face.

They were newspaper headlines, along with the dates on which they'd appeared.

Jesus, I must really be losing it, she thought, reaching for her coffee and gulping down a big mouthful. Maybe a massive caffeine boost would make her brain start working again. Ozzy the cat, who was sitting at the other end of the table watching her, gave a disdainful flick of his tail as if dismissing her weakness. Clearly he didn't need stimulants to keep him sharp.

Beneath the large and elegantly looped Fontayne's logo, PLANS FOR NEW LOCAL SPORTS CENTRE had a date around two years ago. RESIDENTS' FEARS FOR BEAUTY SPOT was a year before that. MASSIVE REDEVELOPMENT was only last year. Clearly they were from local papers too, judging by the wording. Probably the *Sentinel*. And if they were headlines from *Sentinel* perhaps Alex could get her back copies. It would be quicker than going through a great palaver at the public library. Big nationals had online archives mostly nowadays, but local rags like the *Sentinel* were still in the Dark Ages and the hard graft of old-style journalism was still required: struggling with the actual papers bound in huge, unwieldy files, or scrolling through microfiches until you were cross-eyed and heading for a migraine.

She'd ask Alex first.

But a vision of him as she'd last seen him last night made Natalie's hand shake and coffee splosh all over the list. She blotted it furiously with a tissue, but couldn't stop thinking of the red lips of that middle-aged dominatrix encircling his shaft while the blonde had leaned over him, first raping his mouth with her tongue, then offering her nipple for him to suck like a baby.

Why did I just let that happen? He arrived with me! Shouldn't I have been the one to play with him?

Natalie felt herself getting hot again. How could she have just sat there and watched an orgy going on and not participated. Wasn't she supposed to be the proactive one, the girl who just took what she wanted? Maybe she could do that only one on one, with submissive wimps like her bashful schoolteacher on the train?

She tried to imagine what it might have been like if she'd had the bottle, found herself any man, if not Alex, and just had sex. Where would she have woken up this morning? Some of the participants had looked pretty well heeled. Even if they were only playing around, and couldn't have taken her back to their matrimonial homes, she might have been in a suite in the Churchill Hotel right now, sipping Buck's Fizz instead of a cup of coffee at Patti's.

Speaking of Patti, Natalie wondered what time her sister had arrived home. She was surprised that Patti even *was* home. Judging by the way things had been going last night it might well have been Patti who was in a suite at the Churchill, being pampered.

Or being fucked again.

What's happened to her? What's happened to us both? It's sex wherever we look now, whether we're actually looking for it or not. How long has Redwych been like this? It's as if there's something in the air or in the water. Everyone here has turned into a pervert while I've been away.

But God, hadn't Patti looked amazing last night? And so full of confidence and into everything that was happening . . .

Unbidden, Natalie saw her sister now, instead of pictures of Alex and his cock and his women. Her head filled with an image of Patti on that man's knee. Then with a zoom of their joined crotches: Patti's sex stretched over an anonymous man's cock; Patti bouncing on his erection, gripping her own breasts, reaching down to finger herself.

Oh Christ, what am I doing?

Almost choking, Natalie realised that she was holding herself as she sat at Patti's kitchen table. She was squeezing her quim and thinking about her sister – wanting her.

Natalie leapt to her feet, sending her coffee cup flying and Ozzy scrambling from the table and out of the room with an outraged hiss. She had the presence of mind to snatch up her mobile before it got a soaking, but otherwise all thought was blanked by the enormity of what she'd just realised.

God almighty, Nat! She's your sister!

But only a half-sister, a subversive little voice whispered. And anyway, it's not like you're going to fuck each other and produce mutant babies, is it?

Snatching up the pink list, she ran like Ozzy for some dubious notion of safety.

'Why doesn't this stupid fucking place have a Tube?' muttered Natalie, glaring at Patti's car where she'd parked it, in the multistorey, at great expense to herself.

She supposed she could have walked to the public library, but, as everything in favour seemed against her this morning, she'd decided to ask her sister if she could borrow her little red hatchback. She hadn't expected Patti to agree, but it was either that or beg a lift in Dyson's van – which was both cringingly awkward and the absolute pits of slumming.

'Yeah ... OK ... take my car ... But just leave me alone,' Patti had muttered from beneath the duvet when Natalie had looked in on her and told her she was going to the library and needed transport. She would have liked to quiz her sister on the presence of Whitelaw Daumery in Fontayne's last night. But it hadn't sounded as if Patti was planning on getting up for a long while yet, and, considering her sister's athletic efforts the previous night, that wasn't surprising. Natalie knew of old how difficult it was to get Patti to wake up before she was ready. And if Patti was embarrassed and couldn't face her ...

Do not go there, Natalie told herself, hoisting her mini-rucksack and making her way quickly out of the car park. If she started brooding about last night again, she'd never get anywhere! She had to focus!

Outside the main library building, Natalie tried Alex's number again, just in case there was still a chance she could cut some corners off her research time.

'Hi, this is Alex Hendry, please leave a message –'

'Blah-di-blah-di-blah! Fuck!' hissed Natalie stabbing the cancel button in the middle of the message she'd already heard about six times this morning.

What kind of fucking idiot of a journalist is he if nobody can ever get hold of him?

Natalie considered trying the *Sentinel* again, but couldn't face a second wrangle with the stupid prissy receptionist – who'd already been downright obstructive once this morning.

But, then again, if he's getting kickbacks, maybe he

doesn't need to work all that hard. The words 'not in my interest' rang in her mind again. On whose payroll was Alex besides the *Sentinel*'s? The man lived far too well for the type of salary a provincial newspaper was likely to be paying him.

'Screw him!' whispered Natalie as she began to climb the steps of Redwych's Belvedere Library building.

In spite of her years away, and her confidence in herself and her achievements, there was still something about this place that made her feel small and very young again. She supposed it was the lofty ceilings, the self-important neoclassical statuary in the entrance hall and the sombre coloration of dark wood and grey and black floor tiling. It was cold in here, too, despite the warmth of the day outside, and Natalie felt goose bumps form on her bare arms as she stood looking around, wondering where to get started. There had obviously been major rearrangements here since the days of youthful visits.

Some of the library staff were just as snotty as ever, though, she soon discovered, on receiving a cool reception at the enquiries desk to her request for back issues of the *Sentinel*. Was I like this? Natalie wondered, trying to remember her days as a Saturday helper at the Belvedere. She didn't recall being consciously arrogant, although she supposed there was a certain sense of power involved, even when you were right at the bottom of the library food chain.

The female assistant's eyebrows went up when Natalie showed her the pink piece of paper. Natalie was puzzled for a moment by this reaction, but then she realised that Fontayne's was probably infamous in a place like Redwych as the seedy underbelly of sleaze and perversion. The impression was confirmed when the library assistant crinkled her nose, as if the sheet of paper smelled of something bad, and held it very delicately by a corner between finger and thumb.

'Some of these papers are on microfiche and some are bound. I'll have to fetch them for you,' she said rather doubtfully.

She obviously thinks I'm a hooker or a stripper or something, thought Natalie, wishing she'd worn something more outrageous than a simple black T-shirt and chinos. A plunging neckline or something with plenty of slits and cut-outs would've really made their eyes pop in here!

While the assistant still hovered, frowning, a male librarian came up behind her.

'Problem, Susan?' he enquired, even though he was actually looking over the disapproving Susan's shoulder and smiling at Natalie with obvious interest. When he saw what his colleague was reading, his eyes lit up even more.

'I'll see to this,' he said, prising the sheet of paper from Susan's hand and still smirking at Natalie. Natalie could almost see him preening and mentally reviewing his chat-up lines. As he came out from behind the counter, she couldn't help but let her glance drift down to his crotch and got the satisfaction of seeing him blush and look a good deal less sure of himself.

'If you'd like to go through to the main reading room, where the fiche viewers are, I'll bring the papers and fiches to you.' Natalie had to admire him. In spite of his embarrassment he still seemed extraordinarily helpful – and keen.

The main reading room hadn't altered much, except for the addition of the public fiche viewers and a number of open-access computer terminals. There were the usual selection of students, academics and people with nothing better to do with their time sitting around at various desks with their heads down, trying not to attract too much attention to themselves, even though the old SILENCE signs had long since disappeared. Natalie wondered what they would all do if she were to leap on the table and tell them – at the top of her voice – about her adventures at Fontayne's. The students might get a kick from it, she supposed, but some of the more donnish types would probably have a heart attack.

Natalie was just wondering if the Belvedere had moved into the twenty-first century and now served coffee as the bookshops all did, when her pet librarian appeared in the doorway carrying the materials she'd asked for. Maybe if she asked him, he'd bring her a coffee. She could certainly still do with some – to clear her mind of her incessant thoughts of sex.

'Here you are,' said the librarian. 'The most recent article is in this binder –' he laid a huge heavy bound collection of papers on the reading table '– and the older ones are on microfiche.' He set the fiches in their protective envelopes down too. 'If there's anything else you need, or if the fiche readers play up, please come to the desk and ask for me. My name's Roland Dale by the way.' He gave her a winning smile.

'Thanks for your help, Roland,' Natalie said, rewarding him with a smile of her own. One could never tell when a tame librarian may come in handy for research. She may be able to get him to look things up for her – even on the Internet perhaps. Information technologists often had all sorts of obscure resources bookmarked. Which may end up saving her having to pay a dubious acquaintance of hers, Gareth the hacker, to search for things.

On top of the pile of newspapers lay her piece of pink Fontayne's paper, and she paused for a moment to try to remember when it might have been slipped into her bag. And by whom.

My God, I wouldn't have noticed if someone had been trying to stuff twenty volumes of the *Encyclopaedia Britannica* in there! She'd slipped her bag down behind her chair and, what with all the partner swapping and general sexual exhibitionism last night, any one of the people in that private room could have slipped the paper to her. Of course the prime suspects were Alex and Stella, while she'd been in the toilet, but she couldn't swear to that as she hadn't looked in her bag before joining the gathering.

She decided to tackle the bound papers first as they were most quickly accessible, and contained the most recent article. The binders were unwieldy and she ended up making quite a bit of noise when she lost control of one of the covers and it slapped down on to the table.

'Sorry!' she murmured, glancing around to see faces staring at her, some disapprovingly, and some – probably students – disproportionately amused by her mishap. Only one person, deep in study down at the far end of the room, and with his back to her, didn't look round. Natalie stared at the studious one and frowned. Was there something familiar about that figure? It was difficult to tell because he was beyond a big group of students who were gawking at her and sniggering. But maybe it was just someone who was hard of hearing or so engrossed in his studies that he hadn't heard the commotion?

Soon Natalie was engrossed too.

PLANS FOR NEW LOCAL SPORTS CENTRE was a thought-provoking piece. Apparently the centre in question had been put up on land whose use had been hotly contested for environmental reasons, and, as far as Natalie could see, the construction firm who'd got the tender to build it had faced very little competition. There was no mention of Whitelaw Daumery, and there was only the scantiest of information about Ainsley Rose Building Systems, the construction company involved, but somehow that name made Natalie's story antennae quiver. She jotted it down, ready to look it up in the various business directories and on the Internet. Good money said that Daumery either owned Ainsley

Rose or had some kind of interest in it. Or why else would her unknown helper have set her on to it?

What to do next? Hit the directories, or check the fiches for those other articles? Natalie decided it would be logical to see whether Ainsley Rose cropped up again, in the older reports, or whether other companies were involved. If they were she could check up on them all at the same time.

The fiche readers were just as cranky as Roland the pet librarian had warned her they might be. The first didn't light up at all when she switched it on; the second flickered intermittently in a way she feared might soon produce a headache; and the third and last one lit up, but the mechanism for moving the fiche around under the lens was sticky and kept jamming. After a moment or two, Natalie felt her patience – which was always short with anything mechanical – dissipating fast. Her usual way of dealing with such frustrations was a choice selection of good, healthy swearwords, but she didn't think even the accommodating Roland would look kindly on a string of loud profanities in the sacred Belvedere reading room.

'Fuck! Fuck! Bugger!' Natalie mouthed as the fiche viewer stalled for about the dozenth time when she wasn't even anywhere near the first of the relevant pages. She slumped back, gripping her own wrist just in case the temptation to smash the screen got too strong, and suddenly felt the hairs on the back of her neck prickle. She'd never been superstitious or believed in ESP of any kind, but she very definitely sensed a presence of some kind in the close vicinity.

She turned around, then gasped, 'Bloody hell!'

Standing just behind her she found the tall and slightly nervous-looking figure of Steven Small.

'My God, it's you!' exclaimed Natalie, immediately wishing she'd reacted less obviously.

Steven Small gave a shy little smile, a slight yet

strangely sexy quirk of the lips, then looked beyond her to the offending fiche viewer. 'Can I be of any assistance? I've used these monsters quite a bit and I know their foibles.' He looked back at her, and his eyes seemed to skitter over her body, as if he'd suddenly allowed himself to look and acknowledge areas of flesh he'd once visited in intimate circumstances. Swallowing like a hormone-crazed schoolboy, he looked away again, then back at her and blinked once or twice. A warm pink glow began to creep up his neck from the collar of his black piqué polo shirt.

'Look ... um ...' he faltered, then swallowed again. 'If you'd prefer it, I'll just go back to my books. I'm sure one of the librarians can help you. Probably much more ably than I can.'

Oh no they can't, Teacher, thought Natalie, feeling a smile start somewhere in her solar plexus and begin to warm her whole body even though it barely reached her face. She felt the inexplicable attraction she'd felt on the train begin to rumble through her again; the desire to lay waste to this bashful man and gorge herself on the delights of the exceptional body beneath his modest, unremarkable clothing. Not that he was badly dressed, she noticed suddenly. He looked quite cool and stylish in his polo shirt, black jeans and lightweight black linen jacket. The contrast between the dark clothing and his angelic blond curls and pale complexion was dramatic and consciously sexy. There was no way he hadn't chosen those clothes deliberately.

'No. It's OK. I'd be grateful for your help.' She let the smile out, but kept it free of predatory overtones. No need to frighten him off. 'If you can tame this brute, go ahead. Please do!'

There was a moment of tension-dancing, while Steven pulled a chair next to hers so they were both sat down, elbow to elbow in front of the viewer. She showed him the pink sheet of paper, and indicated the two dates she wanted to look at, then felt slightly disappointed when he didn't turn a hair at the notorious Fontayne's logo.

Maybe he's never heard of Stella Fontayne, she thought, as he rested one long, neatly manicured hand on the control lever of the viewer and started to scroll around trying to find what she wanted. Maybe in the realms of academe they've never even heard of such things as drag queens.

Miraculously, Steven seemed to have the measure of the fiche viewer. Natalie found herself hypnotised not by what slid by on the screen, but by the delicate precision of Steven's mastery of the controls. The lightest of light touches seemed to be the key to keeping the temperamental lever from jamming, and Steven Small's touch was as nimble and accurate as a surgeon's.

It was only a tiny step to imagine that touch on her body. To remember brief impressions from a couple of days ago. The smell of his delicious cologne made it oh so easy.

God, it seemed like a decade since they'd gone at each other like animals in that train toilet cubicle. Or, mainly, she'd gone at him like an animal. She'd been the one that had grabbed at as much of him as she could get hold of, made the running, called all the shots. But now she couldn't help wondering what it would have been like if she'd granted him more scope to extemporise. She'd been afraid at the time that he'd bottle out and run if she'd let the momentum slacken even in the slightest, but maybe he wouldn't have, after all. He'd been a surprisingly good lover when he'd got going. A revelation in fact. What would it have been like if she'd allowed him to explore her – and use those beautiful, accurate fingers between her legs?

'There. Isn't that the first of your headlines?'

Natalie jumped, and focused with difficulty on the screen. She'd been so engrossed in her fantasies about how good Steven Small's long, flexible forefinger might feel circling her clit that she'd almost completely forgotten the service he was currently performing. Up there, in a reversed black-and-white image was the article about the local residents and their threatened beauty spot.

Natalie read the article carefully, making copious notes in shorthand. Again there was no mention of Daumery, or even of Ainsley Rose, but again a big, faceless developer – Hotten Construction Services – had snagged a huge construction project and in the process ridden roughshod over the Joe Public of Redwych. It tasted bad somehow to Natalie, and again her sixth and seventh senses detected the fugitive flavour of corruption and Whitelaw Daumery.

The second fiche article could have been a carbon copy of the first with slight variations. The building company, unsurprisingly, wasn't either of the previous two. This time the culprit was Technobuild 2000.

'What are you looking for?'

Steven Small's voice made Natalie flinch, and send the viewer control skidding, just when she'd got the hang of controlling it. It wasn't that she'd forgotten his presence – far from it. The scent of him, his proximity, and even what felt like subliminal heat coming off his body were all driving her crazy – it was just that, for almost the first time since she'd arrived in Redwych, her professional self had gained ascendancy over her hormones.

She turned to him. Should she tell him? Could she trust him? She decided 'yes'. It was certainly far safer for her to discuss her research with a cloistered academic who probably hardly lived in the real, modern world anyway, than it was with a fellow journalist like Alex Hendry. Or even a notorious public figure like Stella Fontayne.

She looked again at the sheet of pale-pink paper,

amazed again that Steven obviously had no idea what Fontayne's was.

She began to describe her job, her goal in Redwych, and her progress so far.

'My goodness, Whitelaw Daumery, eh? That's rather interesting,' Steven murmured, a rather odd, shuttered look coming over his face for just a second, as if he were hiding a reaction. Intrigued, Natalie wondered what it might be. 'I'd rather gathered that he was one of the few genuinely squeaky-clean public figures. Shows how much I know.'

'I don't have concrete proof yet,' Natalie conceded. It was becoming increasingly more difficult to concentrate on the job in hand, and her brief moment of clarity was over. She was too close to Steven, and to her alarm, and yet also, in a very exciting way, she could feel herself responding to him, just as she had on the train.

He was so quiet, so restrained, so deliciously ready to be shocked. Most other men would have referred to their previous encounter, and made a joke about it, or wanted to act on it. But Steven Small seemed almost terrified to even mention it. He was probably still in denial that it had ever even happened.

'I've got enough here for the time being,' she lied, thinking of the business directories she'd intended to pore over. She could probably check the same information online, or perhaps shell out a bit more to Gareth the hacker to do the searching for her. 'It's time for lunch now. Are you hungry?' She stared squarely into Steven Small's eyes and almost forced him not to look away from her. It happened, she silently said to him, just admit the fact. And it'll happen again if I have anything to do with it.

God, she needed a man to give her some confidence back. Some validation of her own 'girl power'! Alex Hendry was too buccaneer with her to do that; he had a dangerous facility for getting her into compromising and vulnerable positions. But Steven Small was someone she could make the running with. She'd done it before, and she could do it again.

'Lunch?' she repeated in the face of Steven's flabbergasted stare. 'You and me? What do you say?'

'Um ... yes ... but I usually go home and get a sandwich,' he stammered, pulling at his collar as if it were too tight.

'Great, a sandwich it is. Lead the way to your place.'

'I – I usually walk. It takes half an hour,' he offered doubtfully as Natalie was already rising and gathering her things.

'Can't we get a taxi? I'll pay if you're worried about the expense.'

What's got into you, Croft? Natalie asked herself as they left the Belvedere library. It was a silly question, though, as she knew what had got into her. That old demon lust, the same mad sprite that had possessed her on the train when she'd first seen this shy but strangely addictive man.

Steven, she suspected, was speechless again in the grip of that same pervasive sprite – one he was far less accustomed to handling than Natalie was.

But once they were outside, he touched her arm. 'I must make a phone call. I was going to meet a colleague and discuss a tutorial programme.' He hesitated, as if asking permission, and Natalie nodded impatiently. To her surprise, he did not whip out the ubiquitous mobile phone, but stepped into one of the old-fashioned phone boxes that stood outside the library.

Steven's call took but a moment, yet even so Natalie was almost dancing with impatience by the time he'd finished. 'You should have called a cab while you were in there,' she said, reaching for her own phone.

'I ... yes ... I suppose I should,' he stuttered, then seemed to look beyond her. 'There's a taxi over there ... shall I hail it?'

Natalie spun around and spotted the cab. Before Steven could raise a hand, she flagged it down with all the confidence of a London taxi habitué. A second later it had pulled out of the traffic and drawn to a halt beside them.

'Small world,' said the butch cab driver Natalie had ridden with before.

Natalie frowned, momentarily fazed by the coincidence of being in Ruth Hamer's cab again, and then bundled Steven unceremoniously into the back seat with her. It occurred to her as the cab pulled away that Patti's car was still sitting there in the multistorey car park.

What the hell! If she broke the flow now Steven might lose his nerve and she might lose her prize and the fun that lay ahead.

'This is a very nice house. Teachers must be far better paid than they let on in TV interviews,' said Natalie as Steven let her into a very large, well-maintained Victorian villa in what was probably the most sort-after area in north Redwych.

The journey had been short, and fraught with tension for everyone except the cab driver, it seemed, but, during one of her tense attempts at small talk, Natalie had managed to confirm her suspicions that Steven Small was indeed a teacher. A part-time supply teacher in various elite Redwych schools, who specialised in English and also coached private pupils on a one-to-one basis.

'Oh, they're not,' said Steven quickly as he let them in. 'It's a family house. It was left to me.'

And is there a Mrs Small? Natalie thought suddenly as she admired the gracious proportions of the hall and the fine polish on what was clearly an antique hall stand and mirror. It had never occurred to her that her shy teacher might be married. He wore no ring, but then a lot of men didn't.

Not that it mattered. He would never have brought her home if there were a little wifey in the kitchen cooking. In spite of his shyness, there was no doubt that he knew as well as she did why they were here.

'Come through to the kitchen. I usually eat in here at lunchtimes.'

Natalie followed him closely, and found herself in a beautiful, old-fashioned but well-appointed kitchen. She'd never felt less hungry for food in her life, but, when Steven turned and looked at her with fear and longing in his eyes, other far keener hungers flared.

'I . . . I don't know what to say . . . The other day,' he stammered, rubbing the fingers of one hand nervously against the palm of the other. 'I don't know what happened . . . I don't know what made me do it. I've never done anything like that before in my life.'

Neither have I, Natalie wanted to say, but didn't. She had to let him believe that she took her pleasure in such circumstances all the time. That she intended to take it now. The totality of his discomfort made her think of last night, and the naked man in the leather mask who had also been nervous and uncomfortable. But that was what that man had wanted. Would Steven want that too?

Well, fuck, he's going to get it! Natalie felt a surge of exultation that shot through her like an electric current. She knew what *she* wanted, and, if Shy Steven didn't want it, well tough luck!

'You took a great liberty there, Steven,' she said, blatantly lying as she advanced on him. She'd been the one taking liberties. 'Do you always break into the lavatories on trains and fuck women you've only just met?'

'No! Of course not!' he flared, then looked horrified by his own outburst.

Right in front of him, Natalie looked up into his eyes. He *was* scared, she was sure of it, but again, she saw the complexity within him. He also wanted this every bit as much as she did. And he understood where she was going. There seemed no need to waste time explaining things.

'Take your jacket off,' she commanded, at the same time moving even closer. Crowding him.

Steven opened his mouth, then closed it again, his eyes huge and dark in a face that seemed paler and more angelic than ever. Natalie reached out and touched his cheek. 'Come on,' she whispered.

Clearly rattled, he obeyed her, then looked around as if wondering what to do with the jacket. Natalie took it from him and tossed it in the general direction of a kitchen chair. It fell on the floor, but she ignored it and plucked at Steven's polo shirt, pulling it out of his waistband and then sliding her hands beneath it. She pressed her palms against his ribcage for a moment, then sought out his small, hard nipples and twisted them.

Steven yelped, and Natalie responded purely on instinct. She whipped one hand out from under his shirt, then slapped his face as hard as she could. While he had the breath still stunned out of him, she grabbed the back of his neck and kissed him savagely, her tongue stabbing into his mouth while still pinching his nipple hard at the same time.

She could feel him moaning around her tongue as she continued to torment him. His hips jerked forward as she subdued him, reacquainting her with the erection she remembered so clearly from the train.

God, he was big! One of the biggest men she'd been with. It was so unexpected in such an unassuming character. She abandoned his nipple and squeezed his crotch threateningly. He started to whimper and plead against her lips.

'What do you want, Teacher?' she asked, moving her mouth across his face, licking and wetting him as she went. Sliding lower, she sucked his neck, feeling an evil pleasure in marking him with a love bite. How the fuck would he explain *that* to his eagle-eyed pupils?

'I don't know,' he groaned, his pelvis working in synchrony with the squeezing and relaxing of her fingers, 'I don't know . . . Oh God!'

Well, I know what you need, thought Natalie looking into his face as she handled him. His whole right cheek was bright pink where she'd hit him, and his eyes looked as if they were on fire from within.

Releasing his genitals, she took a step back, her eyes firmly on him, forbidding him to move an inch. A large, American-style fridge stood nearby, and she opened it up, reached inside and found a bottle of water. She took a long drink from it, all the time watching Steven. He remained quite still, only his heavy breathing betraying the turmoil inside him.

'Unfasten your trousers and drop them to your knees,' she said quietly, not looking at him now, but studying the frosty bottle.

Steven complied, pushing down his snug-fitting jeans with some difficulty as his hands were visibly shaking. Beneath his jeans he wore close-cut trunks-style underwear, the black cotton hugely distended by his risen penis.

'And those,' she indicated, nodding at his trunks.

Looking as if he were almost fainting with a combination of horror and joy, Steven pushed down his knickers and let his cock bounce free. Stiff and red and swollen, it swayed obscenely in front of him; and, tortured, he looked down at it and then at Natalie.

'Oh, yeah,' she murmured. God, he was such a temptation!

Her first urge was to order him down to the kitchen floor so she could leap astride and impale herself on that beautiful monster. But what she'd seen last night had piqued her imagination. She wanted to try something a little less straightforward. What with seeing Patti tied up by Dyson, and then the games played at Stella Fontayne's private party, Natalie had had her first glimpse down sexual byways she'd never entertained before.

And she wanted to travel further down that road.

'Touch yourself, Steven,' she said evenly. 'Hold the tip. Tease yourself. Go on, do it! And hold up your shirt so I can see everything clearly.'

Making a sound halfway between a moan and a gasp, her victim obeyed. He took the head of his penis between the tips of his long, sensitive fingers and began to roll it a little. His hips bucked gently, but otherwise he remained admirably in control of himself, despite the sheen of sweat that appeared on his chest and belly where he'd dragged up his polo shirt.

'That's nice. Now smear that juice all over your dick. Don't let it drip on the kitchen floor. It's not hygienic.'

As Steven self-anointed his penis, Natalie was unable to stop herself clasping her own crotch. She caught her breath at the intense jolt of pleasure, but fought the desire to pull down her own jeans and pants and play with herself too. No, she had to retain the high ground here.

He's enjoying this too much, she thought, watching Steven's hips swaying in time to his efforts, and his beautiful face twisting with the intensity of the sensations. She looked quickly around the kitchen for some item that might suit her needs, and saw just the thing poking out of a utensil container.

'Stop. Hands by your sides,' she instructed, watching Steven's eyes widen as she took possession of the kitchen tool that she'd chosen. 'Stand still. Perfectly still.' She advanced on him.

'No!' he cried as she raised the slender wooden spatula in a high arc.

'Stand still! And shut up!'

His mouth working, his cock a quivering red pole, he complied, but screamed like a girl when she brought the spatula down hard on his long, white-skinned thigh.

'Oh God,' he groaned a second or two later, as a bar of angry redness appeared across the smooth pale expanse. But, impressively, he moved neither his hands nor his body. Nor did he climax, spontaneously, from the blow.

Natalie felt the devil rise in her.

'Press your dick against the red place,' she told him, unable to keep herself from smiling.

'Oh no . . . Oh please . . .' he muttered indistinctly, but still, again, he complied. Natalie could see the tension in his body as he held his glans against the rosy weal. Every muscle was like wire, and she could imagine his buttocks clenched tight as he fought for control.

Suddenly, she wanted to see those buttocks, and see them as red and sore as the lurid stripe across his thigh. Hefting her spatula, she whispered:

'Turn around.'

Chapter Nine
Kitchen Sink Drama

'*T*urn around,' she repeated when Steven didn't move.

For several long seconds, he stared at her, wide-eyed, like prey before a hunter. Then, abruptly, he obeyed and turned to face the sink in front of which he'd been standing.

Natalie's confidence wavered a second. Just as he'd been galvanised into action, right on the point of turning away, she'd seen the strangest and most complicated expression on Steven's face. It took her back to the train and moments when she'd seen the same enigma. Fleeting as it'd been, she could swear she'd seen humour and a subversive knowingness there. As if this were something Steven wanted and was deeply familiar with – and which he knew at the same time she hadn't the slightest fucking idea about!

Darting towards him, she took hold of his curly hair and twisted his face around so she could study it and look for the fugitive expression that had so sideswiped her. But it wasn't there. He was terrified. His face was white where it wasn't still glowing from her slap, and his eyes were now huge black pools of confusion, fear and yearning.

She slapped him again. 'Don't look at me!' she cried, releasing his head with a jerk. 'Don't look at me unless I tell you to!'

Shit, I'm losing it! she thought, wishing for a moment that she smoked or something and could fill time elegantly while keeping him waiting and letting her own composure settle.

She could see his back trembling. 'Yes, mistress,' he whispered.

'And don't speak either! And don't call me "mistress" unless I first give you permission!'

God, she was rattled now. What was this 'mistress' business? Had he actually done this before? Was that what the hidden smile was about?

Steven bowed his head, but obeyed her dictate not to speak.

Natalie retrieved the bottle of water, and sat down on one of the kitchen chairs. She considered opening her bag, pulling out her notebook and reading what she'd written – just to make him wait. But the idea didn't appeal. She had no interest in Whitelaw Daumery, investigative journalism, or anything at all, at this moment, other than what was going on in this room. That strange, transitory expression of Steven's had released a demon in her. She knew now that she had to beat it out of him, whether it had ever even existed in the first place or not.

But first, another matter needed attending to. Putting aside the bottle, she reached down and unzipped her jeans; then, making as little sound as she could, she thrust a hand down into her fly and inside her knickers.

As she expected, she was soaking. Her clit was unbelievably sensitised, and she bit her lips at just the slightest touch there. If she masturbated now, she would shout when she came, that was a given. So reluctantly she withdrew her fingers, and consoled herself with the thought that, when she did let go, the climax would almost blow her head off.

Drawing up the zip seemed to resound around the room and, to mask it, Natalie tapped her foot on the tiled floor. But, when she stood up and advanced on Steven, he was still shaking.

She picked up the spatula, swished it around a bit, and the shaking increased. He looked almost as if his knees were going to buckle.

'Tuck up your shirt,' she said quietly, keeping a hold on her own shakes. 'Bare your arse. Bend over the sink. You know what's coming, don't you?'

He nodded, pulling at his shirt, then rolling it up and wedging it beneath his arms to reveal the pale, firm, and surprisingly sculpted rounds of his bottom. The skin was very smooth, not at all hairy, and Natalie felt a profound, sweeping urge to bite him there. To attack the perfect surface and leave her mark on it. She wanted to defile him because he was so clean and white and saintly.

How? How do I do it? she thought as he bent over, just as she'd instructed.

Oh, screw it, Nat! Just get on with it! Use the fucking Force!

Letting go of any idea of what the right way was, she raised the spatula in a high, wide arc and brought it down as hard as she could on Steven's backside.

He screamed. Natalie gasped herself, surprised by the intensity of the impact as it travelled up her arm, and astonished by the breathtaking surge of excitement. She *did* feel the Force. Her heart was pounding. Her cunt was tingling. Literally tingling as if Steven's cry had sent an electric charge straight through it.

Oh, God, I like this! she thought, loving the deep, crimson swathe she'd cut across the milky skin of his bottom, and using it as a guideline for her second blow, just above it.

He squealed again, then bounced on his heels as if to somehow shake some of the pain out of his flesh and make it bearable. Natalie punished this with another blow and another and another, not really aiming but just putting all her heart and strength into them. Each strike went first white, then coloured crimson, deepening and spreading.

She whacked him particularly hard, and he groaned out, 'Oh, please! Oh, God, please help me!' His feet kicked and scrabbled against the floor tiles, and for a moment Natalie thought he was going to collapse and slither to the ground – but then he righted himself.

'Don't speak!' she said, gritting her teeth, wanting to scream it out, she felt so excited. Summoning strength she didn't know she had, she hit him again, once on each buttock, and, despite sobbing and spluttering, no further words came out of him.

Pausing for a moment, she marvelled at the red glow she'd raised in the cheeks of his bottom. There was fire there – she could almost feel the heat – but she couldn't begin to imagine what such an intense inflammation must feel like from the inside. She stepped forward and pressed her fingers firmly against his left buttock and he made a low, broken gurgling sound in his throat.

Was he turned on still? She poked the other buttock and he gurgled again. She ran a fingertip up the rose-tinted, slightly fuzzy cleft and let it hover over his anus. His hips began to jerk, slowly and rhythmically – and suddenly she felt angry.

'Oh no you don't!' she cried, grabbing the back of his shirt and hauling him away from the sink. As he turned to face her she saw that his erection was as huge and red and proud as it had been before. Huger even.

He clenched his hands and almost as if he were trying to contain them, and stop them flying to either his crotch or his bottom, they shook and the knuckles went white. She looked into his face and saw it was wet with tears, and far more beautiful, in torment, than any man's had a right to be.

When she looked back down at his dick again, his fingers unclenched, his arm moved slightly.

'No way, buster! That's mine,' she growled at him, flinging aside the spatula and scrabbling at her zip again. 'Get down on the floor.'

He slid down to his knees.

'On your back.'

His mouth trembled, and she saw his lips shape the word 'please' again, but he didn't speak. Ponderously, and with many flinches and a deep, ragged indrawing of breath as he settled down, he obeyed her. When he was horizontal, his penis stood out from his body like a fat red spear, vivid against the pale skin of his belly and the fuzzy, sandy hair at his groin.

Oh, yeah! thought Natalie, kicking off her shoes and wriggling out of her jeans. As she dragged off her pants a delicate, silvery string of juice adhered to the sodden crotch, and when her eyes flashed to Steven's she saw him watching the delicate filament hungrily. 'One taste then,' she muttered, then caught some of the silky stuff on her fingers and offered it to him. He fed off it hungrily, sucking and kissing her fingers with slavish enthusiasm.

'Enough! Now keep still,' she ordered him as he began to wriggle despite the suffering in his bottom.

Naked from the waist down, she crouched over him, inching into position, holding her sex above his, and savouring the moment. She felt as if her pussy were as wide as a field, and yet the target beneath her needed a critical approach. It seemed important to slip down on to him like a poem of motion; to acquire him with accomplished accuracy, like a being from a superior race possessing her subject. Hands free.

His penis touched her. The opening of her sex. Contact. She slid down. Hard dock.

'Holy shit!' she cried, feeling as if she would never stop sinking down, never stop being filled. He felt like steel inside her. Enormous. She was almost choking, so completely did she feel stuffed with his flesh.

Eventually she settled and she could hardly breathe. Steven's cock was an unyielding presence inside her, a welcome invader. The way he stretched her was dynamic and a force of nature, even though he lay completely prone and passive on the kitchen floor. Even his hands lay still on the tiles, like a pair of long, white birds nestling on either side of her knees where she was squatting on him. His eyes were closed, and the only external sign of life in him was his throat slowly working.

Natalie hardly needed to move. She hardly dared move. Her pussy was already fluttering around the living obstruction lodged inside it. The slightest trigger would tip her over, send her spinning down the escalator of a wrenching orgasm. She could almost feel it already, like the aura of some terrifying event, something so energetic it played tricks with time.

'Oh, God,' she murmured, afraid of it, yet longing for it, famished for it. Sliding one hand beneath her top, she massaged her tit with her fingers, and began blindly searching lower to touch her clit and bring on the pleasure.

'Let me,' whispered Steven, not lifeless at all as he gently but firmly nudged her hand aside and went in search of her clitoris for himself.

And he was just as accurate as she'd been. His fingertip found her with no fumbling, no problem, no miss-hit.

The trigger was engaged. The lift dropped beneath her. She came, shouting and laughing and holding on to Steven Small for dear life lest she tumble over the edge of the world in the process.

Natalie stood on the pavement and stared around her. Wasn't she in science-fiction land and hadn't there been a transporter malfunction or something? Or a timeslip? The street here – outside the multistorey car park – looked perfectly normal and sunny and innocent while she felt just the opposite. It was as if she'd just beamed in from a dark and parallel universe.

And if I have, how come *you* live in it?

She aimed her silent question at the retreating shape of the black Mercedes she'd just got out of. How come a supposedly penniless schoolmaster could afford a delicious vehicle like that? Or was that a 'family' car? Bought with money he'd inherited, not earned.

Fuck him! she thought, then grinned. Yes, she'd done just that. Twice. On the kitchen floor. Once with her on top, and then again – unexpectedly, but not unwelcomed – when he'd summoned jaw-dropping powers of recuperation and just flipped her near-inert form over on to her back, then pushed into her for a second coming together. She'd got her own back, though, by clawing his tender, red bottom.

After that, they'd tidied themselves up, and while exchanging only the bare minimum of conversation he'd given her lunch. A beautiful sandwich of fresh crusty bread and real butter enrobing slices of thick, hand-carved ham. Even the coffee had been exceptional.

Nothing but the best for you, eh, Teacher? She smiled again, feeling quietly pleased with the fact that she fell into that category herself. Steven hadn't said much, but his whole demeanour was that of a man who'd been given a massive electric shock – but in a good way. She suspected that even the beating had been exactly what he wanted.

And in return he'd given her more than just a bit of

help at the library, a delicious lunch and a couple of first-class orgasms. He'd looked at the company names she'd uncovered and said, 'I know someone who works for Ainsley Rose Building Systems. He's an office manager. I'll get in touch with him and ask him to contact you.'

Natalie thought about this as she searched for, and found, Patti's car. She didn't suppose any friend of Steven Small's would be a major-league whistle blower, but even the tiniest bit of background information would be useful.

'Shit! Bloody hell!'

A salient fact dawned on her as she slid into the driving seat, and as she hadn't yet closed the car door, her exclamation rang around the parking area, earning her a filthy look from a young mother loading a couple of tots into the car beside her.

Steven Small had never asked for her phone number and she'd never told him where she was staying. Clearly the pair of them had been far too doped out on sex to consider that little difficulty. How could he get his friend to ring her if he couldn't give the friend a number to ring?

Swinging Patti's car out into traffic, Natalie considered driving straight back to Steven's place and giving him the number. But, when it came time to choose her route out of the city centre, she found herself driving back home to Patti's. What had happened between her and Steven Small needed some space leaving after it. She needed time to think and to analyse what had happened and why she'd liked it so much. And, after all, at least she could trace him via the phone book or directory enquiries. It would be so much easier to ring him rather than go and see him. Being face to face with Steven Small always ended up with her fucking him. And, as she did have a job to do, wasn't it about time she concentrated on that rather than falling prey to distractions? Like men? And having kinky sex with men?

When Natalie drew up outside Patti's, she breathed a sigh of relief that Dyson's van was nowhere to be seen. Another distraction out of the way. And it was time for a serious chat with Patti about a few things.

'Thank you, my dear. Mission accomplished. At least one part of it.'

'Good! Does that mean I'll be getting my car back soon? I could have done with it. I've been stuck here all day!'

'A thousand pardons, Patti my love,' said the familiar voice, sounding not in the least contrite. 'But I've told you before: you can have another car any time you like. Two cars. Anything you want. You certainly work hard enough for it.'

'Bullshitter,' said Patti cheerfully. It was hard to stay annoyed when she was so curious. 'So, this "mission accomplished" malarkey – does that mean you've had sex again?'

'I'll say . . .'

Patti detected a note of deep satisfaction, almost dreaminess – which added to her curiosity. What had her sister been up to? She'd looked so thunderstruck last night . . .

'Hey, more details please!'

She listened carefully while the creamy, sexy voice described a scenario that soon she wished she'd been a part of. In any capacity. Even just as a watcher.

'You jammy old fuck! That sounds amazing . . . I never realised she had it in her.'

'Oh, she does. I recognised it immediately. As soon as I saw her. Even before we screwed the first time.'

'Well, yeah,' Patti conceded, thinking of what she'd been told – but not by Natalie. 'But I didn't think she'd go so far so fast. I'd better watch my step in the kitchen

from now on!' She chuckled, making a mental note to
rearrange her utensils immediately.

'Now that's something I *would* like to see!'

'What do you mean?' she asked.

'Either you spanking her, or her spanking you.'

Patti thought about it. She knew it was something
she'd like, but what about Natalie? She obviously
thought she was a sophisticated city girl, but could she
really break off the shackles of convention – of an
ingrained fear of primal retribution? That biblical thing
about blood kinship – even if it was only half a bond,
and between women?

'Oh, I don't know,' she said. 'I'm not sure Nat will
ever go for it. For her and me, that is. She might watch,
but more than that I'm not sure. She's far more uptight
and conventional than she would ever admit.'

'She wasn't very conventional just now.'

Patti heard low, happy, deeply filthy laughter and it
made her feel instantly and almost painfully turned on.

'Don't laugh like that! You know it gets to me,' she
complained, sliding her hand to her crotch and gripping
herself through her jeans.

'Oh goody,' murmured her friend, voice lower, more
breathy and more arch now, 'I love to get to you, Patti
my dear . . . What are you going to do about it? Call on
the services of the delicious Dyson?'

'He's not here. And if Nat's got the car she'll be back
any minute. What *can* I do?'

'Oh, I think that's obvious if your sister is about to
arrive. I'd call that perfect timing. Synchronicity. Just
what you've both been waiting for, regardless of what
dear Natalie *thinks* she thinks.'

'I don't know. I just don't know . . .' said Patti, seeing
a parade of images and wanting them real.

'Well, I do. I sincerely believe it'll happen. And sooner
than you think.' Even through the filter of the phone,
Patti suddenly detected a complete change in mood.

'Anyway, my sweet, I can't gossip to you all day. I've things to do. Lots more important phone calls to make. This "thing" of your sister's is really hotting up. Getting delightfully labyrinthine. I rather wish I were in her business myself.'

'You're in *every* business,' said Patti with a smile.

'True. Now I must go, my love. Ciao! Have fun!'

You're a monster, you old faker, thought Patti affectionately. She squeezed hard, pressing her jeans seam into her pussy. But that's why everyone who gets to know you adores you.

'Where the hell have you been with my car? I've been frantic. I thought you'd had an accident. I tried to phone you but your phone isn't working.'

'Sorry . . . I'm really sorry. I lost track of time.' Rummaging in her bag and trying to look contrite at the same time, Natalie fished out her mobile and discovered that it was dead. Attempts to revive it revealed that the battery, which had been low when she'd tried to call Alex, had given out sometime during the day. Perhaps a good thing, considering what had happened.

'Oh, great,' snapped Patti with a shrug. Natalie sensed that her sister's heart wasn't in the complaint. She appeared more curious than irate, somehow.

'I met a friend. Well, an acquaintance, really . . . Someone I met on the train down here. I had lunch with him.'

They were in the kitchen. Natalie was sitting at the table, flicking through her notes, but not really looking at them. Patti was pottering about, not really doing anything except give Natalie the third degree, it seemed.

'That's a long lunch, sis,' she said softly. Natalie could see she was smiling now. A knowing smile.

'What's that supposed to mean?'

'Just what I said,' Patti said, turning away to put the kettle on. 'When lunch with a man lasts until teatime, there's usually more than pizza or a sandwich on the menu.'

She knows! She fucking knows!

'For you, maybe,' she countered.

Patti set out mugs, popped in teabags.

'For any woman, Nat.'

Natalie watched her sister pour boiling water on to the bags, then poke them with a spoon. Patti looked so calm, so smug. Anger filled her with the urge to go on the offensive.

'Look, when are we going to talk about what's going on here, Patti? About last night, and Stella Fontayne, and about you doing it with all sorts of different men, and going out looking like a prostitute when you used to be Mrs Incredibly Respectable Marks and Spencer woman?'

'I told you when you arrived, Nat, I've met some new friends, broadened my horizons.' Patti placed a mug of tea before Natalie and sat down facing her. She seemed unfazed by the questions and unembarrassed by their context. Natalie grew more astounded and irritated by the second. She took a sip of tea, burned her lip and muttered a profanity.

'I didn't think you were all that interested in my life,' Patti went on. 'You've always let me know – without actually saying so – that your life is so much more exciting and significant than mine.'

True, thought Natalie. True that she'd done that, but clearly not true – now, or maybe ever – about their lives.

'I'm sorry. Clearly it isn't,' she conceded.

'I thought you'd probably pour scorn on my . . . my "activities". Everybody in London is supposed to be doing everything, anyway.'

'I'm not. Well, not until a couple of days ago.'

Patti grinned. 'When Redwych took you by surprise?'

Natalie nodded. Patti tut-tutted.

'Yeah, well, Redwych may seem like a backwater to

Londoners but in some ways it's far from that. The old place is a hotbed of iniquity under the surface.'

Natalie forbade herself to remark on the mixing of metaphors. She was about to speak when Patti cut her off.

'Anyway. A couple of days ago, you say? What happened a couple of days ago? What started your renaissance?'

'Well, I met this guy on the train. And I just wanted him . . . I don't know why. I don't know what got into me.'

Patti laughed, and Natalie paused.

'Go on, Nat, spill it!'

Haltingly at first, then starting to enjoy herself, Natalie told the story. The entire, sleazy, sordid account of what she'd thought was her zipless fuck on the train with Steven Small.

'Outstanding, sis,' said Patti when the account was just about finished. 'Truly outstanding.'

Natalie looked at her sister for the first time since she'd started, and suddenly felt really hot and embarrassed – far more so than she'd felt while describing Steven Small's dick and how it had felt inside her.

Patti was slowly caressing her own breast, teasing the nipple between finger and thumb through the thin stuff of the pink T-shirt she was wearing. Her face was as pink as the cotton and her eyes were bright and a little spaced. She'd looked the same way last night while sitting on her hooded paramour's penis.

Natalie took a sip of her tea. It was quite cool now. She'd completely forgotten it.

'The thing was, it seemed so easy to pick up a guy on a train. Really liberating. I thought I could just shag him senseless with no consequences.' In her mind, she turned around again, beside the fiche viewer in the reading room. 'I thought I'd never see him again, then there he was this morning – in the Belvedere Library. God, I nearly wet myself!'

'Now there's a scene to conjure with,' said Patti with a round grin, and Natalie was forced to smile back at her, albeit ruefully. That too was sex, it seemed . . .

'So, proceed, what happened next,' urged Patti, all business.

'He helped me look some stuff up, then we went to lunch,' said Natalie, casting a cursory glance towards her notebooks. Digging up financial dirt on Whitelaw Daumery seemed so far away at the moment, as if it were someone else entirely who was working on the story, not her.

Patti made a dismissive gesture, as if the concept of eating lunch were irrelevant, and she didn't know why Natalie even persisted in mentioning it.

'When we got to his place, I couldn't stop thinking about what I saw last night. The man in the hood getting beaten. I wanted to know what it was like . . . And Steven seemed to know just what I had in mind. He fell right in with it.'

'He spanked you?'

'No, I spanked him.'

'Really!'

Natalie looked quickly at her sister. Patti's voice had been full of astonishment, of awe, even. She'd even stopped fondling her breast and was leaning forward, elbows on the table.

'Come on, Nat. Details!'

It seemed all a white blur now. A dream. As if she'd taken a hallucinogen of some kind. What the hell had she done?

'I – I made him drop his trousers and show me his dick.' It was coming back to her now. Bringing the sensations and the pure, strange excitement with it. 'Then I had him bend over the sink while I beat his arse with a spatula.'

Patti laughed out loud, shaking her head. 'Oh, bravo, sis! That is priceless . . .'

Natalie looked at her sister and saw a rather curious expression on her face. It was more than just amusement: there was an element of memory to it, of irony. Had Patti taken part in something similar herself? Had Dyson given her a dose of the same in her own kitchen?

Pleased by that image, Natalie smiled back at her sister. 'Yes, it was pretty priceless. And so was the fuck we had afterwards.' She felt colour rush up through her face again, but she charged on anyway. 'I made him get down on the kitchen floor and just climbed on top.'

'Oh excellent! Jesus Christ, Nat, you're a quick study! You see one scene and you're out there and at it the first opportunity you get!' Patti paused, and Natalie felt her scrutiny sharpen. 'Did you enjoy it? *Really* enjoy it?'

'Enjoy' seemed a fairly inadequate word, but Natalie supposed it would do.

'Yes. I did enjoy it. I think . . .'

Patti leaned back in her chair, her hand at her breast once more, fingers working. Natalie wanted to tell her not to do it, but she felt hypnotised. She imagined the nipple beneath the cloth: red and tumescent, sensitised.

'And what about the flip side of it? Do you think you'd enjoy that, too?'

'What do you mean?'

The fingers paused, then in a swift, impatient movement, Patti grasped the hem of her T-shirt and hauled it off over her head. 'There, that's better,' she said, and, bare to the waist, she resumed her caressing. 'Does this bother you?' she enquired, as Natalie's eyes helplessly locked on to the spectacle.

Natalie shook her head. It bothered her mightily, but she didn't want it to stop. No way.

'What I mean,' Patti went on, beginning to shift around on her chair now, 'is, do you think you'd enjoy taking it rather than giving it? Pain . . . you know . . .

humiliation. Submission. In its own way it's just as exciting as being dominant. Sometimes more so.'

No way am I going to tell her about Alex, thought Natalie. He didn't hit me but he certainly humiliated me enough. He really put me through it. She could still feel the heat in her body as she'd squatted in that yard and pissed, as she'd writhed on his lap with his hand at her cunt and Stella Fontayne listening intently.

But that isn't me. Surely. It was such a different mindset, a million miles from the confident, take-charge woman she was. How could she enjoy it? Be turned on by it? And yet she was. Even now. Just from the thoughts . . .

'I don't think that's me, really,' she said, aware that Patti wasn't really listening to her any more.

Her sister was lost in a world of internal pleasure, her eyes closed and her long seamstress's fingers working hard at her breast, and below, Natalie now saw, at her crotch. After a few moments she gasped, her eyes popped open and she bounced a little in her seat.

'Oh, wow! Sorry about that, sis,' she said, clearly unrepentant. 'You were saying?'

'God, Patti, I don't know you any more!' cried Natalie, jumping to her feet. 'How can I have a serious conversation with you while you're masturbating? This is ridiculous!'

It wasn't really Patti she was appalled by, but herself. Either way, she had to get out of the room, away from the superheated atmosphere that had suddenly built between them. She was about to run when Ozzy the cat popped in through his flap and seemed to deliberately stand in her path, blocking her way. He looked up at her, his expression clearly – fur notwithstanding – indicating that he'd like her to feed him.

'Where do you keep his cat food?' she asked, turning to Patti.

'I'll do it.' Her sister rose from her seat, and, still bare-breasted, fetched a tin of Whiskas from a kitchen cupboard and attended to the big black-and-white's needs.

Why am I still here? Natalie thought as she watched Patti fondle the cat's head. I should have got out while she was distracted.

As if she'd heard the thought, Patti straightened up and looked Natalie straight in the eye. 'Are we just going to let this fester?' she asked challengingly. 'Just ignore all we've just discussed? After all, it was you who started it. You were the one who wanted to talk about what's going on.'

'I know. I did. I still do,' said Natalie, aware that Patti had abandoned Ozzy, was now far closer than she ought to be, and that her nipples were erect and very pink.

Her sister was standing right in front of her, half naked, warm and sweet, and all it would take was for Natalie to reach out and touch her. Reach out and sample the unknown but the not, she admitted, unwanted. Patti leaned towards her and slid a hand behind Natalie's head. Exerting only the slightest force, she brought Natalie's face to hers and kissed her.

It was only the lightest kiss yet it felt like fire. Patti's lips were so soft, much softer than a man's. Softer than Alex's, softer than Steven's . . . Their delicate velveteen texture was enticing and called for more pressure, more exploration. Not really thinking, and not knowing how she was still on her feet, Natalie felt her own lips open in an invitation to Patti's tongue. As her sister took up the invitation, she also took hold of Natalie's hand and cupped it around her bare breast. The nipple felt like a red-hot stud against Natalie's palm. Her fingers flexed automatically, cradling and cupping. She felt Patti's had slide downwards, cup her crotch and begin to squeeze in the same rhythm as her jabbing, probing tongue.

An extraneous sound filtered through into Natalie's

drugged brain. The noise of the front door slamming and booted feet proceeding along the hall towards the kitchen.

'No!' she cried, shoving Patti away from her and staggering backwards. Her sister was panting as hard as she was, her bare breasts lifting and falling.

'I can't! I don't want this!' Natalie said wildly, grabbing up her bag and her phone and her papers, then nearly knocking Dyson over as he appeared in the doorway.

'Are you OK?' he said, but Natalie ignored him and pushed past into the hall, leaving Patti to the explanations.

'I don't want this!' she whispered, once she was back in her room, the door slammed behind her.

But, as she threw herself down on the bed and sobbed tears of weakness and confused recrimination, she knew she was lying.

Thank God for work, thought Natalie, what felt like hours later. After lying on the bed for a while, staring blankly at the ceiling and listening to every tiny noise in the house, she'd got up, fired up her laptop and plugged it into the telephone jack and thrown herself into Internet research. She'd been aware of the fact that Patti could probably have cut her off at any moment, by the simple fact of lifting a receiver elsewhere in the house, but she'd logged on anyway.

Probably too busy shagging Dyson senseless, she thought now, tuning back into the noises in the house and hearing something that sounded suspiciously like a giggle. Ignoring it, she reviewed what she'd discovered.

After some digging about, she'd discovered that not only did Ainsley Rose, Hotten Construction and Technobuild all mysteriously have their main offices here in Redwych, but that they all had similar addresses. Natalie's suspicions soared, knowing how often this happened in business. Slightly different postal addresses and sometimes post-office boxes, when really this was just one concern, operating out of the same building. Even more incriminating was that all three of her named firms were subsidiaries of a further company – the same one – the Black Gate Group. There was plenty of flash-looking promo stuff for the individual companies, complete with paeans of praise for the various projects each one had been responsible for – but no hard details about any of them. The Black Gate Group didn't appear to be listed in any of the usual sources. She tried the *FT* and various others but there wasn't a byte of information anywhere. Natalie sent a quick email off to Gareth the hacker, and tried ringing Alex Hendry again – but his mobile still wasn't answering and, although there were still people in at the *Sentinel* offices, he wasn't one of them.

'Fuck it!' muttered Natalie as she began a quick written summary of what she'd discovered so far.

This didn't take long, as she had achieved far less than she would have liked to *and* taken far more time over it than was usual for her. It's all the bloody distractions, she thought grimly, realising that not only was she tired, emotionally off balance and angry with herself, she was also desperately hungry and prepared to murder someone for a glass of wine or something stronger.

But Patti and Dyson were still giggling, she discovered when she crept out silently on to the landing. Correction, they weren't actually giggling any more, but she could hear Dyson speaking in low, intense tones, down in the kitchen.

Listening intently, Natalie could hear nothing of Patti at first, but then, suddenly, she heard her sister's voice ring out in a high, clear cry.

Oh, God, thought Natalie, simultaneously recognising another sound. One she'd been suppressing, but one that, now she heard it, was terribly familiar. It came again, and, as it did, Patti cried out again, the sound broken and falling in a plaintive groan.

Don't go down there, Nat, she told herself, even though her foot was already on the top step. Patti moaned again, and Natalie hurtled down the stairs as fast as she could without making a sound.

The kitchen door was ajar.

Now why doesn't that surprise me? Natalie thought as she edged closer to it. They put on a show for me before, the day I arrived – and now they're doing it again.

In the kitchen, someone seemed to have carefully arranged the scene like a piece of performance art. A chair had been place parallel to the doorway, and over its back was draped Patti, her hands fastened behind her back with a tea towel. She was completely naked apart from an incongruously glamorous pair of black high heels, and both her bottom and her sex were crimson and glowing. Her legs were parted, offering Natalie a perfect view of her sister's glistening slit.

Dyson, standing to the side, raised his arm, and in his hand Natalie saw a wooden kitchen spatula, almost identical to the one she herself had used on Steven. A second later it came swishing down and caught Patti squarely across the tops of her thighs. She squealed out loud, then wriggled around as if trying to rub herself against the chair back.

Natalie watched in fascinated, obsessive horror as Dyson continued to spank Patti and Patti continued to wriggle in search of a climax. The spatula was a message to her, Natalie realised, but, hypnotised as a part of her was, there was still an element of resistance in her nature. She would not be reeled into their kinky little games and manipulated by her own sister – either figuratively or literally. She still had a mind and will of her own, and when she did, eventually, succumb again to games of dominance and submission – especially submission – she would select the time and the circumstances for herself!

Chapter Ten

Suspicions

'*A*re you ready to go through with it?'

It was the call that Simon Natwick had never expected to receive, and now it had come he could hardly breathe from fear. And from excitement. The voice at the other end was kind, and yet he couldn't overcome the sense of awe he felt.

'Er ... yes, I think so. What's happened? I thought you said I'd probably never have to do it? Is it because of that think tank? That Committee for Morality in Business or whatever?'

'In part,' answered the strange, vibrant, ambiguous voice. 'And also because certain circumstances have arisen. If you blow the whistle it will add, shall we say, a little spice to a new game I'm playing.'

'You want me to jeopardise my livelihood just for one of your games?' The power and asperity in his own voice astounded Simon. He'd never had the guts to speak to his unusual sponsor in this way before, had always worried that the useful 'retainer' he received would be withdrawn as suddenly as it had been granted.

His sponsor laughed – a deeply unnerving, but not

entirely unpleasant sound – and said, reassuringly, 'If you're fearful of repercussions, my friend, don't be. I'll take responsibility. And –' a long, tempting pause '– remember that little business you wanted to start? Down in the West Country? Your new beginning? Well, just say the word and it's ready for you. I'll set it up.'

The golden dream formed before Simon's eyes. The idyll . . . Free and clear, away from the tedium of being a financial officer and being trapped in a job that he'd realised was killing his soul. Free to live creatively with a nice cushion of capital to make the early days much easier.

'What do I have to do?' asked Simon, feeling almost gleeful now.

'Talk to a journalist. I'll give you her number. Her name is Natalie Croft. All you have to do is answer her questions. Show her the same information you showed me. I'm sure you won't find it in the least bit of a hardship to talk to her.' Simon could almost hear the demonic, scheming smile. 'And when she's done with you perhaps I'll point her in the direction of some of my little friends who work for certain councillors.'

When his sponsor had rung off after giving him more detailed instructions, Simon stared at the name and number he'd just written down and pondered. He had a suspicion that the person he'd been speaking to was perhaps experiencing far more complicated feelings for this Natalie Croft woman than just those of someone who wanted to use her to take a hypocrite like Daumery down. There had been a slightly fond note in the way that name had been spoken.

My God, that pervert really fancies her!

His mind filling with the lurid fantasies produced by *that* notion, Simon smiled, for once feeling that he had the tiniest bit of an edge over his Machiavellian sponsor.

* * *

Stella was ready early. Far too early, to be honest.

With time on her hands, temptation was often diffi-cult to resist. She ran her fingers through the silky fall of her shoulder-length wig of copper-brown hair, then smoothed a fingertip along the line of her right eyebrow. The arch looked natural, but not too natural – it was dark, exquisitely symmetrical with its twin, and slightly feathered. Moments like this were a love affair with her mirror and Stella smiled at her reflection, thinking momentarily of one of her favourite films.

'You're a handsome devil. What's your name?' she asked of her own glamorous, yet slightly intimidating image.

What *was* her name? Was she Stella? Could she really lay claim to that? Or, even looking as beautified as this, would she always be that other and very male person at heart?

'Don't go all philosophical on me, girl.' Rising from her seat in front of the dressing-table mirror, she turned and looked over her shoulder to check the seams on her stockings.

They were perfect, too. Just like her brows. She adjusted the way her French knickers sat across her bottom and gave her right cheek a loving little squeeze. The touch was light but the flesh there still burned and smarted, sending a frisson of reaction to her penis. As it stirred and began to lift, she glanced towards her watch which lay on the dressing table. She was ready early, but was there time for that? Perhaps there was . . . She cupped her crotch.

The doorbell shrilled as if it were wired like some Victorian anti-masturbation device.

'Fuck!' hissed Stella, snatching up her kimono and belting it around her as she went downstairs to answer the door. A peek through the security viewer revealed a familiar face – another 'handsome devil', she thought wryly – and all at once being interrupted was no longer an irritation. A sense of happy evil jerked her cock to stiffer attention.

'Good evening, Alex. Do come in,' she said, throwing the door open with a flourish and enjoying the way Alex's eyes widened and seemed to pop in his head. She watched him glance around nervously to see if there was anyone in the street who might observe him being greeted, effusively, by a half-dressed drag queen.

'What can I do for you, my dear?' Stella asked once Alex had darted inside. She made her voice intentionally low, and intimate, and touched his shoulder solicitously. Alex, in turn, looked like a lost puppy that didn't know where to go. Stella noted that he was wary and edgy, and that his usually immaculate *GQ* turnout was crumpled and slightly dishevelled. There were heavy shadows beneath his fine dark eyes, and his lips looked moist as if he'd been licking them nervously. It was obvious he'd been drinking.

'I don't know. I don't fucking know, do I?' he snapped, still immobilised. He ran a hand through his thick black hair and messed it up even more.

'Come on. Let's sit down and talk. Come through here.' Stella laid a hand lightly on his arm again and he flinched as if she'd burned him. His glance skittered around the hall, and he seemed about to bolt. She took a firm hold on his arm – using a man's strength this time – and steered him into the comfort of her softly lit lounge.

'Sit,' she commanded, directing him energetically towards the sofa. 'I'll bring some wine. Just relax and make yourself at home.'

Hidden from Alex, Stella smiled creamily. Her young associate was about as far from relaxed as it was possible to be, but that was precisely how she wanted him. The tauter the string the sweeter the note it played.

From the refrigerator, she chose a light, dry white wine – nothing too strong, as it was obvious that Alex had already had several drinks. Reaching towards a cupboard to one side of the sink, in order to get glasses, Stella found herself distracted for a moment. She closed her eyes and relived the delicious scenario that formed behind her painted lids. Glasses forgotten for a moment, she cupped her cock in one hand and stroked her bottom with the other, sliding her silky lingerie across the pink and sensitised skin.

Oh, yes! So nice ... So unexpected and yet welcome all the same.

Snapping back to reality, Stella retrieved a pair of fine-stemmed glasses and the bottle of wine and returned to the lounge and the waiting Alex.

He had removed his jacket and was leaning against the back of the sofa, his head stretched back, his tie loosened, his bare throat elongated. It should have been a pose of total relaxation, of abandonment, but Stella could see tension in every line of him. He wasn't a man at ease with himself: he looked far more like a martyr waiting for the most grievous of punishments.

Stella's heart quickened and her cock rose up eagerly. She stood before him and clicked the wine bottle lightly against one of the glasses. Alex's eyes flashed open and his glance settled immediately at the level of Stella's crotch.

Yes, I have got a hard-on, beautiful boy, she thought, letting Alex take a glass from her, then hold it up to be filled. His eyes kept trying to look anywhere but at the front of her loosely tied kimono, and his hand shook a little of the wine from his glass before he'd even touched it.

'Steady on,' murmured Stella, sweeping down to put aside her own glass, and the bottle, and to still Alex's trembling hand. Their fingers touched around the glass, and Alex's skin was very hot. Stella wanted to fling the glass aside and fold Alex's fingers around her cock immediately; but, with reluctance, she released him. There was plenty of time.

'What's troubling you?' she asked quietly, taking her seat beside him and putting her own glass momentarily to her lips.

'Do you want the entire list?' Alex said sarcastically, swigging down his wine and topping up his glass again himself. 'I can't earn what I need on my own. I take money *not* to do my job properly. I can't break free and be an honest journalist because every time I think I'm getting close to paying my own way and getting out of debt, something *else* happens!' He looked at his glass of wine as if he hated it, and put it to one side, on the floor. 'And I've pranged the fucking jeep now, haven't I?'

Stella felt a rush of genuine concern. She took his hand in hers and felt it shaking finely. 'But you're all right, aren't you? Not injured in any way?'

'I'm OK,' he said tightly, and she could feel the coiled spring quality in him. He wanted to pull his hand away, but he daren't do it lest he offend her. She was his meal ticket. His ticket to designer suits and state-of-the-art sound systems and all the other expensive trappings of good living. 'But it's going to cost at least a grand to fix the jeep, probably a lot more. I can't believe it!' He leaned back again, eyes closed, as if making a conscious effort to ignore the way Stella had begun to gently stroke the back of his hand to soothe him.

'Don't worry,' she murmured, unbuttoning the cuff of his shirt and sliding her fingers a little way beneath it. 'You're not hurt and that's what matters. What's a thousand pounds between friends?'

For a moment, Alex looked as if he might cry, and Stella felt a sudden sadistic yen to put him under even further pressure. She turned his hand palm upwards and her thumb circled over the veins in his wrist. 'Come on, what is it? There's something else, isn't there?'

'Bloody Natalie Croft, that's what!' he snarled, his body rigid with stress, but still not pulling away from her.

'But I thought you liked Natalie,' said Stella ingenuously. 'That you liked fucking her. You certainly seemed to be enjoying her in my dressing room last night. One doesn't put one's hand inside a girl's knickers if one doesn't really like her, does one?' Slowly, discreetly, like a high-class thief, Stella slid her hand from Alex's forearm and let it fall on his thigh.

'It's not the sex,' said Alex, his voice uneven, his breathing even more so. 'It's the other thing: the Daumery business. Why the fuck couldn't I have been the one to expose him? I'm just as good a writer as she is. Or at least I could be if I was given a chance!'

'I know that, Alex,' said Stella softly, her hand flexing and appreciating the musculature of Alex's thigh. For all his self-perceived shortcomings as a journalist, there was no denying the beauty and fitness of his body. 'And your time will come. I promise that . . . And I promise that it'll be worth waiting for.' She let her fingers slide upwards. Not too quickly, but with purpose. 'But for the moment it suits my schemes to let Natalie move ahead with the downfall of dear Whitelaw.'

Alex glanced down at Stella's hand, then looked up again. His face was a picture of confusion. It was all there: lust, fear, anger, disbelief and a dozen other ravelled-up emotions.

'Do you fancy her?' he demanded, the long muscle of his thigh like iron beneath Stella's fingertips.

'Relax,' she murmured again, beginning to massage him. Each stroke took her fingers closer to his cock. 'Of course I fancy her. Who wouldn't? She has a sort of brittle, nervous quality I like. But it's just a shell. Armour I want to crack wide open. Beneath, she's vulnerable, pliant, the perfect submissive.'

As she spoke, Stella inclined herself yet closer to Alex,

and looked straight into his eyes. 'The perfect submissive,' she repeated softly, her questing fingers sliding even closer to the critical zone. She flattened her palm over Alex's hip, pressing the fine silk-mix fabric of his trousers against his pelvic bone, her thumb inwards. She still wasn't touching his cock, but she circled her hand to drag the skin and caress it by proxy.

Alex made an almost inaudible croaking sound. His eyes were black and Stella could see sweat on his brow. 'I thought you liked women,' he whispered, 'not men.'

'Oh, Alex, Alex, Alex, I like both! Hadn't you realised?'

Alex tried to struggle, but somehow, to Stella's delight, it turned more into a kind of slow yet reluctant grind of pleasure. He closed his eyes again, turned his head away, swallowed as if his mouth were parched. 'But I – I'm not ... I don't ... Oh, God!' he gasped as Stella slipped her hand neatly across him and cupped it around the fast-hardening cock beneath the fine fabric of his trousers.

'I'm not gay!' protested Alex, his voice rising and cracking in a way that seemed to suggest otherwise. When Stella clasped him harder, he wailed, 'Oh, God, no, I'm not gay!'

'Neither am I,' Stella whispered, reaching over with her other hand to turn Alex's face back to hers. 'I don't like labels. I just like sex. With people who are interesting and hot and adventurous.' She paused, then laid her mouth delicately over Alex's, slipping out her tongue for just a moment to lick along the line of his lower lip.

'I'm not adventurous,' Alex said, his hips lifting even as he spoke. 'I'm not gay,' he reiterated, tears in his eyes. 'I don't like this.'

'Oh, but you do,' Stella said, emphasising the point by clasping the outline of Alex's thick, stiffened penis between her finger and thumb, '*This* likes it. I have a suspicion that *this* likes it very much,' she went on, running her delicate grip up and down the length of him.

'Please ... No ...' Alex panted, shaking his head and wriggling.

Stella smiled. Alex was young and strong and in good physical condition. He could have pushed her away easily, got up and gone. But he stayed exactly where he was. His body was telling the stone truth even though words of denial still fell from his lips.

'Please. Yes!' she said firmly, rolling the tip of him carefully between the pads of her finger and thumb, using the cloth of his trousers and his underwear as a supplementary sex aid. She continued to manipulate him until his heels kicked hard against the carpet and she knew that he was reaching a point of criticality.

Not yet, she thought, releasing him, yet at the same time finding the thought of his coming inside his clothes extremely titillating. It was the ultimate humiliation, the ultimate shame for a man. How vulnerable would that make him to her? She considered grasping him again, and wanking him quickly and mercilessly to a huge climax.

But no, there was more fun to be had with him than that. Finer games to play. She edged back a little, moving away from him in order to give him breathing space. Alex opened his eyes, asking a silent question. Was she going to let him get away now? Before anything really serious had happened? Before they'd crossed the Rubicon he clearly sensed lay before them?

No chance, sweetheart! Stella thought exultantly. She reached out and touched his face and said softly, 'Come on, Alex, get it out for me.'

He begged with his eyes this time, but Stella felt implacable. 'Alex,' she prompted, glancing down at his crotch where the fine silk fabric of his trousers was obscenely tented.

'Oh, fuck,' Alex muttered, but his hands went to the

buckle of his crocodile belt and began to unfasten it. At the same time, he made as if to heel off his highly polished loafers, but Stella shook her head.

Alex looked confused. 'Leave them,' Stella ordered softly.

He continued to work on his clothing, hands rendered clumsy by his shaking and his nerviness. Like a little boy at a first and very dreaded medical, he looked to Stella imploringly for guidance.

'Push your trousers and your underpants down to your knees,' she instructed him, relishing the look of horror in his eyes. She was asking him to exhibit himself, not in the full, clean honesty of nakedness, but in some partial, furtive, deeply sleazy way instead.

And yet he obeyed her and Stella felt a rush of admiration for him. For someone who she sensed was subconsciously somewhat homophobic, he was acquitting himself with at least a fair degree of poise.

She grinned with pleasure when Alex's penis was released, bouncing upwards as if alive with kinetic energy. Reaching across him, she unfastened his tie and left the two ends hanging free, then unbuttoned his dark shirt and folded it back to bare his chest and belly.

'You're very beautiful, Alex,' she said, then pursed her lips, slightly unsatisfied with the arrangement. She adjusted the panels of his shirt a little, and the ends of his tie. Then she bent over him and pushed his trousers and his black cotton trunks right down to his ankles.

'Very beautiful indeed,' she affirmed, finally satisfied with the way she'd disposed his body.

Alex looked agonised. His hands lay limp at his sides on the settee, as if he instinctively knew that Stella wanted him neither to touch himself nor to cover his bared flesh. His fingers twitched though, the effort of restraining himself clearly considerable.

'Clench your buttocks,' Stella instructed him.

Alex complied and the muscular flexion made his

erect cock bob and sway like a living toy. Stella felt an urge to flick at it, and make it dance, but that seemed somehow just too cruel.

'Lovely. Now relax again.'

She looked into Alex's face. Were there tears in his fine dark eyes? It seemed so. Tears of shame and humiliation at having his genitalia so objectified.

'Why so upset?' she enquired softly. 'You've got a sensational dick, you should be proud to show it off. And it's never bothered you to reveal it before, has it? I've seen it often enough at our gatherings, haven't I?' She glanced down at the organ in question, and felt an answering shiver of delight in her own cock. Alex's was weeping pre-come now, the silver fluid giving his glans an unearthly sheen. 'And I've always wanted to get this close to it.' She edged in towards him. 'Close enough to touch it and to know all its idiosyncrasies.' She reached out a finger and scooped up the thin, silky juice from the tip of his cock. Leading him to believe that she was going to taste it, at the last minute she held the shiny finger out to his lips.

Alex shook his head, but Stella was quicker and stronger. She grabbed him by the hair with her free hand and pushed her finger gently but implacably between Alex's protesting lips.

'Suck it!'

He complied, sucking on her fingertip like a baby. Stella didn't let him see it, but the sensation was delectable and made her own cock stiffen and leap. She felt as if she wanted to melt from the warm wet heat around her finger.

Feeling wilder, she pumped the digit in and out of Alex's mouth suggestively. Looking down into his eyes, she left him in no doubt about the sorts of activities that lay ahead of him. Her dick in his mouth, or her dick in his arse; maybe both, one after the other. Now there was a tempting prospect, if she could keep it up!

'Oh yes, my sweet one,' she purred, removing her finger from between his lips, then, without giving him time to anticipate her, swirling it around the seeping tip of his cock again. As he groaned and wriggled again, she captured his glans menacingly between her finger and thumb.

'Such a pretty boy,' she murmured, manipulating him, measuring the pressure so that it was just enough to tease and drive him crazy, but not enough to tip him over the edge. His eyes were watering now, just as freely as his penis.

'Oh, God, please, Stella – let me come,' he begged, his hips lifting and his pelvis circling. Following his movements, Stella maintained her hold on the sticky tip of his penis.

'Oh no, not yet, sweetheart,' she replied, suddenly releasing him. 'Only on my terms – and with my dick inside you.'

'No!' cried Alex, his eyes huge with fear and revulsion. 'Oh no! Not that! Please . . . Just wank me off. Let me wank you off! Please! Anything but that!'

'But that's what I want,' Stella said, keeping her voice quiet and reasonable as if there were nothing at all untoward or abnormal about what she was proposing. Which there wasn't, really, she thought, recalling times when she'd been sodomised and sodomised others in return. It was a breathtaking pleasure – whether given or received.

'I can't! I can't!' whimpered Alex, his stiff upward-pointing cock making a liar of him. He'd grown stiffer, it seemed, almost visibly, at the very mention of being buggered. Whatever he was saying and denying in words, his hungering body clearly had entirely different needs.

'Relax a minute. Get used to the idea. You know it's going to happen, Alex,' said Stella firmly. The look she gave him was harder now, calculated to remind him in whose debt he was and how difficult life could be if that debt was ever called in.

Alex looked at her. His jaw dropped. His eyes filled with the enormity of revelation. But his cock remained pointing heavenwards, hard and eager. 'Oh, fuck,' he murmured and turned his face away from her.

'I intend to,' said Stella. She felt slightly ashamed at using such blatant terror tactics with him, but consoled herself with the fact that it *was* what he wanted. Reaching to open a large, carved, wooden box that stood on the occasional table set to one side of the settee, she then drew out a long length of silk ribbon, coloured red, and a pair of handcuffs.

Loving the feel of the silk against her fingers, Stella swirled it lightly around Alex's penis, completely enrobing it. She layered on the delicate, feather-light stuff, winding it round and around, covering his cock, yet not in any way constricting it. With each twist she managed to ever so gently caress him.

'Hold that on yourself,' she told him when the silk was arranged to her liking, two long loose ends dangling. 'Now turn over. Slide down, kneel on the carpet and rest your chest against the settee.'

Alex complied, openly sobbing, but offering no resistance or argument. When he was in place, Stella fastened the two tails of the red silk ribbon in a loose knot at the small of his back, then quite roughly grabbed his arms and pulled them behind him. Alex collapsed on his face, the air knocked out of him, and, while he was winded, Stella secured his wrists together with the handcuffs. Alex sighed into the cushions, but still didn't struggle. Was he already resigned to his fate? How long would it be before he would accept this without having to go through the motions of protest? Not long, thought Stella, smiling and admiring his body as she folded his dark shirt clear of his buttocks.

Alex was still tense, even if he was now submissive.

The muscles of his backside were taut, unrelaxed, defensive, and Stella sighed, knowing she had work to do in order to coax him to accept her. Sliding her hand up under his shirt, she began a slow, measured massage of his back and shoulders, working at the knots she found and murmuring endearments as she loosened them.

'Don't worry,' she whispered, leaning close. 'It won't hurt if you don't fight me, and you'll enjoy it.' Momentarily, she reached under him and caressed his dick through the silk. 'And it won't make you any less of a man. It's just a different form of pleasure.'

'God, I wish I could believe you,' whispered Alex, uttering his first coherent words for some minutes.

'Well, think about me,' said Stella, pulling back and concentrating on kneading the musculature of Alex's bottom now. 'I wear dresses, I take it in the arse often enough – and I can still be every inch the stud when I feel like it.' He laughed softly. 'Our friend Natalie can vouch for that, believe me . . . Even though I let her beat me today, I don't think she'd deny that it was a man's cock she had inside her afterwards.'

'Christ! You fucked her?'

'Yes, and she was sensational . . . don't you agree?'

'Well, yes, she's a very exciting woman,' admitted Alex. Stella could feel him relaxing now, as if their talk of a third party allowed him some kind of distance or breathing space. The rounds of flesh beneath her fingers were less tense now: still firm but more malleable, more pliant.

'Does she know?'

'Know what? About Stella and Steven, you mean?' She dug in her fingers, not cruelly, but with more vigour. Alex's moan was indicative of his shift in attitude. His voice was blissful, and appreciative. Not long now.

'No, amazingly enough. I would have expected her to cotton on to it straightaway, as soon as she'd met . . .

me,' Stella said, realising it was true. She *was* amazed that a so-called perceptive journalist like Natalie hadn't sussed her out straightaway, on first seeing and speaking to her as she was now.

'I suppose it's because she's only seen ... um ... seen Stella in low light ... and you're so good with voices ... Oh, God! Yes!'

Stella smiled, her thumbs working in strong circles now, sliding into Alex's anal groove and stretching open the snug little entrance.

'Do you really think I'm good with voices?' she said, deliberately reverting to the voice of a refined, Middle England schoolmaster. She felt Alex flinch and begin to tense again. Aha, he still had some inhibitions about being with a man, it seemed. It was OK while he was being fondled and sweet-talked by Stella, but he clearly wasn't too sure about getting it on with Steven.

'Yes! You know you are!' hissed Alex as Stella threw herself with renewed energy into the handling of his bottom.

'Why, thank you,' purred Stella as 'Stella' once again. She leaned closer, her face close to Alex's ear, her long hair falling across the back of his neck. 'Are you ready to do it now, Alex, my sweet?' She pressed a fingertip against his anus, and jabbed it very lightly a little way inside.

'Oh, God! Oh, God!' whispered Alex, 'I ... I don't know ... Can't you take these off?' he asked, jiggling the handcuffs.

'Oh no, no, no,' said Stella, pressing harder against the tight ring of muscle. It was resistant, almost impenetrable, but a good application of K-Y gel would soon change that, no problem.

'Let's keep the cuffs,' she said silkily, still working him. 'They'll make it better. Trust me. You won't regret it.'

'Do I have a choice?' snapped Alex, his fire returning.

'No. Actually. You don't,' confirmed Stella, withdrawing her finger and reaching back to the box to take out a tube of lubricant. Squeezing out a generous measure, she smeared it up and down Alex's anal cleft, and then, ignoring his renewed protests, she scooped up another big dollop and began to thrust it inside him.

'I can't take it! I can't take it!' he gasped as Stella pushed more and more of the gel into him, packing his anus like some finely machined aperture that needed greasing heavily to protect its delicate structure. 'Please, Stella, no more! I'm going to shit myself!'

'Oh, no, you're not,' she reassured him, thinking all the time that if he thought he was going to defecate now, well in a moment, he'd be absolutely convinced of it. 'It's just the nerves inside you playing tricks with your mind, Alex. You'll be all right.'

'This isn't tricks! It's real!' wailed Alex as Stella probed deeper.

'Relax,' commanded Stella, withdrawing. Pulling aside her loose French knickers, she rolled on a thick condom, then anointed her sheathed penis with the same gel, slathering it on generously. Keeping things friction-free meant fewer traumas for her little virgin.

He was whimpering again, but Stella decided not to waste time. The sooner this was happening, and Alex was enjoying it, the better. Nudging apart his ankles as far as they'd go in the hobble of his trousers, Stella knelt between them, on the trousers, effectively immobilising him. For a moment, she twined her fingers with his reassuringly, then she grasped his slippery buttocks, widening the channel to give her access.

'No, no, no,' pleaded Alex as she pressed into him, and yet at the same time she felt him pushing back against her. The sensation was intoxicating. He did want this! He did want her dick inside him! Once again his vocal protests were a token gesture. His mouth was lying while his body told the truth.

'Easy, sweetheart, easy,' she murmured to him, feeling him yield and let his inner flesh accept her penis. 'Just relax and feel how nice it really is.'

Alex made an inarticulate sound, a low animal keening of surrender and obvious pleasure. Muscles within him tensed and pulsed, caressing Stella within him in a way that was both dangerous and unbearably exquisite. Only the presence of the condom kept her from ejaculating long before she really wanted to, but it was a hard-fought battle – all she wanted to do was come.

Oh God, this isn't going to last long, thought Stella happily as Alex began to writhe beneath her, his tight channel flexing and embracing her. There was no resistance whatsoever now in the young man who moved eagerly beneath her. He was wriggling about, rubbing his silk-swathed dick against the sofa beneath him, and obviously revelling in every second of the experience. Even his shouting voice finally admitted his enjoyment now.

'Oh, hell, yes!' he shouted and Stella forged in deeper. She could feel him pushing back against her now, instinctively syncopating his movements to hers for maximum sensation. Critical overload would come at any second now, and feeling an almost tearful affection for the man beneath her, and wanting to share the moment with him completely, Stella reached around, under Alex's belly, and grasped his cock.

'Come, baby, come!' she implored him, working the marvellous young shaft between her fingers and caressing it with the silk ribbons as her own hips began to jerk.

With an indecipherable cry of his own, Alex obeyed her. Hot come pumped out of him into the silk, just as Stella's own ejaculation spurted inside him. Blind, deaf and delirious, all Stella could focus on was the strange, high, white place that seemed to exist, somehow, both up in the stratosphere, yet at the same time in the depths of Alex's body. Then, falling over him, she clutched him to her like a child. Bathed in warm pleasure, she heard him murmur, 'Oh, Stella, thank you . . .'

'Well, that wasn't so bad after all, was it?'

Alex stared at Stella, then laughed out loud at his strange friend's everyday, conversational tone. 'You make it sound like a trip to the dentist's,' he said, accepting the large drink – whisky, this time – that Stella handed to him.

'Oh, surely not quite such an ordeal,' said Stella with a grin, sitting down beside him with her own drink, and crossing her long and sensationally stockinged legs provocatively. 'Although if I were feeling crude I could point out certain similarities incorporating the concept of "drilling" and "excavating".' She looked at Alex over the rim of her glass and winked.

'For a lady you are sometimes a very dirty bitch, Stella,' replied Alex easily. He was amazed at how relaxed and comfortable he felt. No remorse. No guilt. No feelings of dirtiness or shame.

'Why, thank you. I take that as a compliment,' Stella said. 'But seriously, Alex, how do you feel? Any regrets?'

She seemed to have read his mind again, but for once it didn't bother him. 'No, none at all. I feel better than I have done in ages. I don't know why.'

'Good. And it doesn't change things, does it?' said Stella, her hazel eyes dark and penetrating. 'You still like women too, don't you? I haven't corrupted you or bent you in any way, have I?'

Alex considered. Yes, Stella was right. He was the same person that he'd been before he'd had sex with her. Relaxed and sensualised, he considered the thought of being with a woman and found it infinitely appealing. Especially someone foxy and challenging like Natalie Croft. He imagined her on her knees, now, in front of him, taking his cock into her mouth, and as he did so that organ – now safely tucked up inside his clothing – gave a little leap of response.

'Nope, nothing wrong with me. I still like girls,' he said cheerfully, taking a sip of Stella's fine whisky and at the same time reaching down to cup himself.

'So do I,' murmured Stella, doing the same, her long, manicured fingers squeezing and relaxing around the bulge in her silk French knickers.

They drank in companionable silence for a while. Alex felt calm and lucid and strangely philosophical. He wasn't drunk now, not in the slightest, despite the fact that he'd been intoxicated to some degree when he'd arrived here, and had wine and whisky since. Things seemed to be back into perspective somehow, and his life had possibilities.

'About that other matter,' said Stella thoughtfully. 'Maybe you should have been the one to pursue Daumery, but Natalie is on the trail now, so there's not much we can do about that. However –' Stella's eyes were full of the bright, wicked gleam that Alex could almost love her for '– he's not the only one with dirty washing to be aired. How about our dear mayor, and Councillor Peat? When someone hands out bribes, there's always someone else accepting them, isn't there?'

'Hmm.' Now there was something. The *other* end of this sordid trail of sleaze. Let Natalie Croft have the national figure, and take the local villains for himself. That seemed fair.

'Think about it, eh?' Stella said, setting down her glass. 'Let's see how things develop.'

'I'll drink to that,' said Alex, feeling not only his spirits lift, but his penis too.

'Well, I wasn't actually thinking in terms of a drink.'

Something in Stella's voice made Alex turn sharply. The drag queen was leaning back now, her legs splayed, and she was playing with herself openly. Alex could see the clear outline of the very male cock against the delicate feminine fabric of her underwear.

'What did you have in mind?' he said, feeling a frisson of fear return. An exciting fear that stiffened him even further.

'Well,' said Stella, licking her freshly lipsticked mouth, 'I was wondering how you felt about moving on to the next lesson on the gay sex curriculum.'

Guessing what she meant, Alex gasped. He wanted it. He really did. But he was still a little scared. 'Which is?'

'Oh, I think you know.' In a quick, surprisingly graceful movement, Stella slipped off her French knickers to leave herself bare from the waist down apart from her sheer hold-up stockings.

His heart pounding, and his body rigid inside his designer trousers, Alex slid to his knees on the carpet, knelt before Stella and took her cock deeply and lovingly into his mouth.

Chapter Eleven

Connections

'*F*uck! What now?' muttered Natalie, slamming down Patti's phone. She'd just discovered that Steven Small's number was ex-directory, and the officious cow at directory enquiries had refused to yield any help either – even though, if required, Natalie could have described every last quirk of Steven's sexual preferences and his taste in tea, bread and kitchen décor!

The only thing to do now was go round and visit him again, which, even if she'd felt like it, required borrowing Patti's car again, shelling out for a taxi, slogging there on public transport or, in the last resort, walking!

Dear God, why was everything in this stupid jumped-up town so difficult? And especially when other aspects of the chase were beginning to hot up.

Gareth the hacker had come up with the truly critical information that Natalie had been hoping for. Just as instinct had told her, Whitelaw Daumery was the secret owner of the Black Gate Group, which meant that the three controversial and probably obscenely lucrative projects she'd researched in the library yesterday had all poured cash into his no doubt already overflowing pockets. And these, she suspected, were only three deals

out of many, many more. Even now Gareth was trawl-
ing the cyber-ether to find them.

Moral practice in business, my arse! Natalie thought
with a satisfying sense of 'I knew it!' The next obvious
step was to discover how these deals had been secured.
Surely it wasn't coincidence that his companies had
been the successful bidders. She thought back to legend-
ary investigations in the past that had yielded up webs
of national and local government corruption and bribes
and backhanders flying about all over the place. Presumably, these hadn't been – and weren't to this day –
made in the form of cheques or electronic payments that
were traceable. She'd also charged Gareth with the task
of contacting an even more unscrupulous and talented
hacker he sometimes had dealings with to look into the
possibilities there, but she didn't hold out much hope
for it.

No, it was more likely that such payments were
transacted in cash, or in goods or services perhaps –
which would make them much less likely to have been
documented in any way, shape or form, and consequently difficult to the point of impossibility to trace.

But, goddamnit, she was bloody well going to try!
And maybe that was where Steven Small's acquaintance
may well come in. Someone on the inside of one of
Daumery's companies, a mole, so to speak, may have
access to revealing documents that had never been part
of the ever-widening electronic net. It would be absolutely perfect if this person was a disaffected employee,
happy to blow the whistle, but even the most innocent
of company titbits might be helpful and lead to further
discoveries. Which meant she was going to have to
contact Steven again in order that he could pass on her
number.

Natalie closed her eyes. Why did the job and her sex
life keep intersecting like this? First with Alex, now with
Steven. It made everything so complicated, so muddy.

She couldn't focus on the pursuit of Daumery when erotic encounters and discoveries kept appearing enticingly in her way.

You're conveniently forgetting the biggest discovery of the lot, aren't you, Nat? The most perplexing and the scariest one . . .

Even as she thought that thought, the source of her qualms called out to her from the kitchen.

'Breakfast, Nat! Come and get it!'

But get what, Patti? thought Natalie, seeing a mad humour in the situation despite everything.

'Coming,' she called out in reply, but, as she did so, her mobile phone trilled. Pulling it from her pocket she flicked it open, stabbed OK and said crisply, 'Hello. Natalie Croft.'

'Er . . . yes. Hello,' said the rather diffident voice at the other end of the line. 'My name's Simon Natwick and a mutual friend of ours has asked me to contact you.'

Bingo! Natalie thought, but, as she took down the details of where she might meet this potential whistle blower of Steven's, she couldn't help but wonder how and when her shy but pervy teacher had obtained her mobile phone number.

She found out later, when Steven himself phoned her. While she was drinking a second cappuccino in the city-centre coffee bar where she'd met Simon Natwick, her recharged phone suddenly rang, and to her surprise the caller was Teacher himself, calling to ask if she'd been approached by his friend yet.

'Yes, actually. He just left,' she answered cautiously, wondering how much she dare tell him of the stunning disclosures Simon had made.

'And was he helpful?'

'Yes. Far more so than I'd even dared to hope. He gave me precisely the information I need, and he can get documents, too,' she said, deciding to confide in him. After all, she now had some 'dirt' on Teacher, too, didn't she? 'All I need now is video tapes of that slimeball handing over cash bribes and I'm laughing,' she joked.

'I wonder who might have such tapes,' said Steven thoughtfully.

Natalie laughed. Did he seriously consider that such tapes might really exist? Perhaps he was even more naïve than he already seemed to be? At least in the area of the mechanisms of corruption . . .

'Natwick is a strange bird,' she said, thinking of the meeting she'd just had. 'I offered him a fee for his services, but somehow I got the impression he wasn't really interested in the money very much.'

She hesitated, thinking that Simon Natwick was even more peculiar, in some ways, than Steven Small. He'd never even mentioned payment himself, and yet he'd offered no other explanation for passing her the information. There had certainly not been much evidence of reforming zeal or a desire to expose a wrongdoer, either. His motives had been impossible to fathom, and yet, as she'd just told Steven, the information he supplied was explosive.

'I'm sure he has his own reasons,' said Steven vaguely.

'Yes, I'm sure he does.' Natalie decided to change tack. 'Another thing that puzzles me, though, is how you obtained my phone number. I sure as hell can't remember giving it to you! And you must realise that, with you being ex-directory, I couldn't ring you!'

'Yes, that dawned on me after you left yesterday . . . In the . . . um . . . heat of the moment, I'd completely forgotten . . .' For an instant, he sounded much more like nervous Teacher from the train. 'Then it occurred to me that another acquaintance of mine might know you and perhaps have your phone number,' he said lightly, his confidence clearly returning. 'A fellow journalist, actually – Alex Hendry. And of course, I was right, wasn't I?'

Does he expect me to award him a merit badge for initiative? thought Natalie briefly. She was really too high on the information she'd received from Simon Natwick to be irritated with Steven for long, yet something about his attitude made her feel uneasy.

'How do you know Alex Hendry?'

'Oh, just socially. We met at a party,' Steven went on, his voice becoming more consciously casual.

Natalie's ire flared again, in spite of her excitement over recent developments. For a couple of seconds she wished she were back in Steven's kitchen, beating the living daylights out of him, then shamelessly exploiting him for her own satisfaction. She could almost feel his large, beautiful prick inside her as she rode him to a huge climax while concentrating solely on her pleasure at the expense of his.

Just wait until next time, Mr Smart-Arse Teacher, she thought when he'd rung off.

His farewell had been casual, almost dismissive: 'Well, I must fly ... Maybe we can get together soon when you've finished your story.' And, though Natalie had been equally noncommittal, she nevertheless relished the prospect of a repeat performance of their kitchen adventure. What were the chances that she could get Patti to borrow some 'equipment' of some kind for her? Her sister's perverted friends must have all sorts of instruments of punishment and degradation. Natalie imagined going after Steven with a whip or something. Maybe even a cane. Now wouldn't *that* be fun? Especially on a teacher. The very idea of it made Natalie feel almost light-headed and sent a surge through her belly.

Yes, that was it! As soon as she'd worked out how best to interpret and present the information Simon

Natwick had supplied, she'd see Steven again, and let her imagination run wild with him.

Maybe Patti had access to books and magazines too. Special S/M paraphernalia. Natalie imagined chaining Steven up naked and abusing him somehow. Tormenting his cock until he came helplessly ... She could just picture it. Him grovelling; herself magnificent and dominating. Maybe wearing high heels, leather, possibly even a menacing mask, like some of the participants at the orgy at Fontayne's had been wearing.

Yes, that would be the perfect reward to give herself for breaking the Whitelaw Daumery scandal! A session as a dominatrix with Steven Small. What a blast! And the beauty of it was that a bashful schoolteacher was hardly likely to know that she was inexperienced and didn't really know what she was doing. With someone like Steven she could just make it up as she went along.

But just who *was* someone like Steven?

Natalie frowned. Did she *really* know what Steven Small was like? How many times during their brief and tumultuous encounters had she got the impression that he was hiding something from her? That there was much, much more to him than met the eye?

And Simon Natwick had been strangely coy and evasive about Steven, too, come to think of it. Reviewing the hushed conversation they'd had, here in this coffee bar, Natalie realised that the man had not once referred to Steven by name. He'd been mulishly obscure, on reflection, saying things like 'our mutual friend' and 'my contact'. Natalie had thought it odd at the time, but, excited by the vindication of her suspicions about Daumery, she'd put Simon's affectations down to a desire to be overdramatic.

Still, weird nevertheless ...

But for the moment, Steven the kinky academic would have to wait; and she could have another go at pumping Natwick about him, anyway, when they met again so she could collect the copied documents she'd been promised. Sexual dalliance, no matter how intense and satisfying, had to take a back seat for now. She had a story to develop, and the next step was to investigate the final link, or links, in the chain – the crooked councillors who had taken Daumery's money to grant him pot-of-gold contracts.

The town hall and resources such as the register of councillors' interests and other biographical details should be her next logical destination. Thank God it was within walking distance, as Patti had put her foot down over the car today, and taxis were putting a severe drain on Natalie's limited finances. Draining her cup, she stood up and walked out on to the pavement, looking around to orientate herself. The town hall was away to her left in the academic area of the city, but just to her right was the august, gracious building in which the *Sentinel* was housed.

What were the odds that Alex was available today? Surely he knew some good background info on various councillors – if it was 'in his interest' to share it with her, that was. Not feeling terribly optimistic about the result, she tapped his number into her phone.

As she listened to it ringing, she thought that even if he wasn't all that forthcoming about the possible mal-practice of members of Redwych City Council she could at least ask Alex about Steven Small.

'I didn't expect to be able to contact you,' said Natalie, a short while later, when she was sitting with Alex on a bench overlooking the bank of the river. There were no punts or pleasure craft out at the moment to admire, and Natalie realised that was because the sky above them looked decidedly dark and ominous.

'For a journalist, you're a pig to get hold of,' she complained, trying to stop herself thinking how good Alex looked in today's designer offering. Black from head to foot, much as Steven Small generally wore, she realised.

'Yes, I keep meaning to do something about that,' said Alex distractedly, as if he too had many other things to think about than the purpose of their meeting.

'Right! Councillors! Where can I get the lowdown on them? The mayor and a certain Councillor Peat in particular ... I've been given information to the effect that Whitelaw Daumery has been bunging them bribes to get various construction projects. Dodgy projects for that matter ... Stuff built where it isn't in the public interest to be built.'

Watching Alex's face as she spoke, Natalie saw no real surprise cross his handsome features. It was more a sort of 'oh, well, I knew this was coming' sort of a look, as if he'd been hoping she wouldn't get to this place in her search, and yet also knew it was inevitable.

'Well, do you have dossiers on them or what?' she persisted when he remained silent and stared up into the grey sky, looking disgruntled.

'Well, not exactly dossiers, but I do have information that's, well, relevant to your line of enquiry,' he said obliquely, holding out his hand as if testing for raindrops.

Natalie stared at him. If he had the information, why the devil hadn't he ever used it himself? It didn't make sense. Well, not unless, as she suspected, he was taking bribes himself – to keep quiet about what he knew, and maybe suppress coverage of it in the *Sentinel*.

'Who's paying *you*?' she demanded on impulse, and the wild look in Alex's eyes, as he swung round to face her, told her that she'd been right on the money with her suspicions.

What if this was an even bigger story?

'It's ...' He hesitated. 'It's not in my interest to disclose that.' His face was a picture now. A strangely alluring amalgam of shame, superiority and humour. At her expense.

'But you are on someone's payroll, aren't you? How else could you afford clothes like that?' she said, pointing to the beautiful black suit he was wearing. This time she was almost certain it was Armani.

Alex nodded, looked down at his trousers, then frowned furiously when he saw an even darker spot on the dark fabric. It was just starting to rain.

'Right. If you won't tell me who's paying you, can you at least tell me how you know someone called Steven Small? He told me that he got my mobile-phone number from you.'

'Look! I can't talk about all this here!' cried Alex, leaping to his feet and shaking ineffectually at his jacket, which was fast becoming dappled with the big fat raindrops that were suddenly teeming down. 'This suit cost a fucking fortune and it'll get ruined! Let's get inside somewhere!'

'Where, though?' Natalie was on her feet, too, and began to run behind Alex, who was already off in search of shelter for his precious designer clothes. No doubt his elegant shoes needed protecting, too.

'Follow me! My flat's nearby!'

A town-centre flat, too, thought Natalie as she jogged behind him, aware of the irony that her own clothes wouldn't really suffer from a dowsing at all. Since arriving here in Redwych, she'd really been dressing down, her sleek city suits abandoned with her prestigious job at the *Modern Examiner*.

Within a couple of minutes, they were at Alex's flat, and, just like his suits and his wheels, it seemed well beyond the income of a badly paid provincial journalist.

The wages of sin, thought Natalie as she followed him into the exquisite, sparsely decorated area that was his living room. The building was old, but the interior design was modern. Not brutally so, though, and not entirely out of step with the exterior. The walls were white, and the furnishings were of light but highly polished wood and with flashes of warm colours such as red and tan and ochre.

'Get yourself a drink or something,' said Alex ungraciously before disappearing to fuss over his suit and its possible damage by raindrops.

'I will,' said Natalie to his disappearing back. The tray bearing a variety of spirits and some very fine and rare-looking pale dry sherry appeared tempting.

Natalie poured herself a gin, but topped it up generously with tonic. There were no identifiable sounds coming from the direction of Alex's bedroom, so she looked around the lounge.

He had a huge wide-screen TV, an elaborate sound system and a variety of other expensive boy's toys such as a games console, a top-of-the-range DVD player and digital satellite decoder. A rather deluxe PC with all the trimmings stood on a desk in the corner.

I wonder how many corruption stories he's had to bury to earn this lot, she thought, sitting down on the deeply upholstered sofa.

Taking a deep sip of the silvery, balsamic gin, she set aside her glass and relaxed into the cushions, letting her head tip back until she was staring up at the pure white expanse of the ceiling.

How bad was it really to take money for services rendered? Or, in Alex's case, services *not* rendered? And what about Daumery and his pet councillors? OK, so a rich man got richer, and some buildings got built in places that weren't quite the best ones for certain local interests. It wasn't the end of the world, surely? Not as bad as being a mass baby murderer, or being a psycho-path in power in the Middle East or the Balkans?

She tipped forward again, reached for her gin and drank more, as if the clear fluid might also clarify her thoughts – specifically those concerning Alex.

What was so reprehensible about what he was doing? Accepting the quiet, easy life, the comfortable life, instead of doing what she tried to do and getting fucked over by some prima donna of an editor. In the words of Bob Dylan, everybody's 'gotta serve somebody' and whoever it was to whom Alex owed allegiance was certainly generous to their servants.

As she sipped the last drops of her drink, a notion occurred to Natalie out of nowhere.

What if, somehow, Daumery were to offer to pay *her* off? God, how would she respond to that? If the money was really significant? Would she bend over for the cash or sacrifice her journalistic high principles?

What high principles? she thought, laughing out loud. She'd never been that much of a crusader, and anyway, in this case, it would be a win–win situation. Take the money, she'd be comfortable and could freelance or even write that novel she'd always threatened to; go with the story, and get a high, high profile and enjoy the doors that would open up to her in consequence. Either way, since starting this thing, she'd been thinking purely of herself and not of any concept of 'the common good'. She was as self-serving as the next person – if not more so.

'Good God, this is an epiphany, isn't it?' she muttered, jumping up and darting across to check the contents of that gin bottle. Surely it contained some extra ingredient? A hallucinogen or some sort of truth drug? But all she found was a good-quality but unadulterated spirit.

As she poured herself another small measure, she heard soft, padding footsteps approaching from the passage.

And why am I doing this? Alex asked himself as he approached the living room, wearing nothing but his towelling bathrobe. The whole suit thing was a total con. If the rain had done any damage, his specialist cleaner would sort it out. After all, he hadn't cared much when he'd been rolling about in the back of a van in another, equally good, suit, had he?

No, it was sex again, wasn't it? And proving to himself that he could still make it with a woman after being fucked by a man. Well, a sort of man . . .

'Hi!' he said, entering the lounge and seeing Natalie's eyes widen when she saw how he was dressed, 'Sorry . . .' He nodded down at the robe. 'Thought I'd hang up the suit and maybe have a shower. It's been a muggy sort of day. Hope you don't mind.'

'No. Not at all.'

She was clutching a drink, obviously her second, and had an odd sort of expression on her face. A strange glow, almost a contentment that underlay her immediate reaction to his appearance. What the hell had she been doing or thinking while he'd been away?

'I think I'll have one of those,' he said, wondering if he'd made a mistake. The atmosphere between them was strained to say the least. The last time he'd seen her, prior to today, he'd been having sex with two other women in the private room at Fontayne's.

'I'll do the honours.' Natalie seemed keen to have something to do.

Taking the drinks to the settee, they sat down beside each other, looked at each other, then both laughed.

'God, we've only known each other less than a week and already we've got "history"!' said Natalie, holding up her glass.

'Here's to "history",' replied Alex, clinking his glass to hers.

'Is it this place, do you think? Redwych, I mean . . . It's really become the strangest place. I can never remember it being such a hotbed of depravity and corruption when I lived here.'

'Maybe you just weren't looking for it then.'

'True. I firmly believed there was nothing going on. That's why I left.'

'I'm glad you came back.'

Natalie laughed again and shook her head. The relaxed gesture seemed to take in all that had passed between them in the last few days and say 'c'est la vie'.

'So, how do you know Steven Small?'

Ooof! The relaxation dissipated a bit. He couldn't yet tell her the whole story until he'd been given permission.

'I met him at some poxy little function I was reporting on at St Crispin's School. Cheese and wine . . . Bleugh!' Well, that much was true. 'He was a relief teacher there then, and had got roped in somehow, and we just got talking because he looked just as bored and pissed off with the proceedings as I was. We split, went for a pint and then exchanged cards, and we've met for a drink now and again since.'

Only partially true, this time. He could still remember the softly spoken, luring tones when Steven had said, 'Let me take you somewhere that'll really knock your socks off!'

There was silence. When Alex looked up at Natalie, she was staring at him in a really intense and curious way.

Oh, fuck! She thinks I'm gay for him!

Oh, fuck, of course, I am . . .

They both laughed again.

'Well, there's a turn-up for the books,' said Natalie, looking slightly shaken. 'What a weird triangle this is.'

You don't know the half of it, thought Alex, experiencing a strong urge to tell Natalie everything, and to hell with Steven and Stella and his/her never-ending mind games.

But to do that might screw up everything. 'Stella' in particular was capricious, and, if crossed, might turn nasty. Alex thought of his outlays and his debts and knew he had to bide his time.

Natalie was still staring at him. 'You're full of surprises,' she said, her eyes narrowing, as she was thinking rather hard about something. 'Gay lovers and transvestite friends, eh?' She frowned, seemed to be elsewhere. And putting two and two together.

Oh, God, she's nearly got it and, when she does, Stella will blame me!

Without thinking, he put his glass down, snatched Natalie's out of her hand to join it, then grabbed hold of her face in his two hands and kissed her. Kissed her as hard as he was able, pushing his tongue into her mouth to still her protests with sheer force.

A second later, his libido caught up with his flight-or-fight response and his cock reared up beneath his robe. Probing with his tongue, and mashing his lips to hers, he didn't quite forget that he was making an interference run, but suddenly it seemed less important. He could feel Natalie fighting him, and flailing at him with her fists; but by adjusting his grip – one hand behind her head, and the other tightly around her – he held on, almost flying on being a big, bad, unreconstructed and dominant male again.

Holy fuck, she's delicious! he thought, feeling the beginnings of her yielding. At least she'd stopped thumping him, which was a relief.

'What the hell is your game?' Natalie demanded when Alex felt her finally break free of him. 'Trying to prove to me that you're a real man and not a queer?'

'Something like that,' admitted Alex. Honesty was probably the best policy, where feasible.

A sensation like a crack of lightning knocked him out of himself for a moment, and, after a heartbeat or two, he realised that Natalie had slapped him. They stared at each other for a couple more beats, then, astonishingly, she burst out laughing again.

'What is it? What's so funny?'

'I've got to stop doing this,' she said, smiling at him. 'Hitting my lovers, that is ... I slapped Steven across the face yesterday, funnily enough.'

'Are you a feminist, then?'

'Not particularly ...'

'A dominatrix?'

The look she gave him was very revealing. He would really have liked to have been in Steven's kitchen yesterday, and seen the evidence of such tendencies for himself.

'I don't think so ... Although ...' Absently, she picked up her drink, and sipped it. 'I think I might quite like to be one. I ... I don't suppose you'd ...?'

Oh no, not again, not after yesterday with Stella!

Natalie smiled at him. 'Well, it's obvious from the look on your face that you're not into that.' She paused, looked him in the eye, her expression speculative. 'How about straight sex, then? You know, nothing particularly fancy or kinky, just sex.'

'I thought you were mad at me for wanting to prove I'm a man,' said Alex, feeling surer of himself. She did want him, and suddenly the prospect of simple, uncomplicated fucking with a beautiful and intelligent woman was very appealing. His body surged, beneath his robe, affirming the thought.

'I've changed my mind.' She rose to her feet, unbuttoning her simple black blouse. 'Where's your bedroom? Shall we go there?'

Oh, yeah! he thought, a short while later, in bed with Natalie. She had her fingers around a cock that was reassuringly hard and domineering. Yes, even though he'd realised there was nothing wrong with him, and that being bi was perfectly natural and normal and probably the best of both worlds, there was still a primitive caveman segment of his mind that adhered to the 'old ways' ... When men were men, and women were women, and men fucked women's brains out!

'Oh, yeah,' he murmured, rolling over to face her and sliding his hand down her naked belly. Her pubic hair was lush and fuzzy and not quite the same dark, polished chestnut shade as that on her head. Women, they always gilded the lily – but he had no beef with that, bearing in mind his own bathroom cabinet full of grooming products and the high cost of his haircuts. He supposed he probably spent much more on his personal appearance than the average woman did –

Oh fuck!

From left field came an image of himself being right royally shafted by Stella, and his hand froze in the act of parting Natalie's legs.

'What's the matter?' she whispered, her fingers still moving encouragingly on his shaft. Thank God, at least *that* hadn't suddenly lost the plot, too!

'Nothing. Just random thoughts,' he whispered, sliding his hand along its original track. Natalie opened her legs accommodatingly, and Alex's fingers encountered a delicious well of wetness. Oh, lovely!

'Were you worried ... uh ... Oh, God!' Natalie faltered and her hips rose to him. 'Were you worried about the other thing?' she said, her voice light and panting as he circled her clit. 'Because you don't have to be ... really ... If it's any comfort, I've been having some pretty crossover thoughts myself lately. You know ... Oh, yes!' She paused again, her pelvis clear of the bed, working ... Sliding his fingers back to her cunt, Alex felt it fluttering ... Hot damn, some women came so easily!

After a few seconds, she subsided, letting herself fall back against the bed. Alex allowed his hand to settle on her belly, gently curved, little finger nestling in her bush. 'Yes,' she said, sounding amazingly thoughtful and in control of her faculties considering she'd just climaxed, 'I've been having some pretty dykey thoughts lately myself. Found myself fancying women. Well, woman, really.'

'Wow,' said Alex, thinking of some of the scenes he'd witnessed at Fontayne's and other less salubrious venues. Women together. Women caressing and sucking ... Women punishing each other ... 'Do I know the woman, by any chance?'

Natalie tensed. 'That's the dodgiest thing, really ... The fact that it is who it is ... There're other issues to consider.'

Patti, thought Alex, feeling his cock twitch. Now that would be really something – especially with the added twist of incest involved. He was so hard now it was agonising. He was suddenly almost blind with lust, and found the urge to push himself into Natalie immediately difficult to resist.

With a massive effort of will, he contained himself. 'It's your sister, isn't it?' he said gently.

'*Half*-sister,' she corrected immediately, all trace of her release gone. She sounded stiff, tight, inhibited, scared.

'Don't worry,' he said, as she rolled away from him and on to her front. 'I don't think the taboo counts when there's no likelihood of having each other's babies.' He hadn't the slightest idea what he was talking about but it seemed to help. As did his hands on her shoulders, slowly massaging.

'Rationally, I know that,' she said, pushing her shoulders towards his fingers. 'But my subconscious just says "No! You shouldn't want this!"'

'Like me with having sex with a man,' pointed out Alex, seeing how similar their quandaries were. 'I want it, and I know that fundamentally, according to what I think I believe about life, it's fine! Yet part of me still says, "You're just a nasty little poof, Alex!"'

Natalie laughed, and flexed her shoulders again. It occurred to Alex that Stella's assault on his arse had begun with a shoulder massage, and a parade of naughty images passed through his mind's eye. Oh, no, she probably wouldn't like that, but oh, how he would have liked to try. And to find out what it had felt like for Stella ... He glided his hands lower, over Natalie's ribcage, her hips and finally her buttocks.

'Have you ever had it that way?' he whispered into her ear, cupping the firm flesh of her bottom cheeks and circling it suggestively.

'What way?' she demanded, tensing again.

'You know ...'

'Yes, I think I do ... and I don't want it that way, thank you very much!' She tried to turn over, but he held her down, his hands returning to her shoulders as he threw a thigh across hers and pressed his erection against her bottom. He had no intention of forcing anything on her, it just wasn't his way, but the simulation of it was hugely exciting.

'Are you sure?' he enquired, massaging his crotch against her backside.

Natalie was still tense, but he could feel her responding, surging up against him.

'Absolutely,' she said, adjusting her position beneath him. He had a feeling she'd slid a hand between her legs. 'Just because you buggered Steven, it doesn't mean you can bugger me just because you've got a taste for it!'

Relaxing against her, Alex laughed out loud at the way she'd misconstrued things. 'Oh, no, Natalie, you've got it so wrong there. I've never buggered Steven. It was the other way around. Why do you think I was so worried about my masculinity being compromised?'

Natalie was silent for a moment, her body still. 'Really? Oh my God ... I just never imagined that ... I assumed that Steven would be ... um ... well ... the passive one. He's so quiet and sort of effete ... I never realised.'

She seemed to drift then, and Alex guessed that she was thinking about Steven again. Which was dangerous. Any second now the penny might drop.

'Natalie ... please ... Are we going to do it?' He rubbed himself urgently against her, rubbing his cock against her inner thigh and feeling his pre-come flowing like silk against her skin. 'I'm not made of stone, you know. I can't last much longer like this. All turned on and nowhere to go.' He jabbed his cock against the slope of her buttock for effect.

For a second, he felt her tense and bunch up like a coiled spring, ready to throw him off, but then she laughed, her voice low and throaty.

'And I'm not made of stone, either,' she said huskily, and, instead of bouncing him off her, she rose up on to her hands and knees, offering him the delicious view of her bottom, her juicy, rose-tinted quim, and the shapely columns of her taut thighs. Looking over her shoulder, she said, 'Well, go on then, Alex, prove you're a man.' Falling forward again, low on one forearm, she reached beneath herself, and Alex saw her begin to stroke her clitoris. 'But not ... well ... you know ... Just keep to the regular diplomatic channel, eh?' Her breathing heavy now, she turned her attention solely to her own efforts between her thighs, her fingers working furiously and her bottom weaving slightly.

'Yes, ma'am,' replied Alex. His heart was tripping. He was so excited he had a feeling he might not last long and hoped that she was already halfway there. Kneeling behind her, he gripped her thighs and positioned himself. There was still a moment of excruciating temptation. She was so dripping wet it wouldn't be too difficult. He could draw up some of her juices and massage the tighter entrance. He could be in there almost before she knew what he was doing. It was there, the forbidden way, the dark side, the tighter, more dangerous, far more challenging fuck ...

Dear God, what was he thinking? It had felt like having a poker of iron jammed into him – fabulous, but terrifyingly exacting. How could he possibly countenance doing that to Natalie without her permission?

With a sigh, and the knowledge that his good deed would be more than amply rewarded, he pushed forward, using his fingers to guide his cock into the slick welcome of her warm, sweet cunt.

Chapter Twelve
Incriminating Evidence

'*O*h yes!'
Natalie punched the air, unable to believe her eyes or her luck. The thick wodge of photocopied documents in the padabag that Simon Natwick had sent her contained the sweetest incriminating evidence she could have imagined. She couldn't believe how stupid someone so supposedly astute as Whitelaw Daumery had been, not shredding astonishingly candid letters and financial statements like these. Or destroying the fawning letters he'd received from equally stupid city councillors, who appeared to be just as grasping and acquisitive as he was. It couldn't be naïveté, in this day and age, surely? So it had to be arrogance that had led to such carelessness. An unshakable belief that no one would ever suspect him and that he was completely fireproof.

Well, Whitelaw baby, you're going to burn to a crisp if I have anything to do with it! You and your nasty, creepy friends on the council, too.

She couldn't wait to whip all this into shape and write the final draft of the article. Some actual documentary evidence of the handovers of cash would have been nice. She thought of her quip about the transactions being caught on video and grinned. Surely Daumery wasn't quite *that* stupid! But even so, when put together with information she'd found herself, and the stuff that Alex had thoughtfully had biked around to her this morning, she had more than enough for an excellent 'allegedly' story. The sort of piece that would sow seeds in all the high places and stop Whitelaw Daumery's meteoric but hypocritical rise to prominence.

Despicable slimy bastard! How cool would it be if she could have produced some evidence of his perverted sexual preferences too?

Natalie smiled wryly. Now who's being a hypocrite? Most of Daumery's transgressions were probably things that she'd now discovered she enjoyed herself!

Booting up her laptop, she prepared herself to work. Patti was out somewhere – an unspecified somewhere; she hadn't volunteered the information, and Natalie hadn't asked – and with Dyson out washing windows, presumably, Natalie had the living room, and the big table in there on which to set out her materials. It would be a doddle – one of the easiest pieces she'd ever done.

But it was while she was making herself a cup of coffee to accompany her work that the doubts set in. The doubts and disquiet that she realised had been there, underneath, all along.

It was all *too* easy.

How had Simon Natwick put all this together so fast? Gathered precisely the right documents? It was almost as if he'd already had the dossier ready to roll. And, if he had, why hadn't he used it himself, for pity's sake? The impression she'd gained was that he had precious little respect and fondness for Whitelaw Daumery.

Distracted from the focus she'd enjoyed earlier, Natalie found her attention bouncing around all over the place when she sat down to work.

There were plenty of places to bounce – or, more correctly, people to bounce to . . .

Alex.

Steven.

Patti.

Patti and her mysterious and rather menacing friend Stella Fontayne.

Which linked back to Alex, who also knew Stella.

It was all getting worryingly circular. Even Daumery himself was part of that particular equation, too.

'Too fucking weird,' muttered Natalie, wishing not for the first time in years that she still smoked. And it was far too early for a drink, not yet lunchtime.

'For Christ's sake, Natalie, pull yourself together!' she cried, then settled before the laptop again and flexed her wrists and fingers like a concert pianist. 'Time to get it on, girl,' she murmured, and, banishing the shades of Alex and Steven and Patti the best she could, she began to type.

'So why should I help you help her?'

Patti looked at her companion, hardly able to believe her ears. 'I thought it was you who wanted to help her, not me. I'm only making a suggestion!'

She felt distinctly off balance. It was always difficult at times like these. She was in limbo and not quite sure who she was dealing with. She was sitting in a tastefully decorated north Redwych sitting room with a selection of fabric swatches and designs and she was pitching them, as far as she knew, to Stella Fontayne. Only Stella wasn't wearing any of her existing gowns or any of the wigs and the make-up that went with them. Sitting opposite her, smiling narrowly and looking evil as sin despite his angelic curls, was Natalie's shy schoolteacher, the decidedly male Steven Small.

'Look! This would be a damn sight easier if I knew

who I was dealing with right now!' snapped Patti, losing it.

'Tsk, tsk . . .' said the voice of Stella through Steven's smirking lips. As Natalie watched, he reached for one of his long black Russian cigarettes from the box on the table and lit it with a slim sliver of a lighter. 'Let's not get snappish, shall we? We're both on the same side. I'm just not sure I should make things quite that easy for her.' He paused, took a long drag, then blew smoke in a fine, elegant plume towards the ceiling. 'Or for you, for that matter.'

'I don't know what you're talking about,' said Patti, closing the pattern book she'd been flicking through, looking for elegant women's evening gowns that could be adapted to fit a man.

'Oh, I think you do,' murmured Steven, purely Steven now. It wasn't often he matched Stella's voice with his male appearance – or vice versa – and as far as Patti knew, neither she, nor anyone else, had ever seen the full transition between the two. Visually, he was either one or the other: full wig and make-up, with feminine clothes or lingerie; or Steven's quiet but distinctively sombre sartorial style. 'You want to have sex with her, but you can't quite coax her into it, can you?'

How aggravatingly right he was. As always. She'd nearly drawn Natalie over the line, the other day, but even flaunting her breasts and masturbating hadn't been quite enough to silence Natalie's qualms and make her accept what she really wanted.

Patti admitted her defeat in the form of a mutinous glare at Steven.

'Don't pout,' he said, stubbing out his smoke after only a few puffs. 'I'll make it easy for you. I'll allow the pair of you access to those tapes that are so important to her, but only if you'll put on a show for me. I'll set it up. All you have to do is be there. You can't lose, if you think about it, can you? She'll be so grateful for a look at the tapes that she'll do anything for you.'

He looked at her from the other end of the settee, and his hazel eyes were cool, hard and triumphant. 'You get to help your sister – which I know is what you really want to do, much as you slag her off – and I get to see a delicious little lesbian incest scene. It's not much to ask, is it? Especially when you want to fuck her as much as *I* want you to do it.'

'You are such a bastard, Steven! Stella! Whoever you are!' cried Patti.

But she *was* excited. She'd wanted Natalie for so long, and always known that – despite certain moral notions – it would be right and good between them, and here was Steven/Stella offering her the perfect opportunity on a plate. Goddamn him!

She smiled.

'Good girl. That's right. Now give me a little something on account . . . That's my delicious, beautiful Patti.'

'What do you want?' whispered Patti, her innards melting. She felt a sudden rush of desire that took her breath away. There was something in that cajoling but steely tone that got to her every time – whether it was Stella or Steven who wielded it.

'Oh, just a tiny little performance. Before you phone Natalie and arrange for her to meet you.'

'But what?' Patti could hardly breathe. She wanted to touch herself.

'Pull down your jeans and panties and finger yourself.'

She wasn't the only one who wanted her to touch herself, it seemed.

Quickly, fumblingly, Patti obeyed him, opening her legs wide and baring her crotch.

'Now bring yourself off, as fast as you can, and imagine it's Natalie who's doing you.'

No problem, thought Patti. Reaching down, she found her slippery, aching clit.

I shouldn't be here, thought Natalie, as the taxi pulled up outside Fontayne's Club. The building looked just as grey and menacing in the daytime as it did at night, and gave her just as many goose bumps.

This is all part of the same put-up job, she told herself as she paid off the cabbie – not Ruth the chunky dyke this time – then climbed the steps to the black-painted door. It's all too convenient. Too easy. Evidence shouldn't just throw itself at me like this.

'Er, hi. It's Natalie Croft. My sister Patti asked me to meet her here,' she said into the speakerphone in answer to the gruff enquiry she'd received when she'd pressed the bell.

There was no acknowledgement, but the door clicked open and Natalie entered the gloomy foyer area. There was nobody about, and for a moment she felt at a loss, and inexplicably afraid.

'Don't be a wimp,' she said sternly to herself, and, spotting a door ajar at the far end of the hall, she made her way to it and pushed it open.

Where the hell was she? The last time she'd visited, the place had seemed like a rabbit warren. She'd been up; she'd been down; but she couldn't work out on what floor she finally ended up. She may even be on the same floor as the private room right now.

Even though it was daytime, lamps lit the short corridor she found herself in. The artificial light did little for the shabby-looking wallpaper, though, and hid none of the general dilapidation of the paintwork and the few bits of furniture – a coat stand and two hard chairs – that stood against the wall.

'Is anyone here?' she called out, and felt a rush of relief when her sister answered.

'In here,' came Patti's voice, issuing from a partly open door at the far end of the corridor.

'My God, this place is such a dive,' said Natalie as she joined Patti in a room just as down at heel as the rest of Fontayne's. Lace curtains of dubious age hung at the wide, French windows and the furnishings were haphazard to say the least and appeared to have come from second-hand stores and auctions. There were more chairs than anything, arranged in the form of makeshift rows, like cinema seating, and all facing the only new-looking item in the room. An extremely large television set on a long, low, wooden stand, with a sophisticated video-tape player beneath.

'What's that for? Blue movies?'

'Actually, yes,' said Patti, uncurling herself from one of the sofas and turning around to face Natalie. She looked confident, yet strangely edgy at the same time. Her eyes were bright and there was a sense of energy and purpose about her that made Natalie nervous.

'Well, I hope that's not what you've summoned me here for, Patti,' replied Natalie, advancing, even though she felt like running a mile. This meeting reeked of 'set-up' and she had a feeling that the incriminating tapes Patti had promised to show her – when she'd rung earlier – were nonexistent. She'd been brought here as part of someone's else's agenda, not her own, and she wished to God that she were back at Patti's, writing and shaping her article and making the most of the solid information she did have, rather than chasing the wild goose that Patti had dangled before her.

'I can't believe that even the most half-baked of conspirators would allow themselves to be taped giving and receiving bribes. It's ridiculous!'

'Ah, but if they don't *know* they're being taped . . .' Patti reached down and picked up a video tape, in a plain white box, which had been sitting, with a number of others, in a heap beside her. 'All sorts of people use this place for private meetings – discretion assured – and not one of them realises that Stella has the whole place wired for CCTV and video. I didn't know until she showed me a tape of myself.'

Natalie's heart did a hop, skip and jump. Not only at the thought of tapes of Patti having sex, but at the possibility that Stella may have bugged her own dressing room, and lavatory even. Maybe that was what she'd been brought here to see after all, and not tapes of money-grabbing councillors and their exchanges with Whitelaw Daumery. It was on the tip of her tongue to ask Patti, but somehow she could not get the words out. Something in Patti's knowing eyes suggested that her worst fears were true.

'So, do you want to see this?' Patti said, hefting the tape in her hand, almost as if she were about to throw it.

'What, just the one?'

'Stella thinks ahead,' said Patti, switching on the television and sliding the tape from its case and into the player. 'This is the juiciest edited highlights. All spliced and diced, in case a time should come when she needs to apply a little pressure in certain quarters.'

A thought occurred to Natalie. 'Does . . . um . . . Does Stella know you're showing me this? Surely, if she's holding it in readiness, she won't want anyone to see it just yet. Least of all a journalist who might blow all her schemes to hell and back.'

Patti looked stubborn, and her lovely mouth thinned. 'Look, don't you want to see it? I'm taking a risk for you here, you know that, don't you?'

Oh, Patti, if only I trusted you, thought Natalie, sensing a growing dilemma. It could be that her sister really was running a risk for her, taking chances with a friend, a good contact and customer. But, on the other hand, Patti could be part of some grand and as yet indecipherable scheme to trap Natalie herself. She could still see the unblinking, mascara'd eyes of Stella Fontayne watching her reactions the other night, gauging whether or not she really was a metropolitan sophisticate, then dismissing her as a naïve young ingénue who really knew nothing.

What the hell! Bring on your traps! I've got enough for my story already, thought Natalie, all this is just extra. Just self-indulgence. Doing what *I* want. And I'm up for whatever you can throw at me.

'I'm sorry,' she said, trying to make a contrite face and convince Patti that she was giving her the benefit of the doubt. 'Please, play the tape. It could be really, really useful to me.'

'All right, then,' said Patti crisply. She pressed the PLAY button, and, after a hiss and a phut of static, the screen sprang into life.

What followed was the nastiest of video nasties that Natalie had ever seen, even though it contained no sex, no violence, and only a moderate amount of social swearing. These bastards, they were so complacent, so blissfully convinced that they were above any civil or moral codes of conduct. Daumery, of course, featured in all the clips – all thoughtfully time- and date-coded – passing considerable sums of money, and sometimes other goods, such as share certificates, to various members of the City Council of Redwych. Natalie recognised both the mayor and Councillor Peat, and also several others from the dossiers and clippings that Alex had sent her. Their arrogance astounded her. These people thought they were gods, little tin gods. In the most recent clip, showing a bribe for a council project that she guessed was hardly even begun yet, Whitelaw Daumery even laughed and joked about his appointment to the Committee on Moral Practice in Business.

'What a fuck that man is!' exclaimed Natalie as Patti thoughtfully paused the tape for a moment. 'It will give me the greatest of pleasure to expose him for the shyster he really is!'

'Are you really so moral yourself, though, sis?' Patti said suddenly.

Natalie turned sharply towards her sister. What was she on about now? Was this it? Some sort of sting?

'What do you mean?'

'Well, I can't imagine you having taken a bribe that big, or given one, but surely you're not a spotless lamb of moral propriety. Surely you've done things you're ashamed of.'

Natalie felt for a second as if the breath had been knocked out of her. She prepared a rebuttal, an expression of outrage, then realised, to her cold, cold shame, that on her own small scale she'd done things just as unpleasant and underhand. She'd certainly sometimes slept with men to advance herself. Well, slept with them because she wanted to, but at the same time acknowledging that it would do her career no harm to do the deed.

She also thought of the illegal things she asked Gareth the hacker to do. The fact that, if the opportunity had arisen, she would have badmouthed anyone at the *Modern Examiner* to improve her own status there.

God, I'm horrible, she thought in a moment of agonising clarity. In a lot of ways I'm as bad as Daumery. It doesn't always have to be about money. She thought of the way that she'd always used Patti as a foil to make her own career and lifestyle look superior. The way she'd always slightly despised her.

Which was reprehensible when she cared for her so much, too.

'Yeah, you're right,' she said. 'I'm only really pursuing this Daumery thing because it might put me back on top at the magazine – or in whatever job that might come after it.' She sighed, then looked into Patti's eyes, and saw not condemnation but sympathy. 'I'm just as much a shit as he or any of those councillors is, really . . .' Another sudden flash of illumination came, and it made her laugh out loud at the irony. 'I bet if someone offered me enough money to keep my mouth shut, I would do. It's vile really, but I'd be a liar if I said I wouldn't do it.'

'Oh, how touching! This must be the purest moment of self-knowledge I've ever seen. I'm honoured to be a witness.'

Feeling her stomach drop inside her, Natalie leapt to her feet, spun around and faced the figure who stood in the corner of the room. She had no idea how much time had passed while she and Patti were watching the incriminating video, but it was early evening now, and darkness was beginning to fall. Even so, there was no mistaking the person who now emerged from the shadows. She sensed, rather than saw, her sister stand up beside her, just as on edge.

'You!' Natalie said as Stella Fontayne moved closer.

'Who else would it be?' the transvestite said softly. 'This is my club. My viewing room. My collection of special and particular videotapes.'

Oddly enough, given the gathering gloom, the drag queen was wearing a pair of huge, 'movie star' sunglasses – designer shades – that obscured a good deal of the upper part of her face. A face framed by a beautiful glossy fall of near platinum blonde hair that hung in a thick straight bob to the transvestite's broad shoulders. Stella was wearing a long black coat of some light but satinised fabric. The coat hung open, to reveal beneath it a heavy black silk blouse trimmed with complicated draping, and a pair of loose but elegant black trousers. High, high black shoes adorned her long but quite narrow feet.

Natalie was at a loss for what to say, both because of the stunning appearance of Stella, and because of her own moment of self-revelation – conveniently voiced aloud for the entertainment of her companions.

'Nothing to say?' said Stella, moving past Natalie and Patti to sit down in one of the battered armchairs. She crossed her legs more gracefully than any real woman that Natalie had ever seen, and laid her hands on the arms of the chair beside her, as if displaying the perfection of her crimson, immaculately manicured fingernails.

'Not even a thank-you?'

'What for?' blurted Natalie, all her senses and systems fuzzed by the ersatz woman's strange, commanding presence.

'For providing you with materials pertinent to your enquiries, Natalie.' Stella smiled, looked thoughtful for a moment, then drummed one long, red-tipped fingernail on the chair arm. 'Although I hadn't quite decided to offer you access to the tapes just yet . . .' She turned an obscured glance at Patti, and managed to look stern, even behind the mask of the big dark shades. 'Patti?'

'She's my sister. I wanted to help her,' Patti whispered.

'To help her? Is that all?' Stella's painted mouth quirked in amusement, and for one second her tongue peeped between her glossed lips and she nodded almost imperceptibly.

Natalie looked around at Patti, where she stood just a couple of feet away. Her sister was visibly shaking and her eyes looked a little glazed. She was scared of Stella Fontayne, but there was more to it than that. Patti looked as if she might faint or expire at any moment; she was almost panting. And her nipples, beneath her thin white cotton blouse, were hard as stones and pressing against the cloth. Natalie had never seen anyone look so blatantly turned on, in lust. But she couldn't quite figure out whether it was for her, or for the lounging, smiling Stella.

Either/or, she thought suddenly, when Patti turned to face her, the pupils of her eyes dark and enormous.

'Not all,' Patti whispered, pressing her hand against the front of her jeans.

Oh, I see it now! thought Natalie, almost laughing aloud. She couldn't contain her smile. *This* was the set-up. Between them, Patti and Stella had manoeuvred her into a position of disadvantage, and vulnerability, so that Patti could finally get what she wanted. Presumably Stella wanted it too – although whether as a watcher or a participant Natalie couldn't yet tell. The huge black shades imparted a vaguely reptilian, almost alien, look to the imposing drag queen. With her blonde hair and her sombre top-to-toe black clothing she looked like an icon from a rock video, glamorous, untouchable, a dream almost.

And yet . . .

For perhaps a fifth of a second, the tail end of an idea streamed across Natalie's mind like a comet. What? Surely not? Then it was gone again, as quickly as it had appeared, dismissed as nonsense before it had even been fully assimilated.

The complicit looks passing between Stella and Patti commanded her full attention once more.

Natalie made a decision. She faced Stella, staring at her boldly to make her believe that the shades didn't faze her.

'I know what you two want. And I know you're trying to bamboozle me with some sort of "payment" crap,' she said firmly, watching every nuance of the transvestite's mutable expression. 'It's all a game, though, isn't it? Just a form of words to cover something that's utterly absurd.'

'At the risk of falling into cliché, isn't the whole of life a game?' the drag queen answered imperturbably. 'Daumery plays games with money and power and property. Others of us play games with sex.' She looked down at her hand, then lifted it, scrutinising a single fingernail as if finding fault with the faultless. 'I know which *I* think is the most fun.'

Me too, thought Natalie, to her own surprise.

'I could walk out of here right now, couldn't I?' she said. 'With no repercussions, right?'

The blonde head nodded, silky strands of hair swishing against the shiny coat collar.

'I thought so.'

The three of them remained where they were for a few long seconds: Stella seated, Natalie and her sister standing. She could go now, and nothing would happen. She'd seen the tape. It was enough. To set the ball rolling she need only mention its existence.

'So, are you walking or staying?' said Patti softly. Her pupils were still dilated, her mouth moist as if she'd run her tongue over her lips again and again. It was almost as if she already knew Natalie's decision.

'I think I'll stay,' said Natalie, stepping forward, taking Patti by the shoulder and kissing her roughly. As her sister sucked on her tongue, she heard Stella Fontayne laugh as if from a great, great distance.

This is my choice. I call the shots, thought Natalie, taking hold of both Patti's shoulders and pressing down, forcing her to bend her knees and collapse gracefully on to the small, rather tattered rug that lay between the row of chairs and the television. Once they were both down, she lay on top of her sister and rubbed her body against her. Raping Patti's mouth, she grabbed at her crotch, pushing the denim of her jeans into the V there. Patti moaned around Natalie's tongue, and her hips bucked. Both her hands folded over Natalie's, pressing and encouraging.

Am I doing this right? Natalie thought. Patti seemed to be enjoying it, if her wriggling was anything to go by, and yet it was all so new, so different, so goddamn weird. And it was so hard to think and to concentrate when her blood was clamouring and her entire belly felt like a huge knot of frustration.

'Fuck it!' she muttered, pulling back, aware of Stella's close scrutiny behind the shades.

This is my choice, Natalie told herself again. She gave Patti one last squeeze, then released her. Patti looked up at her, confusion and disappointment in her eyes.

'Don't worry. I'm not chickening out . . . I just don't know what to do, so you'd better do me first!'

As she spoke, she looked not at Patti, but at Stella, who smiled a *Mona Lisa* smile and nodded approvingly.

Oh, how you're going to love this, thought Natalie, and on impulse, she smiled back. A tiny barely acknowledging smirk, as if to say 'Two can play at this game . . . I can take anything that you care to dream up.'

'You asked for it, sis,' said Patti, a hard edge in her voice as she broke the strange connection Natalie had experienced with Stella. A second later, Natalie was gasping for breath, her mouth ravaged, this time, by Patti's. Her sister was ungentle, rough almost, quite unlike anything Natalie had expected. As they broke apart, she felt Patti's hand close around her breast. Gripping cruelly. Twisting slightly.

She started to protest, but Stella cut in, 'Oh, no, Natalie, you asked Patti to do you. You put the power in her hands. Haven't you learned anything yet?'

Natalie felt herself blushing from ignominy and her own lack of resistance to pain. Patti was really hurting her now, first mashing her breasts against her ribcage, then tweaking her nipples. It was horrible. It was nasty. But it was doing astonishing, unexpected things to her body. The ache in her crotch that had nagged a moment ago was a raging maw of need and desire now. Natalie wanted to grab Patti's hand and make her squeeze and grip her crotch, just as she'd gripped Patti's.

But she knew she couldn't do that. Her sister had the

power. She had none. She was the victim, the recipient, the submissive.

Patti rocked back on to her knees, and looked down at Natalie, who still lay on the rug. Natalie felt as if a stranger was studying her. A dark-eyed, intense, almost manic stranger whose entire body seemed to vibrate with sleazy energy. Natalie could almost forget the presence of Stella, so great was her shock at the sight of Patti ascendant.

'Take your trousers off!' Patti instructed her.

Natalie felt some dark ecstatic fear rush down through her innards. Oh, God, oh, yes . . . She kicked off her shoes and then struggled with her cotton trousers, her fingers feeling like swollen, nerveless digits as she first fumbled over the button, then jammed the zip.

With a soft exclamation of impatience, Patti dashed her hands away, and wrenched down the zip herself. Natalie felt humbled, like a fool; she felt so excited and turned on it was almost like nausea.

'Do it! Get on with it!' snapped Patti.

Wriggling and feeling exposed, even though she still had her knickers and her top on, Natalie tugged off the trousers and kicked them away. She was conscious of the thinness of her panties, of stray strands of pubic hair peeking out. Was she seeping already? Could they smell her? Surreptitiously, she tried to part her thighs.

'Now your panties,' said Patti coldly, as if she'd seen what Natalie was up to and disapproved.

Natalie could feel herself shaking as she obeyed her sister. And she'd been right about her knickers: as she eased them away from her crotch, the copious wetness clung for a moment to her sex, then released. Glancing down, she saw a large, dark, diamond-shaped patch of stickiness that extended the entire length of the gusset.

She was sopping. A willing, eager, shameless, horny slut. For her own sister. She tried to turn away, but Patti grabbed her by the jaw and twisted her back to face her.

'Give them to me.'

Feeling as if her entire mind and body were one effervescent mass of emotions, Natalie handed her pants to Patti. She wanted to laugh, she wanted to cry, she wanted to masturbate furiously, but she knew that all these urges had to be contained within, and stoked and stoked and stoked until eventually they exploded out of her. The tears almost did form in her eyes – prematurely – when she realised that, novice that she was, she already understood the game perfectly.

Experiencing a kind of sick delight, she watched Patti lift the panties to her nose and inhale deeply. Her sister gave her a look of amused disdain, then passed the garment to Stella. The drag queen unfolded and refolded the flimsy knickers and then she too inhaled their scent. Their strong, revealing odour ... Natalie knew that much because she could smell herself like a pungent spice in the warm, close air of the claustrophobic viewing room.

'Very choice,' the transvestite murmured vaguely, passing them back to Patti.

Patti studied the scrap of black cloth again, then returned her attention to Natalie, a wicked smile illuminating her face. She grabbed Natalie by the chin, and, before she could protest or draw breath, she began stuffing the little bundle into her mouth.

No! No! No!

Natalie screamed inside, choking and panicking, awash with shame and a deep dark thrill that came purely from the sense of violation. This was disgusting, loathsome, and yet the urge – the grinding need – to touch herself soared higher.

'Relax,' murmured Stella, dropping to crouch beside her. As Patti adjusted the positioning of the cloth inside her mouth, Natalie felt the transvestite's long, pale hands stroking her bare belly and her flanks to calm her. The action was soothing, a caring touch like that of a mother or a kindly female friend, and Natalie ceased to fight her sense of disgust, and began to make low sounds of pleasure in her throat, and to move rhythmically. It was so nice, so sweet; between her legs her flesh was flowing like honey. As Natalie watched the slow, almost hypnotic movements of Stella's hands, she noticed a curious thing. At some time during Patti's little domination trip, the transvestite had popped off every single one of her long, red false fingernails. Her hands and fingers were still narrow and elegant, less feminine now and stronger-looking . . .

The next instant, Natalie jack-knifed up off the rug. With no warning, Stella had slung an arm around her hips, lifted her up, and rudely thrust a finger and thumb into her pussy and anus. Speared on a pincer grip, Natalie now understood that what she'd thought had been violation before was actually nothing of the sort. She was crudely possessed in both orifices, and this was only the beginning. Her belly heaved with lust. Stella pushed at her and forced her upwards. Confused tears seeped from her eye corners as her tormentors laughed together and her traitorous body screamed silently for an orgasm.

'She's very responsive,' observed Stella.

'Oh, yes, she is,' whispered Patti, bending over to place a kiss against the corner of Natalie's mouth, delicately licking her lips where they were stretched by the bunched panties. 'I remember when we were young – just nymphets, really – and we used to share a room. I always knew when she was masturbating, and I used to be so jealous of how quickly she could come.'

'Really,' murmured Stella, her hold on Natalie's genitalia relentless.

I can't bear this! I can't bear much more of this! Natalie thought, her brain filled with the odour of her own arousal and thoughts of herself lying in bed, a randy teenager, diddling herself . . . She wondered why

Patti had never said anything, but realised they'd never been that close. The idea of Patti holding and cherishing the shameful little secret for all these years made Natalie burn with mortification. And, as her mind burned, her besieged quim did also. Kicking her legs, she tried not to free herself, but to nudge Stella's wrist so it brushed against her clitoris.

'Please!' she tried to cry around the obstruction in her mouth, but it came out as a stifled, gargling grunt. She cried out again as Patti fumbled around under her top, pushed up her bra, and pinched one of her nipples. After a second, she began twisting both at once.

Unable to contain herself, Natalie writhed and wriggled like a beached fish. Stella's fingers felt like thick prods of warm, living wood inside her. Hard and unyielding, yet organic and connected with her. They flexed, varying the grip, playing her like an instrument, invading yet not hurting. Driving her crazy ... Her clitoris felt swollen, as if it were ten times its normal size. She redoubled her efforts, calling out with every part of her body for the single stroke that would bring her complete release.

Through a haze, she looked up at the two women who held her and possessed her. Patti, the real woman, looked pink-faced, excited, yet unashamedly happy, as if she were finally getting a treat she'd long been promised. Stella, the *faux* woman, was smiling, her eyes an enigma behind the big sunglasses.

Is she even wearing make-up behind them? thought Natalie suddenly. The drag queen's mouth was red, but her skin seemed bare of foundation and powder. What if she'd been summoned to this tryst at short notice? Had only time to dress, put on a wig and a slash of lipstick? Natalie tried to concentrate on the shape of the jaw, the nose, and the lips beneath their paint. Again, she seemed to almost see something familiar, but then the transvestite smiled, as if recognising the approach of revelation.

Sitting back, Stella spoke huskily to Patti: 'I think our little Natalie is ready for an orgasm, don't you?'

Patti nodded, and Natalie felt her sister's hands slide down her ribcage and her belly, then hover near to the periphery of her pubes.

'You can touch her now,' whispered Stella, hoisting Natalie's hips high with the arm that supported her. At the same time her finger and thumb massaged from within.

Patti leaned over Natalie, obscuring her view of the transvestite who held her.

'Do you want it, sis?'

Natalie wanted to come, but she wanted more than that, more than she'd ever dare admit. Reaching up, reacquiring the will to use her hands, to take action, she plucked the panties from her mouth, flung them away, and cried out 'Yes!' Then she reached for Patti's face, pulled it down to hers, and hissed, 'But I want you to kiss me while you touch me. Do you hear that, Patti?'

Patti smiled her answer, and, as Natalie closed her eyes, she heard Stella softly say, 'Bravo!' After a moment, Natalie felt her sister's lips settle delicately on hers.

The kiss was soft, and sweet, and loving – but in the space of a breath, Natalie was howling and shouting against the gentle lips that kissed her.

A single touch had fired her, and her body was a maelstrom.

Chapter Thirteen
Endgames

Watching Patti as she brewed tea and made other preparations for breakfast, Natalie could hardly believe what had happened in the viewing room at Fontayne's Club. It had been like a dream, another world, something so bizarre it just couldn't have happened. The aftermath and getting home were almost a blur to her now, although the pleasure she'd experienced at the hands of both a real and a make-believe woman still echoed in every nerve end in her body.

My God, I had sex with Patti and it was amazing! But how do I act with her now? What do I say? Should I kiss her and ask what next? Or pretend it never happened?

Patti turned around and put a plate of egg, bacon and tomatoes in front of Natalie. It was a lot more substantial and calorific than the usual cup of black coffee, and sometimes maybe hi-bran cereal that Natalie usually had for breakfast, but somehow today that didn't matter. She was starving!

'Thanks, it looks great!' she said, striving for a tone of voice that sounded normal, but also warm, and yet not too different from the way she'd always spoken before.

It was impossible, and she muttered, 'Bloody hell, Patti, I just don't know how to be with you now!'

Patti put down her own plate, then sat down and reached for the teapot to pour them both tea. 'Just be yourself. The way you've always been.' She paused, then topped up the cups with milk. 'Only maybe a bit nicer and a bit less superior.' She grinned, then stirred her tea, looking steadily at Natalie as she did so.

Natalie laughed. Suddenly she felt completely free, as if a weight had lifted off her. Patti was beautiful. Patti was clever, and had quietly and competently achieved a lot for herself. She was also sexy, and Natalie wanted her to be that way. It was such a relief to have got her hang-ups sorted out at last.

'Yes, I know I've been a bit of a cow to you over the years, haven't I?'

'Well, yes, you have, but I don't mind. I never really did,' said Patti, picking up her knife and fork and starting in on her bacon.

For a moment, Natalie felt the dangerous prickle of tears, but Patti's shrug and smile, and the way she was quietly getting on with her breakfast and not making any big deal or scene about anything, were calming. She looked down at the food that her sister had cooked for her, and the question of what to do in the next few minutes was simply answered. Taking up her knife and fork, she began to eat with real enjoyment.

But when the food was gone, the questions returned.

'What are you staring at me for?' enquired Patti, buttering another piece of toast. 'I'm not going to jump on you or anything. If anything's going to happen it'll happen all in good time. Just because we've made love once it doesn't mean we have to do it *all* the time.'

'Was that making love?'

In all truth, Natalie was still trying to work out what it had been, from her own point of view at least. She'd been a victim, an object for them, and yet she'd brought it on herself and, ultimately, she'd been the one who'd been rewarded. She wasn't even sure if Patti had even had an orgasm, and, while she'd been there, Stella certainly hadn't. And yet both Patti and Stella had seemed well satisfied with the encounter. Elated even. Natalie remembered laughter and gentle banter while she'd pulled on her clothes, then sat – almost numbed by sensory overload – and sipped a big tumbler of whisky that Stella had thoughtfully provided. The other two had watched videos, of other sexual encounters, not unlike the one that had just taken place, and made ribald and occasionally critical comments on the performances, which were sometimes their own.

Eventually, with Natalie half asleep and not really thinking straight, she and Patti had tumbled into the taxicab Stella had called – driven by the now familiar Ruth Hamer, who seemed to be everywhere – and come home and gone blearily, and without speaking, to their separate beds.

'Yes, I'd call it that,' said Patti intently. 'Lovemaking doesn't have to be between marrieds, or life partners, and all nicey-nicey and straight and done under crisply pressed sheets and all that, you know.'

'I do know!' Natalie felt her natural prickliness rising. She hated to be patronised and talked down to. She knew about the byways and low-ways of sexual preference, even if she'd only just begun to actually explore them.

'Yes, yes, I know you do,' said Patti quietly. 'I'm sorry, but it *is* all relatively new to me, too, and I forget that and tend to start preaching the cause.' She reached out and touched Natalie's hand.

Natalie felt a spasm of heat form beneath her sister's fingers. Did she want to 'make love' now? The memory of those fingers moving on her bare skin came zooming back into her consciousness, the feel of them pressing against moisture and sensitive structures. The hot bloom of pleasure they could give, and dark pain of pinching and twisting that in its own way could be just as sweet.

She drew in a deep breath. 'There's a big difference between theory and reality,' she conceded. 'I might have known things, up until now, but knowing without understanding is just a plastic reality, not real at all.'

'But you know now, don't you?' said Patti, her finger-tips moving evocatively, 'You see the way . . .'

'Yes, I do.' Natalie twisted her hand, to hold Patti's in return, to caress lightly with her thumb. She could feel her heart pounding and it seemed rather hard to breathe. 'Yesterday . . . Did you come? You know . . . when I was rubbing you? I got so caught up in what *I* wanted, and how I wanted it, that I forgot all about you. And I feel guilty. And greedy.'

'Oh, I did OK,' said Patti vaguely, giving Natalie's fingers a squeeze, then withdrawing her own. 'Don't you worry about me.'

'I –'

'Yeah, I know – and I want you, too,' said Patti, rising and beginning to collect the plates. She looked Natalie earnestly in the eye, and Natalie had a sudden feeling of places reversed. Patti was so much the older, wiser sister now, and yet it felt OK. Strangely . . . 'But I think we need a bit of space to think about this. Not too much, of course.' She grinned. 'But maybe an hour or two.' Turning away, she stacked the dishes on the draining board. 'I've got a lot of sewing jobs to catch up on, and you've got an article to write. Why don't we just get on with . . . um . . . "normal" things for a little bit, then see how we feel later?'

It made sense, but Natalie felt rejected. And alarmed that she'd so completely forgotten about the Daumery article. Again. It had been her prime goal for coming back to Redwych, and yet she'd now got to a stage where – if someone told her she had to dump the idea and not write it – she really couldn't have cared less about it!

The cups and plates clattered alarmingly in the sink and, a second later, Patti was kissing her fiercely and Natalie was responding. Their mouths clung and mated for what seemed like a long, long time, and then, with obvious regret, Patti drew back.

'Look, this isn't a rejection or anything. We will get together. We just need to breathe. Got it?'

Natalie nodded, knowing Patti was right, and blessing her for her wisdom, but still wanting her anyway.

They left it at that. After breakfast, Patti went off to the sitting room, and Natalie to her bedroom. Patti insisted this wasn't necessary, and that they could both work in the same room, but Natalie knew it had to be that way. She couldn't focus properly with others too close to her. Even in London she'd always done her best work at home in her flat. And Patti was more than just some colleague – especially now.

Natalie had also wondered if Dyson might come wandering in at any time, too. She wasn't sure that she wanted him around and looking over her shoulder. He'd left early, but, being self-employed, he could, of course, keep his own hours.

But in her room, the going wasn't easy at first. Her mind kept flitting away from Whitelaw Daumery, his business deals and his illicit financial arrangements, and returning to thoughts of Patti and Stella and also Alex and Steven Small.

I've had more sexual partners while I've been here than I normally have in two or three years! And done more things . . .

It was astonishing. And bloody marvellous. And a terrible distraction from work. Who even cared what Whitelaw Daumery did – unless it was as part of one of Stella Fontayne's strange sexual shadow plays?

Eventually, after fetching a bottle of water from the

kitchen – and resolving to give Patti a contribution towards the housekeeping as soon as she had some funds – Natalie managed to apply herself to the revelation of the true and twistedly acquisitive nature of the chairman elect of the Committee for Moral Policy in Business.

The first of what would be many 'final' drafts of the article began to take shape. The words that would devastate Whitelaw Daumery's career settled on the screen in a smooth, acerbic flow – light as a rapier yet effortlessly damning. There wasn't much need to dress it up, and Natalie refrained from even the slightest hint of hyperbole. Having done what he'd done, Daumery was his own worst enemy. Inserts from the letters Simon Natwick had photocopied for her said almost everything, without addition. If she could somehow have got stills from the videotapes she'd watched yesterday, that would have been perfect, but Natalie suspected that would be a one-time viewing only. Still, the very hint of their existence would probably be enough.

When Natalie finally surfaced from the world of Daumery and his fellow thieves and charlatans, it was getting dark outside the window. She'd worked hours and hours solid, with just the briefest of breaks for food and the lavatory. Patti, she hadn't seen once all day. The only evidence of her sister's presence in the house had been a beautifully prepared salad left for her in the fridge when she went in search of food, and the steady drone of the sewing machine as she'd passed the sitting-room door. Along with some highly fruity swearing when that drone had suddenly stopped. Presumably designing and sewing frocks for drag queens was just as difficult in its own way as crafting articles exposing corrupt businessmen . . .

Now, though, Natalie could hear voices. Plural. Low, excited voices, male and female. Dyson had come home and she suddenly felt like a cuckoo in the nest, and that the fragile, just-born female bond between herself and Patti was fractured. She's with him now; she won't want me. I'm superfluous.

Nevertheless, she went downstairs, unwilling to be cowed into staying out of the way by feelings of wimpishness.

'How's the article coming along?' said Patti brightly. 'Have you finished it?'

'Almost,' admitted Natalie, feeling stunned by her sister's appearance.

Patti looked wonderful. She was dressed in a tough-looking biker-style leather jacket and a short – very short – suede skirt, but it wasn't just the clothes and the aggressive-looking make-up that she wore with them that created the allure. Patti seemed excited, hyped, alive, and almost fluorescent with a compressed nervous energy. Something was up, obviously, and it was something wonderful that Patti couldn't wait to get to. Dyson was involved, too, it seemed. The young man was waiting by the front door, keys jingling, also dressed in leather.

'You're going out, then,' Natalie said, feeling redundant and unwanted. Just then Ozzy appeared around the corner from the lounge and she was glad of him there, so she could crouch down, stroke him, and hide her eyes from Patti and Dyson.

'Er ... yes, just for a while,' said Patti, and Natalie sensed that her sister felt as awkward as she did. It was almost as if Patti wanted to invite her along, and yet hadn't been given permission to. More games, thought Natalie, but this time they don't want me to play.

'Well, have a nice time,' she said, straightening up, and catching an ironic gleam in Dyson's eye. She wanted to tell him to go and screw himself, and that she could find her own amusement, thank you very much, but that seemed petty and childish. Instead, she just said, 'I think I'll push on and finish the article tonight. I'll be glad when it's done.'

'Are you sure you'll be all right on your own?'

It was Natalie's turn to smile. Patti hadn't asked this on the other evenings she'd gone out. It must be a sign of the renaissance of their affection. She nodded. 'I'll be fine.'

'Well, lock up after us, won't you? There are burglars and all sorts of weirdos out at nights,' said Patti as she and Dyson left.

Weirdos? Well, you seem to know most of them, sis, thought Natalie when the other two had gone and she was left alone with Ozzy and all the notional burglars and thugs that might be lurking around outside. She had no inclination whatsoever to write, and knew that, even if she tried, it would come out as nonsense now. How could she think about Daumery's financial manoeuvring, when even now the man himself might be out there, with Patti and Dyson, and Stella and Alex, taking part in some depraved but highly pleasurable sexual ritual?

After a few minutes, Natalie turned on the television. Then turned it off again immediately, on discovering a no-brain programme about interior decorators. She felt wild and unable to settle, her body wired for action, and for sex, yet mentally unable to decide what to do about it. Masturbation was an option, but it seemed so clinical, so deliberate. What she wanted was to be swept away into something mad and powerful where the pleasure was huge and she was not in control.

Who else do I know who I could get into some trouble with?

She could ring Steven Small, she knew that. But somehow, she didn't want to. It would answer a question inside her, confirm a preposterous idea that was gaining more and more credence in her mind, but that her pride, mainly, did not want to know the answer to.

If the insane thing she was starting to suspect was actually true, that would leave her feeling even more rejected.

The final straw was the exit of Ozzy through the cat flap. Even the cat's left me now, she thought grimly, and began to rummage around for the local papers. If she couldn't get some action, she could at least take herself off to the cinema and escape into someone else's less deviant idea of fantasy.

But as she was perusing the cinema listings, and finding them tedious in the extreme, the phone rang.

Natalie considered letting the answering machine pick up. It would be for Patti, anyway. Hardly anyone knows I'm here, thought Natalie, eyeing the ringing device longingly. Even the human contact of taking a message seemed preferable to hanging around here talking to herself and feeling frustrated.

'Hello, Natalie,' said a familiar voice immediately she held the receiver to her ear. 'I was wondering if you'd like a little adventure tonight. It seems a shame that you're all on your own there and everyone else is here, having fun.'

'What sort of adventure, Stella?' She made her voice sound bold, but just a little blasé and uninterested, even though just the sound of the drag queen's voice had set her blood surging.

'Oh, I think you know,' the transvestite replied archly. The quality of the transmission was a little fuzzy, probably from a mobile, but Natalie could hear every nuance of the excited sexual challenge in Stella's voice. She waited, hoping for more, from which she could divine other nuances, ones that might answer her questions, but for several moments the drag queen said nothing. It was almost as if she were allowing Natalie to hear sounds in the background. There was a swish that might have been a whip or some other instrument of punishment flying through the air. Then there was a sharp, high cry; a woman's voice – it might have been Patti – followed a series of guttural yelps, in quick, rising succession that was the unmistakable music of a helpless rise to orgasm. Whether it was a man or woman coming, Natalie couldn't tell.

'What the hell are you up to there? What are you doing?' she demanded, although she had a perfectly good idea. It was another scene, more of what she'd seen before, and she was being invited to participate. The only trouble was her doubt in her own bravery. It was one thing watching, and maybe playing around with a couple of people – like Patti and Stella – but to expose oneself totally, body, mind and emotions, was as terrifying as it was seductive.

'Are you afraid?' asked Stella softly yet challengingly.

'No, I'm not!' cried Natalie, as much to herself as to convince the distant drag queen of anything.

Of course I'm not scared. I can take whatever they dish out and come back, demanding more. I'm a strong, grown-up, kick-ass woman and I know what I want. And I know that Stella and her court of darkness can give it me. Why aren't I saying, 'Yes, bring it on – I'm ready!'?

As if she'd actually spoken the words, Natalie heard the drag queen answer them. 'In that case I'll send a car for you. No need to dress. The driver will bring you some appropriate clothes.' She hesitated, and Natalie thought she caught the faint sound of a kiss being blown to her. 'We'll see you shortly, Natalie. And we look forward to it.'

We? It? Natalie opened her mouth to ask more questions, but the line had gone dead.

What the hell do I do now? And what do I put on if there's no need to dress?

Her heart racing, she ran up the stairs and into the bathroom. Was there time for a shower? Probably not. Tearing off her clothes, she sponged her body the best she could, aware all the time that, even as she soaped herself, the sweat of nerves was popping out to undo her work. In the end she sprayed on scent and hoped for the best.

Nerves also made her bladder play tricks. She squatted to pee. It wouldn't come. She tried again, releasing only a trickle. Goddamnit! She considered playing with herself, bringing herself off in order to release the tiny locked-tight muscles down there, but there was no time and she might only make things worse.

Her shaking hands made putting on make-up difficult. She lined her eyes and made a mess of it. No time to start again, so she just smudged the result, and found it strangely pleasing. Staring out through dark, smoky eyes, she coated her mouth with lip pencil, blotted, and pencilled again. She repeated the process again and again until her lips were almost dyed with the dark, plummy stain, and yet nothing came off when she touched them. Who alone knew what rigours her mouth might have to endure?

Back on the lavatory again, and at last releasing her waters, she heard the doorbell ring, and had to wipe herself haphazardly with a handful of tissue. Grabbing Patti's towelling robe, she almost fell down the stairs to answer the door. What an idiot she'd look, face all wild and robe hanging open to show her nakedness, if it was only a neighbour come round to borrow a cup of sugar!

'I might have known it would be you!' she said, feeling both relief and disquiet at the sight of Ruth Hamer again.

The sturdy, short-haired woman looked very different tonight, though. Gone was the battered leather jacket and jeans she'd worn on all other occasions, and in their place were a crisp black man's suit, black tie, and white shirt, and dark shades in the style of an American covert government operative. She was a 'Man in Black' and also a woman. Who liked women.

'Put these on,' she said curtly, handing Natalie a white dress bag made of thick, good-quality plastic. 'No, here! Those are the orders,' she added, grasping Natalie's arm to restrain her when she made to take the bag upstairs and change.

The dyke's fingers were cruel. 'Well, shut the door, then,' said Natalie, breaking free with some difficulty.

But the dyke stuck a solid Dr Marten-clad foot against the door and held it open. 'No. Here. With the door open. Those are the orders.'

Natalie felt herself start to shake. What she was being asked to do was appalling, incredible. The street was quiet, but every now and again a car would speed by, and people were out walking their dogs and generally going about their business. There was nobody in the immediate vicinity now, but at any minute a passer-by could appear.

And yet she knew she was going to do it. Not giving herself the chance to chicken out, she handed the bag back to the dyke, then undid the robe and let it drop away, leaving her naked.

The black-clad taxi driver eyed her with real interest, eyes flicking from Natalie's breasts to her crotch, and back again. Without a word, she held the bag open, proffering its contents.

Natalie looked inside it, painfully aware of the bright light from the hall silhouetting her bare body and drawing attention to it.

The bag contained a curious assembly of items. If worn in combination with, say, a little black dress, she would have been charmed by them, even if they were a bit clichéd. But on their own they presented her with a problem.

She'd been given a fake-fur wrap, a glittery paste necklace and matching bracelets, long black satin gloves, and a pair of the highest heels she'd ever seen in her life.

'Where's the dress?' she said, attempting to sound blasé, and bored.

'This is it,' said Ruth Hamer. 'And can you get a move on. They've already started.'

'Oh, well, all right, then. I don't want to keep them waiting – whoever they are.'

First she pulled on the long gloves, which were quite tight, but fitted perfectly. Having her arms almost completely covered – the skin embraced and protected nearly to her armpits – was a most curious and very arousing sensation, when juxtaposed with the nudity of the rest of her body. The exposure of her breasts and her pubic area seemed greater because of it, her bottom and thighs more prominent, and almost immediately she felt a powerful urge to touch herself.

It seemed that the dyke, too, wanted to touch her. The woman's eyes were brilliant, dark and rapacious, devouring every critical curve and cranny of her again, and again, and again. She looked like a little girl at a party, not knowing whether to go for the jelly first, or the ice cream, or the chocolate éclairs. Natalie found such hunger exciting and her need to masturbate strengthened.

Next, she clipped the bracelets around her wrists, over the gloves, and the necklace around her throat. It was a showy and eye-catching set, and Natalie had no doubt that it came from Stella Fontayne's collection. The sparkle and vulgarity of it was perfect for a drag queen.

Now for the high heels.

As she set the shoes down ready to step into them, Natalie heard the sound of voices somewhere close by, then footsteps. Oh, God, someone was going to walk by and see her standing naked and bejewelled on Patti's front doorstep!

In a swift, proprietorial gesture, her driver stepped in front of her, spreading her jacket a little so that Natalie was obscured from the view of anyone on the pavement.

The voices came closer, and a sauntering couple, a man and woman arguing good-naturedly about a television programme, approached. They seemed to be in no hurry, and Natalie willed them to get a move on. Her bare body was pressed close to that of the lesbian taxi driver, and she could feel experienced hands moving over her, fingers cruising her bottom, her thighs, and then her crotch. The laughing couple stopped, almost against Patti's gate, and the woman reached up and began to kiss the man with considerable passion. As his arms went around her, a finger invaded Natalie's quim.

Oh, God! Oh, no! Please don't, thought Natalie, yet she felt unable to stop herself bearing down on the invading digit. It pushed into her quite roughly as the kissing couple devoured each other, then twisted inside her, making her rise up again, on her toes.

Then, as suddenly as they'd stopped, the couple broke apart and moved on again. The intruding finger slid neatly out of Natalie.

'Come on,' said her companion impatiently, her voice giving no indication of the liberties she'd just taken. 'Get your shoes on. They're waiting. We've got to go.'

Natalie struggled to obey, then teetered once the shoes were on. It felt as if she were wearing stilts and her ankles seemed in danger of giving way any moment. Without waiting for her to finish herself, the driver threw the wrap around Natalie's shoulders, then took her by the wrist and led her out on to the pavement and to the car.

The kissing couple's progress had been slow, and at the sound of Natalie's heels clattering on the flags, they turned around to see what the noise was. The man's mouth dropped open, and his eyes bulged with instant lust at the sight of a naked woman in gloves and heels being led towards a car, her skin luridly white in the sodium light from the street lamps, and her pubic mound a vivid triangle of erotic darkness. His companion gasped and then giggled in nervous astonishment.

After one moment of pure horror, the strangest emotion came over Natalie. She wanted them to see her. She wanted them to see more of her, touch her even. Slowing mulishly, and resisting the pull of her captor, she experienced an overpowering urge to call the couple over, press her breasts into the man's hungry, sweaty palms, and take the hand of the woman and put it in between her legs. She imagined standing there on the dingy pavement of Redwych, swaying and gasping while a pair of total strangers who simply wanted to use her for cheap entertainment masturbated her. She wanted to cry out loudly and climax before them, unable to stop herself.

'Come on, slut, get in the car,' hissed Ruth Hamer, pulling harder, her fingers cruelly pressing the bracelet into Natalie's gloved wrist. 'There'll be plenty of that when we get to where we're going.' It seemed that she'd easily understood what Natalie was thinking.

The car was not the bog-standard taxi that the woman had driven before. Tonight there was a limousine parked against the kerb. The driver held the rear door open for Natalie in a mock expression of old-fashioned courtesy, then slammed it and walked around to the driving seat.

What's that perfume? thought Natalie, as she settled on to the back seat. A pervasive scent hovered around the interior of the car, more than just the luxurious odour of leather upholstery. It was familiar and yet exotic, and it fired the senses. She wriggled her bare bottom against the fine hide of the seat and felt an urge to press herself down against it, to flatten her pubes and rub hard, both staining the leather and stimulating herself at the same time. Without touching herself, she knew her sex was oozing.

Her driver put the car in gear and pulled away from

the kerb at an alarmingly high speed. Natalie knew she should be afraid, and that she should comment on this, but it seemed impossible to think about normal aspects of life like driving. All her trepidation should be saved for whatever lay ahead of her at the end of this trip.

'You're allowed to masturbate,' said the dyke, almost conversationally, over her shoulder.

Natalie didn't want to give her travelling companion the satisfaction of knowing how aroused she was, but somehow just the word itself was an irresistible stimulant. Her sex felt puffy and bloated, the membranes suffused with a glut of blood. Her nipples were hard and tingled unbearably against the wrap where she held it closely against herself. Surreptitiously, she rubbed the fur over her skin, circling it against her breasts, then down over her midriff and her belly. It felt sublime and yet almost a form of torture. She wanted it to be fingers that were moving over her. Fingers exploring and stirring her, pulling at her nipples and slipping into her sex, quickly and roughly. Playing along with her game, the fantasy that she was reluctant and modest and appalled to be used in such a way.

Sliding down in the comfortable seat, Natalie ignored the streets of Redwych passing by outside. In her mind there were others in the car with her – men, women, it didn't make any difference to her now – and they were forcing her to expose herself and to touch her own body. Almost on her back, sideways across the seat, she let the wrap fall aside, and her legs splay open in a vulgar display. Examine me, fondle me, she said to her invisible companions. Make me come, even though I don't want to. Writhing against the leather, she rubbed her bottom against its smooth, cool surface, squashing herself down, massaging her anus until she wanted to kick out in frustrated lust.

Natalie gasped, unable to keep quiet now, and she heard the driver chuckle. 'Go on! Do it!' the dyke said cheerfully. 'Let me hear you come. It might be the last time you get to do it in private for quite a while.'

Private? Natalie thought. Private with you listening for every breath, every movement. Why don't you concentrate on your driving and making sure you don't crash this car?

And yet Natalie didn't care. She could think of nothing but her body, and the way it felt. The electric excitement in her belly and crotch that would be eased and satisfied only by her hand or that of another. Letting her thighs drape even more widely open, she began to caress herself, running her fingertips up and down the channel of her sex and taunting her clitoris with near-contact, but not quite touching it. She felt as if a balloon of sensation was swelling inside her, cutting off her breath and making her gasp. It seemed to press on every part of her, increasing the tension in her belly, hyping up her lust.

Just when she thought she could stand it no longer, she seemed to push through to another level of delicious frustration. Lifting her bottom from the leather, she jerked her pelvis, waving her hips back and forth, the very motion a subtle form of stimulation. Dimly, as if from a great distance, she was aware that the car was first slowing, then stopping, and though she could hear voices and sense the presence of people beyond the car, she could do nothing to stop the jungle dance of her body. The only thing that finally stilled her was a rush of cold air, when the car door was opened, hitting her nakedness.

'Well, I see that our new friend couldn't wait to get here to start enjoying herself.'

Natalie looked up through bleary eyes and saw Stella Fontayne, silhouetted by strong light behind her, in the open car-door space. The drag queen was not looking her in the eye, but was staring directly at the junction of her thighs. For an instant, the old, buttoned-up, closed-off Natalie from London wanted to cover herself, and get as far away from this place as was possible, but then the new, hungry Natalie took over. Reaching down between her legs, she stroked herself insolently.

'Oh, you delicious little slut,' said Stella, leaning forward. Natalie thought for one moment that the transvestite was going to reach in and touch her, just where she was touching herself, but then Stella stepped back and nodded to someone Natalie couldn't see.

'Bring her in,' she said crisply. 'It's obvious that she's eager to get started.'

Almost immediately, Stella was gone, and a male figure, bare-chested and wearing a leather hood, trousers and tall boots, reached into the car, grabbed Natalie's arm and began to drag her out into the cold night air. The man's grip on her upper arm was cruel, and Natalie struggled and then stumbled when she tried to stand up in her high heels. The fur wrap fell on to the rough asphalt path they were standing on, and she was revealed as naked but for her gloves and jewels and shoes.

'Where the hell are we?' she demanded, but in spite of receiving no reply, just a long, faceless stare, she realised she was in a park in the suburbs of Redwych. She recognised it as somewhere that she'd used to play as a child, with Patti. Even then it had been underused and not maintained very well, but now in darkness it seemed more of a neglected wilderness than ever. How on Earth could Stella and her friends hold one of their gatherings here? The place was deserted, but it was still out in the plain, open air. Someone might come along and see them about their business . . .

And then she remembered. Her heart fluttered as the hooded man – who already seemed familiar – and the black-clad taxi driver began to frogmarch her along the path in Stella's wake.

Oh, no, not there! thought Natalie, even though a part

of her revelled in the prospect that lay ahead of her. She saw the shadowed entrance, and the filth-encrusted skylight windows, and her cunt clenched in both antici-pation and memory. It was the old, and even then unused, below-ground men's lavatory, where she and Patti, and other children, had once played 'doctor'.

Her hooded 'master' forced her down the steps in front of him, holding her arms tightly together behind her and forcing her breasts before her into almost obscene prominence. When she entered the chamber below it almost seemed as if a light were trained specifi-cally upon them.

'Well. Here she is,' said Stella, sounding triumphant. The transvestite, elegantly clad in a floor-length, long-sleeved black velvet gown, and her sleek blonde wig, gestured flamboyantly towards her like some kind of ringmaster asking an audience to admire a captured savage. 'The young woman who wants to join our group and take part in our games. What do we think of her?'

Figures moved out from the corners of darkness: there were about a dozen, mostly men, but a couple of women. All were either hooded or wearing black dom-ino masks.

'Beautiful tits. I'd like to come all over them,' said one man, stepping forward and grabbing Natalie's breasts before she'd barely had time to draw breath and fami-liarise herself with her surroundings. His leather hood covered all his face and head, but his lips were very red, wet and hungry-looking. His hands were hard, and his rough-skinned thumbs strummed Natalie's nipples enthusiastically. 'Very tasty,' he added twisting one teat cruelly.

'Let someone else get a look in,' said another man, in a more refined voice that Natalie recognised with some shock as Whitelaw Daumery's. He too was fully hooded but wearing a dark shirt with a pair of jeans and a leather belt.

Slumming it, eh, Whitelaw? thought Natalie defiantly as the man she hoped to bring down thrust his hand between her legs and groped her. The experience should have been horrible – masturbation by this man she'd grown to despise – and yet instead she found it piquantly exciting. It amused her that he thought he was using her, and enjoying her. In reality, it was she who was enjoying him – the crude rolling action of his thumb was delicious on her clitoris – and in the days and weeks ahead she was going to use him in a far more drastic way than he could ever use her. She almost laughed out loud when she felt a sudden orgasm gathering.

'Enough,' snapped Stella suddenly. 'Can't you see she's about to come? She needs to wait and learn the meaning of discipline before that happens.'

The words seemed to make Natalie's head go light with anticipation. Her cunt throbbed yearningly and she felt a powerful desire to lie down on the filthy floor of the ancient lavatory and masturbate. She wanted to open her legs wide and expose every bit of her sex to all these people. To defiantly anticipate their desires and take control of the situation, even though they would consider that it was she who was subservient to them.

'Lay her down on one of the tables,' ordered Stella, the only other member of the assembly who wasn't masked.

Her jailers dragged her over to one of a pair of old and very solid-looking wooden tables, set more or less side by side in the centre of the dank and shadowy room. There, she was forced to lie on her back, and, the moment she was settled, two men – the leather-clad man who'd accompanied her from the car and another – took hold of her and pulled her down to the end of the table so her bottom was right at the edge. Handling her as if she were nothing more than meat, they manipulated her legs and made her bend them, pulling her knees right up with her calves, and her high heels were resting on the backs of her thighs. She began to gasp, pant and hyperventilate almost, when some kind of rubber strapping was produced and she was bound – quite tightly – in this position.

'Stay calm,' said the man wearing leather, and, recognising the voice of Alex, Natalie managed to claw back some composure. 'Just relax,' he whispered, leaning closer so no one else could here them. 'You know you're enjoying this, so just relax and get the best from it.'

More straps were produced, from somewhere beneath the table, and Natalie's hands were secured to them, her arms outstretched. Straps on either side of her clipped to the leg bands and she felt an enormous tension as her thighs were drawn wide open. She looked wildly from side to side, searching the hidden faces for some clue to the identities of those who were seeing her so vulnerable.

One of the women was oh so familiar, and Natalie felt her heart surge when she recognised her sister. Patti had lost her jacket and skirt somewhere along the line, and a pair of black crotchless tights framed her pubic bush. Behind Patti and to one side stood the fully clad Dyson, one arm around her, his hand fondling her breast possessively.

It was strange, but one glance into her sister's eyes calmed Natalie, and allowed her to find her place in the scheme that lay ahead of her. There was no need to struggle, to strive, to do anything but receive the gifts these people would give to her. The gifts of effort, stimulation, orgasms, themselves. How clear it seemed to her now. She was the privileged one, and, as Alex had said, the one getting the best of the experience. They were all here to serve her, as well as enjoy her. She laughed out loud. She was unassailable. She was the queen here.

'What's so funny, city girl?' murmured Stella Fontayne, coming to stand beside Natalie and looking down into her face intently. She reached down, cupping Natalie's breast just as Dyson was cupping and kneading Patti's. Natalie felt the threatening touch of Stella's pointed acrylic talons. 'Do you want me to find some new ways to make you laugh?'

Natalie looked up into the bizarre, created beauty of the drag queen's painted face, and finally saw what her subconscious had been seeing for quite some time now. She felt like shouting for joy. All her strange new friends were here after all.

When she smiled, knowingly, a tiny frown crumpled Stella's brow for a moment, and she dug her false fingernails ever so slightly into Natalie's skin. 'What is it, little one?' she asked. Her voice was like silk and Natalie knew the transvestite had understood her.

'I know you,' whispered Natalie.

'Of course you do,' Stella whispered in reply, then kissed her lips.

Chapter Fourteen
Human Nature

*T*he dark world flashed by outside, but Natalie had no interest in it. Her world was the company of the man/woman who sat beside her in the chauffered car.

Images of the gathering kept flicking into life on the screen of her mind. People gathering around her, touching her, their hands exploring her every curve and hollow, their fingers hungrily probing her every orifice.

And not just fingers. Things had been pushed inside her. Delicious, wicked, inanimate things. Vibrators, dildoes, cool, hard spheres on strings, butt plugs. She'd been filled and stuffed and then masturbated until she'd climaxed helplessly. Then she'd been left to rest for a spell, panting and sweating on her sacrificial slab, her body still filled with rubber or porcelain or whatever, while Patti had taken over as the worshipped goddess.

Right on, sister, thought Natalie, stirring now against the strong body of her companion on this journey. She could still see Patti, on all fours on the other table, and hear her shouting and half protesting as Dyson had started to bugger her. A second later, Natalie had heard her sister howling in ecstasy and seen her pushing herself backwards against her violator like a hungry bitch on heat.

'What are you thinking of, my sweet?' A gentle hand brushed the hair back from her forehead affectionately. 'Have we so worn you out that you're nodding off to sleep?'

Natalie looked up at Stella, who looked just as immaculately turned out as she had done at the beginning of the evening. Just a slight retouch of her lipstick was all that it had taken to restore her bandbox perfection, while Natalie felt – and knew – that she looked as if she'd been dragged backwards through a hurricane by her hair.

'I was thinking of Patti being buggered by Dyson,' she said, and, in spite of the overworked tenderness between her legs, she reached down and touched herself, 'and how much she seemed to be getting off on it.'

'Oh yes, my sweet, she was loving it,' said Stella emphatically, 'It's a very stimulating experience – you should try it. Maybe I should do you now. Before you have too much time to think about it . . .' Stella slid a hand beneath Natalie's bottom and began to caress the groove there. 'There's not much time, but if we're quick, I'm pretty sure you'll enjoy yourself.'

It was so tempting. Horrible but tempting. She felt herself melting, growing soft and open, but still a little fear held her back. She would feel much safer in more comfortable surroundings, maybe.

'You're not ready, are you?' said Stella gently, her fingertips delicately fondling and stimulating the tiny entrance. If she didn't stop that soon, Natalie knew she would soon be begging for it. 'Maybe later. When you've had some wine and you're relaxed?'

Natalie made a soft sound of affirmation, but couldn't stop herself from wriggling. She felt Stella's other hand slide down her belly towards her clitoris . . .

* * *

Was it morning? How late was it? How long had she slept? Natalie had no way of knowing what time it was because there didn't seem to be a clock in the bedroom.

Chinks of light were showing through the heavy velvet curtains, so it must be dawn at least, but beyond that Natalie didn't really care. She felt cocooned here, warm and safe and out of the way of the world and all its worries and aggravations. It was a luxurious haven that she'd never expected to find.

Was this Stella's bedroom, or was it Steven's? Where were the boundaries between one persona and the other? The more she thought about it the more the lines grew indistinct.

It had been Stella, last night, who had gentled her and soothed her through the heart-catching trauma of being sodomised. Stella who had massaged her to orgasm after orgasm, until her whole body was so loose that she could have been ravished by Attila the Hun and his hordes with no difficulty. Stella who had lifted her on to hands and knees – just like Patti before her – and who had anointed her anus with a cool and scented gel. It had been Stella who had teased her with first one finger, then two, then three, stretching the pliable muscular ring in preparation . . .

But it had been Steven who had at last pushed in his rigid penis, and brought her choking and grunting to a final massive orgasm, while she'd rubbed herself frantically. The emotions and sensations she'd experienced had been truly astonishing: terrifying and deeply submissive, yet invoking a strange lightness, and a joy and peace that made her weep.

But where was the giver of that joy?

Not the bathroom, judging by the silence beyond the partially open door. There were no sounds of running water or masculine grooming. No off-key whistling or any of the cursing that usually accompanied wet shaving. And presumably Steven did have to shave wet to get his face smooth enough to be Stella's.

Frustrated by her own inertia, Natalie rose from the bed and walked towards the curtained windows. Certain subversive aches and twinges reminded her of a night like no other she'd spent before, but other than that she felt amazing. Like the proverbial million dollars. No, scrub that, she felt more like a billion . . .

'Oh fuck!' she murmured, on letting in daylight.

The sun was high in the sky, shining down on a view of a beautiful, well-tended garden that backed on to a rolling golf course. On the lawn, sitting in a garden chair and talking earnestly into a mobile phone, was Steven. He was wearing a black velour bathrobe, and on the white-painted table beside his chair were the remains of a croissant breakfast.

'Beast! You might have brought me some,' she muttered, but she didn't mind really. He'd granted her sleep instead, which was what she realised she'd needed.

Observing her erstwhile lover more closely, Natalie became intrigued as to the content of his conversation. From the intent expression on his face, the call was serious. She couldn't hear anything through the window, but she got the impression of staccato phrasing and curt profanity. Who the hell was he bollocking? And what about? Knowing his true nature now, Natalie felt glad that it wasn't her.

After a moment or two, Steven flipped the phone closed and then immediately looked around and up towards Natalie. It was almost as if he'd known she was at the window all along, and she felt the craven urge to step back, just in case he hadn't seen her. But he smiled and waved, so she bit the bullet and opened the window.

'Where's my breakfast?' she called out. 'And what time is it?'

'Good morning, Natalie,' he said, his light, pleasant

voice carrying no real trace of Stella's arch, theatrical tones. 'If you wait there, I'll bring your breakfast up in a jiffy.' He consulted a watch that glinted like molten steel on his wrist. 'And it's half past eleven on a bright sunny morning. Will there be anything else?'

'Oh fuck!' said Natalie again, astonished.

'Well, you can have that too, if you like,' said Steven with a broad grin. 'But will that be before or after the croissants and orange juice?'

'Both. Or perhaps during. We'll see,' said Natalie back at him, before retreating from the window.

'Who were you talking to?' she demanded when Steven appeared in the doorway, a few minutes later, carrying a laden tray. His blond hair and pale skin looked stunning against the inky black robe and made him appear handsome, artless and unexpectedly young. Not in the least like a middle-aged drag queen, now defrocked.

Steven didn't answer for a few moments. Instead he appeared to concentrate on placing the tray carefully and securely on the bedside table, then pouring a glass of orange juice from a tall frosty jug. He seemed to hesitate for a second before holding it out to Natalie, and she got the distinct impression he was anticipating some kind of fallout.

'What is it?' she said warily, taking a sip of the juice, which was exquisite. 'Who were you talking to?'

But suddenly she knew.

'It was Daumery! Fucking Whitelaw Daumery you were talking to, wasn't it? You were tipping him off, you shit! Weren't you?'

With the speed of a cobra Steven reached out, took the glass from her the instant before she flung it at him, and set it out of harm's way on the tray.

'Yes, I was talking to Whitelaw Daumery, but I think you should know that it was he who rang me first.'

The hot burn of rage faltered in Natalie's chest. A

second ago, she'd felt furious, ready to kill even, but unexpectedly that urge was already failing. She'd worked hard on the story, and on digging out Daumery's nasty secrets, but suddenly it really didn't feel as important to her as it had previously done. She couldn't even remember what her fervour for it had felt like. So much had happened since she'd boarded the train for Redwych. Not least her finding out that she wasn't really the person she'd thought she was at all.

But she wasn't going to let Steven know that. Well, not just yet.

'About what?' she snapped.

'He was worried,' said Steven with a smirk, he was toying with the sash of his robe as if he were about to take it off in an attempt to distract her. 'About you. He was a bit disconcerted by the way you looked at him last night.'

Yes, well he might be, thought Natalie, remembering the instances in question. She'd taken great delight and gained considerable perverse stimulation from staring hard into Daumery's face while he was touching her. The sweetest kick was when she'd given him a hard, hard look while he was kneeling astride her torso, about to insert his cock into her mouth, and in consequence he'd ejaculated prematurely on to her face. A second later she'd come herself, triggered by the nimble fingers at work between her legs. Stella's, as she recalled. The very same fingers that were twirling the black velour sash right now.

'And what did you say to him? I hope you didn't mention my investigations.'

'I told him everything,' said Steven with a narrow smirk. 'Every last dirty thing about him that had been discovered. I took great pleasure in it.'

'You would, you fuck!' Natalie shot back. 'And now you've ruined everything for me. He'll have a team of lawyers on it now. Spin doctors cooking up some crap that'll refute everything. Lackeys destroying evidence even as we speak.'

'I don't think so. I told him to work out a package for you. An attractive offer to secure your silence . . .'

'You hideous conniving bastard! Do you think I'm as corrupt as he is? As *you* are?'

She'd thought about this – weighed up this very question – and yet hearing it did shock her. Shock her because she already knew what answer she'd give – which was the clearest possible indicator of the difference between the new Natalie and the old.

'No, I think you're a realist, Natalie, and that you're beginning to come to understand the workings of human nature.'

'Fuck you, Steven! Stella! Whatever your name is!' She was angrier more because he understood her than because of anything else. Without thinking, she flashed out her hand and struck his cool, pale face, just as she had done in the kitchen what seemed like a lifetime ago.

Just as fast, Steven grabbed both her hands, then pushed her backwards on to the bed. He forced her arms – quite gently – above her head, holding both in one of his own hands while he ran the other insultingly down her body to her crotch.

'It'll be your choice, Natalie,' he murmured against her neck, his mouth moving there as his fingers did ingenious, rhythmic things to her clit. 'Your choice entirely, but I know the offer will be well worth your while.'

'How so?' she panted, feeling her hips begin to lift and a pool of pleasure start to gather deep in her gut.

'Because you know that I have certain tapes that I'll give you copies of if our friend Daumery isn't adequately generous.'

'You really are a shit, aren't you?' gasped Natalie through gritted teeth. His fingers were moving about now. One, then two of them slid inside her, hooking and searching for her G spot. Her clitoris felt abandoned, but, when he pressed inside her, she groaned with delight.

'The man's your friend,' she persisted, hardly able to breathe, the pleasure pool expanding in her belly, threatening to overflow. 'How can you do this to him?'

'The man's a boor and I despise him.' Steven's tone was light and perfectly conversational. His fingers flexed inside her.

Natalie shouted. Then came violently when Steven released her hands and applied fingers to her clit to complement the ones at work inside her.

Natalie despised Whitelaw Daumery too, and even more so after her phone conversation with him – despite the considerable substance of the offer that he made to her.

A huge sum of money, enough to retire for a while and write that novel, if she wanted to, and a plum job – facilitated through an influential friend – with a media group that was in direct competition to the *Modern Enquirer*. Both facts of Daumery's offer were appealing to her, the latter especially, as it was a way of thumbing her nose at Alan and the magazine.

And yet somehow, even though she'd coolly accepted the deal – and become just as much a self-serving weasel as Daumery himself, she reflected – she had a feeling that she wouldn't be taking up that golden job in London.

'I think I'll stay here,' she said, finally eating the breakfast that Steven had brought her. 'I've had too much fun here to want to leave and I want to live somewhere where I can spend more time with Patti.' She drained her coffee cup, thinking momentarily of her sibling and their startling new relationship. 'I could either take time out to write my novel, or maybe just freelance – or I could even get a job on the *Sentinel*. What do you think?'

Steven turned round to face her. He'd finished his coffee long ago, and had been idly sorting through various cosmetics that were spread out on his dressing table. 'Well, of course, I'd be delighted if you stayed – and I can promise you that the fun's only just begun. But what about that job with the Nexus group? It seems a shame for it to go to waste.' He picked up a pair of tweezers, and, returning his attention to the mirror, he began to pluck his eyebrows.

'Um ... yes, I suppose so,' said Natalie, hugely distracted. She suddenly wanted to see the edges of Steven as they blurred into Stella – even though it was something she suspected he didn't easily reveal. 'Maybe Alex could take that job. I know he wants to do more serious journalism, and it would be his big chance. I'm sure that between us you and I could twist Daumery's arm and force him to make sure that Alex gets the job instead.'

'That's a rather elegant solution,' murmured Steven absently, reaching for a concealer stick and delicately patting a little of it underneath his eyes. 'And I suppose you'd take his place at the *Sentinel*?' He dabbed a little more concealer on his neck to cover the bruised mark of the love bite Natalie had given him.

Natalie rose naked from the bed, and walked to the dressing table. Pulling up a chair, she sat down beside Steven. 'Well, yes, that would be the idea. Although I'd want to investigate everything, and rake up dirt, not turn a selective blind eye the way Alex has had to do. After all, I don't have his expensive lifestyle to support, so I can write what I want.'

Steven grinned, picked up a powder brush, and flicked a little on to set the concealer. 'You'd have to clear this with the *Sentinel*'s owner, you know,' he said, his attention apparently on a selection of eye pencils.

'And who might that be?'

It was Natalie's turn to grin into the mirror at Steven. She had no doubt that she was looking at the newspaper baron in question. Or baroness, she thought, as Steven deftly outlined his eyes with a dark, sooty-coloured kohl and almost at a stroke, Stella Fontayne began to appear.

'Anyway, I think I could persuade him . . . Or perhaps her . . .' she murmured, reaching across to stroke the long muscular thigh so close to hers. As she slid her hand upwards, her companion picked up a mascara wand and applied it unwaveringly to lashes that were already so long that it wasn't fair.

'Really? And how would you do that?'

'Sexual bribery.'

'Oh yes, that would certainly work,' murmured Stella, exchanging mascara for lipstick and beginning to smooth it expertly over the contours of her lips.

Natalie watched, fascinated, in the mirror. With red lips and dark eyes, Stella looked back out of the glass; her short, natural-blond curls were just as flattering as any of her wigs had been.

'How often do you let people see you change?' said Natalie, feeling awe-struck, and also instantly and confusingly aroused again. What was the mechanism here? Did she desire a woman, or a man, or a blend of both?

'I don't, Natalie. You're very privileged,' said Stella softly. Then she swung around on her stool, faced away from the mirror and reached for Natalie's wrist.

'But what do you want in return?' whispered Natalie, sensing a new game and the necessity for yet another trade-off. Her heart began to pound when Stella drew her gently but firmly from her seat, and encouraged her to kneel on the carpet in front of her. With a couple of flicks the dark robe was spread wide open.

'Well, a little sexual bribery will do nicely for a start.'

'Of course,' Natalie murmured.

She gave a little smile, then took Stella's cock into her mouth . . .

Enjoyed *Hotbed*?

Read on for a sneak peek at
Portia Da Costa's scintillating

HOW TO SEDUCE A BILLIONAIRE

Also available from Black Lace

BLACK
LACE

Prologue

He was tall, dark and handsome. Always tall, dark and handsome. A romantic cliché, but who was she to argue with her subconscious?

Dream Lover didn't speak as he climbed into bed with her. He rarely did speak. Her fantasies were visual, not auditory and her own sighs and moans were all the soundtrack that she needed.

Falling back against the pillows, she let her imagined lover take the lead. His smile was enigmatic as he loomed over her, a subtle play of light and shade, but his eyes were vivid and dark with desire. Aquamarine and too brilliant to be natural, they almost dazzled her as he moved in close to kiss her. His lips were mobile and velvety, and the contact compelled her mouth to yield, his tongue demanding entrance, and thrusting fiercely.

Oh yeah!

Fantasy hands settled on her body, the contact firm but not rough as he explored her. He cupped her breast, squeezing lightly, thumb flicking back and forth, driving her crazy even though he'd barely begun his magic. She squirmed, every bit of her coming to life. Especially certain bits . . . The touch of his fingertips was smooth and warm, sliding easily against her skin. It felt lovely and made her wriggle even more . . . until an intrusive memory popped unwelcome into her mind.

A nearly-man, someone she'd once dated and hoped for great things with, he'd had callouses on his fingertips when he'd touched her. They'd felt horribly rough against her skin when he'd tried to sneak his hand up her blouse, and it'd destroyed every chance she might have had of getting turned on.

I'm my own worst enemy. Everything has to be perfect when in real life it probably never is.

As she banished the thought with a furious shake of her head, her hair lashed against the pillow as if she were already in the throes of orgasm. Still without speaking her phantasm-man soothed her, gentled her. His touch both calmed her down and shook her up at the same time, and he stroked her breasts, one then the other, alternating, knowing just when to switch. Then, kissing harder, he drifted that enchanted arousing hand further down, cupping her crotch in a light grip that employed a pinpoint degree of assertion and confidence. Her legs lolled apart of their own accord, making room for his exploration. Seducing him . . .

Of course, it went right. Why wouldn't it? It was all idealised. Questing, he parted the hair of her pussy with those perfect fingertips, dipping in to touch her clit. She gasped, always astonished to be so wet at these times. Lost in her fantasy though, it was easy to get slippery and silky, effortlessly easy.

She cried out, her own voice sounded shockingly loud. Usually she was able to keep the noise down in a shared house, barely articulating any more than wordless Dream Lover did. For a moment, she worried that her house-mate Cathy would hear her, but then told herself not to fret. She'd never heard any sounds of erotic partying from Cathy's room, and her house-mate led a happy, uninhibited sex life with a real, live lover. Cathy was normal, and shared good times with her steady man.

She's younger than me too.

No! Another intrusive thought . . . It was a weird night tonight. Somehow she was more turned on than usual, and yet at the same time less able to concentrate on making Dream Lover real.

What had got into her? Had she lost it completely, from all this incessant brooding on . . . her situation?

Closing her eyes tight, she focused on the dream man who was making love to her. He was passionate and beautiful, and though she still saw no exact likeness of him, he was somehow clearer. She didn't force the issue though. She had other priorities. Something else she needed to keep from slipping away . . . Sensations that could be as fugitive as they were precious and exquisite.

Stroking, stroking, stroking. The pressure, the pattern just right. No man would ever match her own fingers. No man would ever map her own body as she did.

No man had ever even had a chance to try, because no man was perfect.

Stop it! Don't go there. Focus, idiot!

Slipping, circling, swirling, Dream Lover banished her conundrum. His touch and the way it journeyed over the folds and dips and hotspots of her sex was matchless; dominant without being domineering, powerful without being rough. The gathering pleasure made her rock her hips, jerk and thrust against the contact. But Dream Lover was Dream Lover and he didn't miss a beat.

Gasping, she rose to him again, imagination finally taking over, the fantasy and the sensations becoming one. As if sure of her readiness, the man she'd conjured up moved over her, gracefully settling between her legs, his idealised cock pressing for admittance against the entrance of her sex.

The unknown country.

But it felt right. It felt wonderful. Hot. Solid. An iron-stiff rod pushing inside her, yet living and sensitive. Driving, thrusting, possessing, the rhythm divine and metronomic. The way he knocked against her clit with each plunge triggering pleasure that bloomed like fireworks, streaming up into the heavens and taking her with them.

Her teeth clamped hard together, keeping in her shouts, but inside she cried, *Oh thank you, thank you, thank you!*

Whoever you are . . .

Afterwards, she lay still and gasping. Wrung out like a dishrag, sweaty and dishevelled.

This was getting ridiculous.

You need to get a real man, you bloody fool. You need

to find out what it's really like. Nobody but a nun is still a virgin at twenty-nine nowadays, regardless of whatever life 'stuff' happens to them.

Holding out any longer for some crazy ideal of a perfect man was stupid. There *were* no perfect men, and if she kept holding out for one, she'd find herself holding out forever, and end up as a dried up spinster with only her sketching and good works or whatever to keep her occupied. She'd bet good money that any normal woman would be prepared to sleep with more than a frog or two in the hopes that one of them might turn out to be moderately princely.

Waiting for desire was daft. The years were flying by. She had to go half way, and take a risk; *work* to feel passion. Just sitting around expecting lust to suddenly arrive, kaboom, was pathetic.

Next time a nice man with potential crossed her path, she had to give him a chance, and not keep turning away because he wasn't Dream Lover.

As long as he's just a little bit tall and dark and handsome . . .

Shaking her head, she sat up and smoothed down her nightgown.

Time to draw . . .

1

'Oh no! Why today? Why do you have to do this to me?'

Jess Lockhart stared up into the pouring rain and almost shook her fist. She would have done it if there hadn't been cars whizzing by, driven by people who'd think she was a loony; cars that flung up sheets of muddy spray that soaked her shoes and legs as they passed.

Why had this happened just when she wanted to look her best at work? She didn't normally dress up. Smart casual, in fact very casual, was her usual look. But today she wanted to appear a bit more polished, just in case, because of the mighty, exalted VIP who was visiting.

Not that the new owner of the insurance group she worked for was likely to descend from on high to tour the cubicle farm. Why would he? He was a businessman, a tycoon, a financier. He wasn't interested in what the lowly drones at the coalface were doing, just the monetary assets that Windsor Insurance, his new acquisition, represented.

'Why does nobody I know ever drive past?' Jess growled at no car in particular.

This was the busiest part of the city and not everybody was going in the same direction, but surely somebody else was heading for Windsor Insurance? But most likely they wouldn't even recognise such a rain-soaked and bedraggled mutt as their work colleague.

Now, if she'd got up in good time, she could've checked the weather forecast and known that sharp, heavy showers were on the way. But no, she'd been awake half the night, stupidly fantasising about Dream Lover, and then equally stupidly trying to capture his image on paper. Consequently, when it was time to get up, she'd slept in, woolly-headed and weary. If she'd woken up at her normal hour, she could have begged a lift from Cathy, but she'd left it too late. Cathy was an angel, and she'd offered to wait . . . but that would have made her late for work too.

Now you're paying the price for your midnight shenanigans, dimbo, and as you didn't even have the foresight to bring an umbrella, you're going to get soaked to the skin between the bus station and work. Brilliant!

Blinking water out of her eyes, Jess realised that the hair that had begun as a chic and elegant up-do was fast collapsing, its structure undermined by the teeming deluge. With a muttered oath, she pulled out the securing clip, and slung it aside in disgust, to run her fingers through the thick straggles of her sodden hair.

So much for 'maple syrup' low-lights and a twenty-quid conditioning mask.

Just about to retrieve the clip, she darted back from the kerb's edge. Despite the double yellow lines and 'No Stopping' signs, a vehicle actually was pulling up beside her now, its slowing speed only splattering her with a light swish of rainwater this time. Her hairclip was crushed to shards beneath the wheel of a distinctive, retro looking powder blue car. A long, low, classic Citroën. An uncle of hers had driven one once upon a time, and she'd always loved riding in it, because of the way its suspension made you feel as if you were floating on air. Happy, innocent days those had been, when she and her sister had accompanied her uncle's family on sketching holidays to Cornwall.

But what was a vintage 'blue whale' like Uncle Mark's doing here in this neck of the woods, jostling amongst the school run SUVs and the hot hatches and the occasional luxury saloon or hybrid?

Looks like I'm going to find out.

A figure within the blue car leant across the passenger seat and rolled down the window.

'Can I give you a lift somewhere?' said a deep, musical voice, easy on the ear, but very 'not from round here'. The accent was hard to pin down though – basically British, but with bits of other things – especially amongst the drumming rain and the honking car horns.

Jess blinked again. And not just from the water running into her eyes. It was like a double recognition. *Really* weird, making her feel weird too, as if she'd been whirled around several times, far too fast.

No, surely not . . . Surely it's not him *. . . or* him*!*

The man in the car was the spitting image of the pictures she'd seen of today's VIP visitor . . . and he could also have been Dream Lover at a pinch.

The familiar but unfamiliar man grinned, his face lighting up in a sunny, happy, amused expression, glowing somehow, almost dazzling. Eyes that were a bluish green – bluer than his car, but not as green as the actual green of leaves or grass – almost seemed to twinkle at her.

Dear God, it is him! It's the VIP! The new big boss of all bosses!

'Lift?' he prompted, making Jess realise that she must look a complete fool, standing there, wet and bedraggled, with her mouth hanging open, and was probably compounding that impression with every second that passed. Yet still she stood there, and time seemed frozen, apart from the ominous approach of an incoming traffic warden, heading along the street.

But what was this handsome devil, this mighty captain of business, doing cruising along, driving himself in an obviously ancient car when he should be riding in a limousine with a brace of PAs and a chauffeur to look after him? And the VIP's clothing didn't fit the surroundings either. He looked as if he was on his holidays. His suit was light-coloured, fawnish linen, stylish but slightly crumpled, and he wore his flower-patterned cheesecloth shirt with the tails out.

It's definitely him though. Handsome as the devil, but nothing like your everyday average billionaire tycoon. Definitely eccentric.

'Thanks, but it's all right. I'm nearly there. I

wouldn't want to trouble you, and I'll get rain on the upholstery of your car. Thanks . . .'

He laughed softly, cheerful and clearly entertained by her absurdity.

'Sod my upholstery, it'll survive.' He quirked his dark brows at her, and his smile was oddly entreating. 'Please won't you get in? You're getting drenched, and I'll never forgive myself if you end up catching a cold or flu when I could've prevented it. I'm not a pervert or a kidnapper, honestly.' He glanced quickly up the street at the approaching warden. 'I think I'm going to get a ticket any second if we don't move on.'

'Okay then. Thanks.'

Jess slithered into the passenger seat, embarrassingly aware of the slim skirt of her one good suit riding up her thighs. Her tights felt horribly slimy on her wet legs, but she'd wanted to look 'well put together' today and groomed, so she'd worn a pair. Normally she relied on a spot of fake tan.

'Where to?' The VIP arched his eyebrows at her again. And what eyebrows they were! Dark and very firmly marked, they were a perfect match for the near-black brown of his slightly tousled hair and the sexy roguish stubble of his semi-beard.

I don't think Dream Lover has ever had a beard.

'Um . . . Windsor Insurance. It's about two monoliths down, on the left. You can't miss it. There's this silly picture of a castle on the logo.'

And it's your latest acquisition, Mr Beach Bum Billionaire, I think you'll find.

'A silly castle, eh?' he observed, setting the car in gear, eyes on the traffic, yet still making her feel as if he was scrutinising her intensely. 'And what are you then, the lost princess?'

'Nope, just a serf. A minion. A lowly member of one of the claims teams.'

'Oh, not so lowly. Not from where I'm sitting.' Before Jess could even form a response to that, he gestured towards their destination, which now hove into view on the left. She hadn't noticed but he was driving quite fast in the wet and had navigated his way neatly through the hurly-burly of the morning rush hour. 'That it?'

Was he even going to mention who he was? Maybe not. Maybe he wasn't going to bother inspecting the troops, after all, and was just going to hang out with higher management echelons?

'Yes . . . Yes, thanks. You could drop me just here. That's the staff entrance.' She nodded to where some of her work colleagues, most of them considerably dryer than she was, were filing through the double doors.

As she put her hand on the car door handle, he stayed her, his fingers on her arm. It was the lightest contact, but she almost rocked in her seat, imagining the same lightness of touch in another context. A night-time context, slight and gentle, but the beginning of more, so much more.

Jess! What the hell . . . What . . .

Incredibly, her body roused. It was so sudden and so incongruous that she almost swayed in the seat.

Why now? In these circumstances? In the rain, with a man she'd met seconds ago, and would prob-ably never meet again, other than perhaps a nod of acknowledgement as he swept through the claims department on some kind of royal progress.

And yet, it'd happened, shaking her in a way that had always seemed like some magic unknown, a state fantasised about and achieved in solitude, but never experienced out here, in the real world. How could one fleeting touch from this displaced beach bum catch her unawares and take her effortlessly to the domain of Dream Lover?

Staring at him, she could almost see her every thought mirrored in those tropical ocean eyes. As if he knew her. Totally. Understood her lack of experience, and comprehended that she didn't *want* to lack experience, but simply didn't want to throw away something precious in a meaningless act with someone she didn't quite care enough about.

'Are you okay?' He frowned. Looked puzzled. Probably not as completely bedazzled and befuddled as she was, but somehow, amazingly, affected by the moment. 'Do you have towels in there?'

'What?'

'Towels. For drying yourself.'

'Er . . . No, not really, it's mostly hand-dryers.' Now there was a point.

He leant forward, popped open the glove compartment, and fished out a box of man-size tissues, as yet unopened. 'Take those. They'll be better than nothing. Your boss should provide better facilities for his staff than just hand-dryers. Especially in this soggy climate.'

'Oh, I couldn't . . .' Easy for him to be Lord Bountiful. Nobody would get soaked to the skin by dank northern weather on his tropical-somewhere hideaway or any other parts of a billionaire's exalted world.

'Oh, go on. It's just a box of tissues.' He reached over, unzipped the top of her tote bag and shoved in the box of tissues. 'Now, off you go. You'll be late, and we wouldn't want that, would we?'

'No, we wouldn't,' she shot back at him, glad to have retrieved her backbone from somewhere. He'd given her a very brief lift – and the weirdest jolt of pleasure – but he wasn't the boss of her . . . even if he was.

'Thanks again,' she cried, opening the passenger door and shooting out before things could get any weirder.

Soft laughter rang in her ears long after she'd entered the building, echoing as if imprinted on her brain.

2

Portrait of a young woman as drowned rat. I wouldn't want to draw that!

Jess could still see her face in the ladies' room mirror. Her makeup had mostly gone to hell, as had her hairstyle, leaving her looking generally gobsmacked and waterlogged.

And the man who'd given her an almighty shaking up for a variety of reasons had seen that impressive look, and obviously found her a rich source of amusement.

Arrogant bastard! In your world there'll always be a nice dry car to take you where you want to go! No slumming it in the rain like us plebs . . .

Now though, at her desk, an hour later, she felt warmer, better, and at least slightly dryer. His big box of tissues had helped with the blotting, and she'd set it beside her computer, like a talisman. She entertained silly, subversive thoughts about hanging on to it when it was empty, as a keepsake of their 'moment'.

Or at least your moment, Jess. Ridiculously bad timing. Couldn't have been worse.

Silly mare, she chided herself, yet, even as she went through routine tasks, she tried to reclaim the sensations.

Heat, even though she was shivering. Heart racing. The deep, slow, honeyed surge, low in her belly. Astounding . . . alarming . . . wonderful! Everything she could induce in her fantasies, yet never feel here in the real, living world!

Unfortunately, though, the man who'd induced those feelings would never know it. Hell, he'd probably completely forgotten her even before she'd reached the door to the building, even though the smell of his gorgeously spicy cologne was still powerful and exotic in her brain.

Those blue-green eyes. That sunny smile. They were still with her too. And she kept seeing his strong, lightly tanned hands, so relaxed yet sure on the steering wheel . . . and in everything they did, probably. Could this man be the full-on placeholder for Dream Lover? A face she could picture in her fantasies? An avatar to make do with until somebody real came along? If they ever did . . .

Banishing that grim thought, she felt her fingers itch to start doodling, and after a sly look around, she succumbed, pretending to jot notes on her pad, yet in reality pencilling the curve of that smiling mouth, that sexily stubbled jawline. Just elements. She daren't get absorbed in a full face sketch or she'd get no work done and somebody would notice. Not a good strategy at the best of times, but doubly unwise today. Everybody was supposed to look super-efficient, and wholeheartedly dedicated to insurance, for the 'royal' visit: the arrival of the group's new owner to inspect their very humble and fairly insignificant division. Which was weird, but apparently the VIP's eccentric habit.

And management doesn't know the half of it. She grinned to herself while she doodled the curve of his gorgeous lips on her pad. *That stuffy lot upstairs will have a fit when they see your flowered shirt with the tails hanging out.*

So, she'd actually met Ellis P. McKenna, international financier and general all-round filthy rich tycoon. One to one. He was the scion of a billion-dollar entrepreneurial family who'd bought out Windsor Insurance as part of a group along with a large number of other financial concerns, just like someone going out and buying three sweaters in different colours rather than only one. If actual whole companies were so easy to acquire and dispose of to him, it didn't bode well for the little people like her who worked in them.

We all might be just as disposable as cheap jumpers if you decide to keep this operation lean and mean, Mr McKenna.

Jess shuddered. She needed her job, because she didn't have any reserves. Ensuring that her gran had been comfortable at Baxendale Court in her final years had hoovered up every scrap of Jess's modest savings, and she was still gradually paying off the loan she'd taken out to make up the difference. She didn't regret a thing, and would do it again in a heartbeat, but it had left her finances since then a tad precarious, even long after Gran had passed on.

Impatient suddenly, she flung down her pencil, breaking the point and attracting curious looks from Jim and Michelle, who shared her 'pod' of desks.

Oh, come on, Mr McKenna, let's see you again. We'll all sit here tugging our forelocks for a bit, then we can get back to our normal drone activities . . . and I can be sure that Dream Lover is just Dream Lover, a man I once met for about thirty seconds.

Would he even acknowledge her? Or just swan past, barely noticing the faces behind the desks? She pushed his box of tissues to a more prominent place. Perhaps that might remind him?

Even as Jess was thinking that, there was a faint jumble of voices out in the corridor, a small commotion like a looming weather front. People around her sat up straight, fiddled with their ties or smoothed their hair. Michelle even pressed her lips together to refresh her lipstick. Ridiculous! The VIP would come blowing through the office, barely breaking stride, a self-identified deity amongst them, hardly bothering to acknowledge the individual insects he now employed.

The minor hubbub intensified, still approaching. Unconsciously, Jess did the smoothing of the hair thing too. She'd drawn it back now in the best 'do' she could manage at short notice and with her clip smashed and gone, a ponytail at the nape of her neck, secured by a covered elasticated band she'd discovered at the bottom of her bag. She patted at her blouse too, the only part of her ensemble that had more or less avoided getting soaked. Unlike her skirt, which was soggy round the hem, and her shoes, which audibly squelched when she walked. She could have changed into her comfy shoes, but they were far too casual. Ah, the irony, considering that Ellis McKenna was more casually dressed than anyone here.

Jess's heart thudded. Some of those voices were distinct now – those of her bosses – but another one also sounded vaguely familiar.

Oh holy shit, you are *tall, dark and handsome, Mr McKenna!*

The potential candidate for Dream Lover met the height credentials too.

Flanked by the Windsor Insurance bigwigs in their best dark suits, stringently ironed shirts and sober ties, the man with the vintage Citroën strolled into the room, looking like a shabby but dazzling peacock god surrounded by a scuttling murder of crows. Sharp aquamarine eyes scanned the desks and the people behind them, registering, summing up, and passing by with the efficiency of a Terminator. It took but a split second for him to find her . . . and smile.

Oh no!

Without any warning to his entourage, the newcomer abandoned them and strode towards her. Jess had the ridiculous urge to shoot to her feet.

God damn it, he's not a king or anything! I haven't even decided whether he's Dream Lover or not yet.

Sitting tight, she offered him a friendly smile. He had stopped and given her a lift, after all. 'Hello, Mr McKenna,' she said quickly, getting in there first, amazed that she suddenly felt both super-confident and quivery as a jelly inside. He was definitely having Dream Lover effects on her.

His gaze flicked to her nameplate. 'Hello, Ms J. Lockhart. Have you dried out yet?'

'Yes, thank you.'

His brow puckered as he took in her still damp hair, and then, as he peered around the edge of her desk, her wet-hemmed skirt and her sodden shoes.

'Fibber,' he said in a low voice, possibly audible only to her as he leant closer. Jess gripped the edge of her desk to steady herself, made woozy by a sudden waft of his intoxicating male fragrance. It seemed stronger now than it had been in the car.

Who the hell were you intending to impress that you needed to top up your cologne?

His Mediterranean eyes, and the way they flashed, supplied the answer.

I've told you before! Don't be idiotic, Jess, you're nothing to him.

But against all reason, that was wrong. The way he looked at her said she *was* something to him. Something she couldn't completely believe. She could almost imagine she was *his* Dream Lover.

He didn't say more, but his intent expression, and the little quirk of his firm, rosy, biteable lips said their conversation was merely postponed, not over. With a wink, he turned from her, his sharp eyes focusing elsewhere, this time on a step stool against the filing wall, close to her desk. Swooping down, he drew it out, and then leapt lightly up onto it, just a yard or so from where Jess was sitting.

'Right, everyone. I guess you know who I am, and if you don't, I'm Ellis P. McKenna and three weeks ago I took Windsor Insurance into the UK portfolio of the McKenna Group.' He beamed around at every-body. Jess didn't know what the men in the section were making of this, but she could feel a cresting wave of fluttering female excitement building in the room. *Stop showing off,* she wanted to say to him, even though every part of her subconscious and most of her conscious mind loved his display. His body was lithe, but strong-looking, and its proximity was like having some kind of sweet, heady alcoholic syrup bubbling inside her. He was inducing all the reactions that her fantasies managed to trigger, but which never occurred outside of them. Against her will, she found herself zeroing in on his waist . . . his linen clad thighs . . . his crotch . . . Wondering and wondering.

Desiring . . . At last. An actual living, breathing man. It was just like in the car. She was experiencing real female lust for a male who wasn't simply a figment of her imagination. All her adult life she'd wanted this to happen, and she'd believed she was weird and a freak because it hadn't. She'd never experienced the siren call. Never want to give . . .

Blinking, she realised he was speaking again. But there had been a pause. A pause where he'd looked back into her eyes, and, yes, watched the birth of her physical attraction to him. Had he sensed its unusualness?

'What I just wanted to assure you all was that there won't be any redundancies or any cuts in salaries. Well, not at this level.' He winked again, to all the desk-bound assembly in general. 'I haven't decided about this lot yet though.' He made an elegant sweeping gesture to the suits in his retinue, then beamed again, obviously highly amused by their discomfiture.

'Well, that's it really. I'm not one for speechifying. I just didn't want anyone to worry.' He leapt down from his vantage point. 'As they say in the movies, "Have a nice day."'

Yes, please go. I can't think. I need to settle down. Go away, Mr Dream Lover McKenna. Just walk out of my life so I can keep you in my fantasies.

A new emotion sluiced through her, as shocking and intense as the lust she'd felt. It was a black, aching sense of loss and despair. Why feel what she felt now, for a man she'd never see again? Why couldn't it have happened with someone attainable, with whom there might be a future? And more to the point, somebody that she liked, not this clearly supremely arrogant alpha male.

But Ellis McKenna didn't walk. He stayed where he was, scoping her, and frowning.

'You really are still a bit damp there, Ms J. Lockhart, aren't you?' The frown deepened, became layered somehow, as if his attention to her was operating on multiple levels at once. 'We can't have that. I'm not keen on the idea of an employee of mine coming down with pneumonia on the very first day I meet her. I think you'd better come with me.' Imperiously, he held out his hand, as if to draw her up from her seat. 'Please?'

And there it was again, that strange hint of entreaty in his eyes. That very human quality, a need for genuine interaction, however brief.

What the hell is going on? This is just barmy!

Still not sure whether she was succumbing to a consummate manipulator, or a man's real wish for her company, she took the offered hand, snatching up

her bag from the side of her desk. His fingers closed
around hers, firm and unyielding as if he thought she
might flee if he let up on the hold. It was impossible
not to follow him now as he led her the length of
the desk farm, running the gauntlet of dozens of pairs
of curious eyes tracking their every move.

'Where are we going? You can't just waltz me away
somewhere,' she hissed, in the lowest voice she gauged
he could hear without it carrying to the curious ears
of her colleagues.

'I can. I'm the boss,' he said, twinkling at her over
his shoulder.

'You're only the boss of me as an employee, not as
a person. I ought to report you to my union rep for
harassment.' And in any other circumstances, it might
have been harassment, but this . . . this was something
else entirely.

He stopped as they got to the lift, and released her
hand.

'I'm sorry. I'm being a bit of an arse, aren't I? Do
you want to go back to your desk?' His expression
was still that curious blend of provocation and appeal.
He was daring her to walk back between the rows of
avidly gaping faces, yet hoping that she wouldn't call
his bluff.

But what on earth is he planning?

Jess shot into the lift, and almost adhered herself
to the far wall, about as far away from Ellis McKenna
as she could get. After pressing the button for the top
floor, he winked at her, and leant against the opposite
wall. Why did she feel disappointed that he didn't
lunge in her direction?

But, he didn't need to lunge. He just did it with his ocean-green eyes, scrutinising her from head to foot while a little smile played around his lips.

Jess wished, wished, wished she looked more impressive. She lifted her chin and eyeballed him back boldly, but she was all too aware of the soggy hem of her skirt, her squelchy shoes and the stringy wet strands of her hair. Still, pretending she looked fabulous, she stayed strong, trying not to be intimidated by his effortless, scruffy glamour and his sexual aura, an emanation so intense it was like a mist that filled the cabin of the lift.

Oh shit. Oh Lord. I want him. I've no practical idea how to do sex, but I want to do it with him, even if I will be the most hopeless lay.

Ellis tilted his head a little, his eyes narrowing almost as if he'd heard her. For about a fifth of a second, he caught his plush lower lip between his teeth, and looking at him, at that complex expression on his face, she could imagine that it wouldn't matter to him that she was inexperienced. Whatever happened, he would be good enough for both of them. He'd be sensational.

The 'ding' of the lift arriving at their destination made her jump, physically. They'd been in the lift less than thirty seconds but it felt like a lifetime.

'Where exactly are we going?' she asked, following him as he strode out of the lift, then paused to wait for her.

'I've commandeered old Jacobson's office for the day. He's slumming it, in with one of his henchmen.' Ellis winked at her again. 'He says he doesn't mind in the slightest but I can see he's really fuming inside.'

Jess had no idea what Mr Jacobson, the head honcho, looked like when he was fuming. He hadn't even been the one to interview her, and staff on her level never really interacted with senior management.

Looks like I'm interacting with a level of management way above 'old Jacobson' today. It isn't possible to reach a higher level than this.

'I hope he doesn't decide to take reprisals on people like me when you've flitted on to wherever you plan to flit to next,' she said crisply, as Ellis ushered her into the Executive Director's office suite. Jacobson's secretary gave her a curious glance, but only momentarily. The woman barely seemed to have eyes for anyone but Ellis McKenna.

'No interruptions please, Ms Brown,' he instructed, pausing at the older woman's desk to bestow a brain-melting smile.

'Of course, Mr McKenna,' she replied, sounding suspiciously breathy.

You make all women crazy, don't you? Jess accused him silently as he held open the door to the inner sanctum for her.

The way his beautiful mouth quirked seemed to suggest, once again, that he'd heard the thought.

It was a large office, with a very fine leather-topped desk, banked computer workstations to one side, and an 'informal' area over by the floor-to-ceiling windows that looked out over the busy street below. Across the rooftops, in the distance, there was a tantalising view, between two high rises, of the city park, a bit of breathing space amongst the built-up metropolis. There was even the faintest glint of the boating pond, the glitter of water.

Two long settees faced each other at right angles to the triple-glazed glass, with individual armchairs drawn up to the sides and a couple of small, low tables strategically placed.

But wasn't really the seating arrangement that caught Jess's eye. It was the collection of items assembled, some on one of the tables, some on one of the couches.

Ellis led her to the nearest couch.

'I think you should take your skirt and your shoes off.'

Jess gasped. What the hell?

The dazzling, roguish god laughed, his white teeth glinting.

'No, I'm not planning to ravish you . . .' He paused, and for a moment a more saturnine expression crossed his face. 'Well, not unless you absolutely insist. But really, your skirt is still wet at the hem, and I swear I can hear your shoes squishing as you walk.' He nodded at the offending footwear. 'It's bloody cold today, considering it's supposed to be summer round here at the moment, and like I said before, I'd never forgive myself if you ended up catching a chill.'

Thunderstruck, Jess said the first thing that came into her head. 'Why? It's not your fault.'

'Oh, I think it is, in a way. The big boss is visiting, so you chose to wear a smart but rather flimsy suit and insubstantial shoes. It *is* my fault.'

'That's nonsense. I always dress smartly for work.'

He narrowed his sea-blue eyes.

'All right . . . Yes, this isn't my usual work suit. It's my interview suit. And these are my best dressed up shoes.'

'Well, take them off for a while then. I've had the heating turned on, so we can slip your skirt over the radiator and your shoes beneath.' He leant over and patted one of the curious items on the nearest settee: a thick, fluffy bathrobe in navy blue. 'You can wear this while they dry off, and we can have a nice little chat and drink some hot chocolate. That'll warm you up.' He nodded towards a tall vacuum jug standing on one of the tables, with china cups and saucers, and a basket with what looked like home-made cookies nestling in a white table napkin. How had he assembled all this stuff in just an hour? Had he decided the moment he'd first seen her that he'd hijack her from her desk like this?

'I can't take my clothes off just like that. It's . . . um . . .' She clasped her bag, as if it were a weapon with which to defend herself from him. 'I mean . . . you're like the super duper boss of me. I only met you for a few minutes less than an hour ago, and this is an open office, for God's sake!'

'Who do you think is going to ogle you? It's just storage across there, as far as I can tell, and I don't think the birds are particularly interested in us.' He gestured towards the building across the road. He was right; the only living creatures that could overlook them were a few pigeons roosting on the windowsills across the way. 'I'll turn my back, of course.'

The situation was hurtling into the surreal. Jess

shook her head. It was as if she'd stepped through a magic portal at some time since the blue Citroën had drawn up beside her. Or maybe that was the event horizon, entering his car.

'Okay then, if you don't trust me not to look, Jacobson has a small executive bathroom.' He waved towards a door at the end of the computer bank. 'You can change in there instead.'

Stop acting like a ninny, Jess. Just treat this like a game, a hoot. Pretend it's all a big giggle and an adventure. He'll be gone in a few hours, and he'll most likely never come back. You'll laugh about this afterwards and he is fabulous fantasy material . . .

'I trust you not to look, but I think I'll still change in there.' Kicking off her wet shoes, she swept up the thick, luxurious robe and then hurried off towards the door to Jacobson's bathroom.

This was the weirdest situation she'd ever found herself in, and she needed a moment to regroup. To think and to look at her reflection in the mirror and convince herself she wasn't in an extended and augmented version of one of her own erotic fantasies. A freaky dream that she'd wake up from in a minute, and then have to drag her half-asleep body out of bed, to go to work.

And she needed a minute away from the challenging, macho aura of Ellis McKenna . . . The only man she'd ever met who actually honest to God turned her on.

Ellis pursed his lips as the door slammed.

What the hell are you doing, man? Being Mr Impulsive and playing up to your reputation for eccentricity is one thing . . . but this, this is different.

She's different.

Jessica Lockhart. What was it about her? Everything about her initial impression upon him had been unpromising, and yet, oh dear God, he'd been aroused the minute she'd slid into the Citroën in her soggy suit and her waterlogged shoes, and with her dark, saturated hair hanging in thick, wet rat's tails.

Frowning, he retrieved her shoes, imagining the shapely feet they'd protected. He wasn't a foot fetishist, but it was easy to imagine the lovely legs those feet were attached to. And the luscious thighs. And the lithe yet curvaceous hips.

His mind flashed a vision to him of those enticing legs and hips naked, and the mysterious grove of her sex, fully revealed to him. If she were a natural brunette – as he had every reason to believe – she'd be dark-haired down there too, the contrast against her creamy skin stark and stunning.

But great legs and an enticing little pussy were characteristics of a thousand girls. What was it about this particular girl . . . this woman . . . that had hooked him? Still musing, he placed the shoes close to the radiator, but not close enough to ruin them by cracking the leather.

Maybe it was the fact that he *did* perceive her as a girl?

But she isn't one. She's a woman. Later twenties. Not all that much younger than me, if truth be known.

But his journey through the valley of grief had aged him prematurely. Not physically, but emotionally. He felt as if he was a thousand years old in loss and regret, but in reality, thirty-six was no age at all. And he'd found a way to deal with his life as it was. A set of workable parameters . . .

But even so, that still didn't explain why Jessica Lockhart shook him up like this. She didn't remind him of Julie. Not in the slightest. They were entirely different types, except perhaps for that elusive quality; that of being untouched, yet curious. The way his wife had been at the dawn of their relationship.

A sudden image of Julie in her wedding gown pierced him like burning spear, hitting so hard he almost cried out, his excitement and arousal instantly forgotten.

No. No. No. That's the past, a paradise that can never be revisited. That state, that love that I once had . . . That's a closed book now, and never to be reopened.

He turned away from the window, and the vision

of the waterlogged metropolis and its unknown humanity, all hurrying about their business. Not that he'd even been seeing them.

The room, for all its sterile utilitarianism and lack of real character, was warm now, both physically and in an obscure, discreet sense that had everything to do with the woman he'd brought up here.

Perfection was a thing of the past for him now, but he could still have something different, something distracting. The pleasures of the flesh in all their delightful forms were still available to him, and some amenable company for a strictly limited while would be welcome.

Hmm . . . flesh. He was back to musing on her thighs again, and back to considering the mouth-watering curve of her bottom as she'd walked away in her trim but damp skirt. His fingers flexed, anticipating soft skin and firm musculature, as he imagined touching and squeezing, not to mention exploring and perhaps even a bit of judicious spanking, should things develop along those lines. She hadn't ever played any kinky games, he'd wager the entire income from this rather mundane company on that certitude.

What will your cries of surprise be like, Jessica? Will you moan with pleasure when I touch you? Will you whimper and cry out my name when I'm between those silky thighs of yours, thrusting?

Ellis McKenna smiled to himself. Life still had the potential to be good, even for him, and as he unscrewed the top of the vacuum flask, the hot, rich cocoa smell only added to his excitement and the gathering thrill.

His cock leapt, as he imagined those deeper pleasures, better even than the luscious taste of chocolate.

He always felt better when he was planning a seduction.

Also by Portia Da Costa:

The Accidental Call Girl

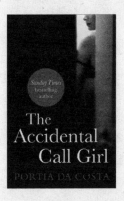

It's the ultimate fantasy:

When Lizzie meets an attractive older man in the bar of a
luxury hotel, he mistakes her for a high class call girl on the
look-out for a wealthy client.

With a man she can't resist...

Lizzie finds herself following him to his hotel room for
an unforgettable night where she learns the pleasures of
submitting to the hands of a master. But what will happen
when John discovers that Lizzie is far more than she seems...?

**A sexy, thrilling erotic romance for every woman who
has ever had a "Pretty Woman" fantasy.
Part One of the 'Accidental' Trilogy.**

BLACK
LACE

Also by Portia Da Costa:

The Accidental Mistress

Seduced by a billionaire…

After being mistaken for a high-class call girl when they first met, Lizzie now enjoys a fiery relationship with John, her gorgeous and incredibly rich older man. Devoted, romantic and devilishly kinky, John knows exactly how to satisfy her every need.

But John has a dark side – and a past he won't talk about. He might welcome Lizzie in his bed – and out of it – but will she ever be anything more than a rich man's mistress?

Part Two of the 'Accidental' Trilogy.

BLACK
LACE

Also by Portia Da Costa:

The Accidental Bride

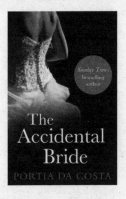

Marrying a billionaire?

It's every girl's fantasy but ever since meeting brooding sexy tycoon, John Smith, Lizzie has never been entirely sure of his true feelings for her.

Has he proposed marriage because he truly loves her or just to keep her in his bed?

Part Three of the 'Accidental' Trilogy.

BLACK
LACE

Also by Portia Da Costa:

In Too Deep

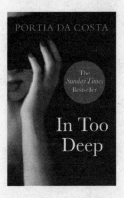

I just want a taste of you. Or a touch. My fantasies about you plague my every waking hour. My only comfort is imagining that similar fantasies might obsess you too.

When young librarian Gwendolynne Price finds increasingly erotic love notes to her in the suggestion box at work, she finds them both shocking and liberating.

But who is her mystery admirer and how long will he be content to just admire her from afar...?

The *Sunday Times* bestseller. *In Too Deep* is a dark sensual romance to fuel your fantasies

BLACK LACE

Also by Portia Da Costa:

The Stranger

Once she had got over the initial shock of the young man's nudity, Claudia allowed herself to breathe properly again...

When Claudia finds a sexy stranger near her home she discovers that he has lost his memory along with his clothes.

Having turned her back on relationships since the death of her husband, Claudia finds herself scandalising her friends by inviting the stranger into her home and into her bed...

BLACK
LACE

Also by Portia Da Costa:

Entertaining Mr Stone

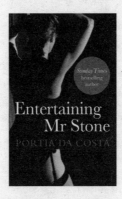

She's a good girl gone bad...

When Maria Lewis moves back to her hometown, the quiet life she is looking for is quickly disrupted by the enigmatic presence of her new boss, Robert Stone.

A sexy, powerful older man, he seduces Maria into a deliciously erotic underworld. But will she ever be more than Mr Stone's plaything?

BLACK
LACE